# MORE BY THE AUTHOR

## Universal Defender

Book 1: Today I Save Myself

Book 2: Fire to Burn the Stars

Book 3: Enter Unmaker

## Blue Flash

Miles Radien and the Cult of the Chaosmaker
(Universal Defender)

Veralis Stratenheim and the Bridge Across Fire
(Universal Defender)

Reticent (Angels of Anarchy)

Talenostrum

Night of the Whapwolf

In Combat with Time

www.BlueForgePress.com

# Miles Radien and the Gauntlet of Doom

## Gregor Fjellrev

**Blue Forge Press**
Port Orchard, Washington

Miles Radien and the Gauntlet of Doom
Copyright 2023
by Gregor Fjellrev

First eBook Edition December 2023
First Print Edition December 2023

ISBN 978-1-59092-918-6

Cover art by Jasper Martin AKA Jupiter Menagerie



For information about film, reprint or other subsidiary rights, contact: blueforgegroup@gmail.com



Blue Forge Press is the print division of the volunteer-run, federal 501(c)3 nonprofit company, Blue Forge Group, founded in 1989 and dedicated to bringing light to the shadows and voice to the silence. We strive to empower storytellers across all walks of life with our four divisions: Blue Forge Press, Blue Forge Films, Blue Forge Gaming, and Blue Forge Records. Find out more at www.BlueForgeGroup.org

Blue Forge Press
7419 Ebbert Drive Southeast
Port Orchard, Washington 98367
blueforgepress@gmail.com
360-550-2071 ph.txt

# Miles Radien and the Gauntlet of Doom

GREGOR FJELLREV

# 1

# The Gauntlet of Doom

The Fortress ran as per usual, Torvaltyne Bastion. With the war against Demons having become more 'up and running', and the incursions happening more often, everyone had something to do.

"Tactician, requisition order from the High Commandant. They want another twenty-five percent of Manufactorum Two for infantry gear production," was the report from Arakai Selendica, the Cynofrax Vulpian and level-headed blademaster who was taking to an administrative position within Torvaltyne. Though Radien had been appointed its leader and commander being that the entire place was his brainchild, Arakai was the one being told the matters that needed deciding on, while Radien was the one who made the decision, if Arakai didn't already have a pretty good read on what Radien would decide. It was most helpful that Arakai didn't mind his role as a silent workhorse, as he was never overworked.

"They've already got *half* of Manufactorum Two!"

Radien said. "Tell them that, in case they weren't aware! As for Arcturus's request for first dibs on the Archonium shipment we just received, that's denied! Tell him 'horde reasons' are *not* a valid requisition justification!"

Arakai nodded as he transmitted the message. Radien flung the door open to the Artificer's Wing subsection of the Fortress's Manufactorums; sets of high-precision and often hand-operated apparatuses for imbuing specific properties onto weapons or armors, stuff that mass production and industrial-scale equipment simply couldn't cut it for. He then headed over to the machine that he had been alerted wasn't functioning, and quickly assessed it. The process had thankfully only been paused rather than stopped, so all he needed to do was impart a low-level Psionic Resonance Wave into the mechanism to kick it back into gear.

In layman's terms, he just did the telekinetic equivalent of smacking it to make it work again. He then glared at the machine as if ordering it to stay put as he then backed away to deal with the next thing.

"Okay, what else?" Radien asked Arakai.

"Dorg and Jarrek wrecked another sparring ring."

"I've told them to use the *Hurlath* arena for their spars! You'd think that Redarian would learn by now that Dorg likes to throw people, so he should be prepared to get thrown!"

The specific arena to use was the Fortress's resident arena for the traditional Death World Vulpian sport of *Hurlath*, where competitors take turns throwing each other across the room, into walls, through terrain emplacements, and against ceilings until one of them yields. "Anyways, run the Repair Matrix on it, that worked last time."

The two were then approached by Micah Jorvask, a Redarian herself like Jarrek, but where Jarrek Wöllschlager was Arch-Militant of the Redarian Interplanetary Battlefleet, Micah was a Disciple of Shadow, Second Degree in one of Nathineyl's intelligence corps, the Eyes of the Daggers. However, the proper name of such a corps within Redarian circles translated as 'Houses of Shadow', or 'Shadow House'.

Micah did not hail from Redaria Prime or Omega herself, but rather from the binary planet system of Koros-Nathineyl. Specifically, the latter planet, in case it was not obvious by which planet's intelligence corps she was a part of. "Radien, my organization's got the scoop on a potential SWEEPS base being constructed, planned to be larger than the one on Turazin. I'll let you know the important details afterwards, but expect that report."

"Got it, good," Radien said as the two continued on.

"I've got a shipment coming in I gotta deal with, Radien, you're good from here?" Arakai then informed.

"Aye! Go for it!" Radien approved. "Miirkae, remind me when we're to spar next?"

"One hour!" the Hykentiu responded as he practiced on a training dummy in the courtyard with his spear. Though he was from an amphibious species, Miirkae passionately swore off ever using a trident as his weapon. So instead, it was a double-pointed spear that could separate into a pair of pointed Bastons. It was considered to be disjointed enough from the weapon of stereotype to be valid.

Radien then exited the courtyard and passed by the Science Station Wing, where Veralis was exiting one of the labs.

"Ah, good," Veralis said as she noticed Radien. "I wanted to get back to you on that power diversion we need into Lab Four, we need the extra routing from labs five through eight, in order to speed up the process of the serum we're developing."

"Five through eight are in use, though!" Radien said. "I know Pyrhea's got that excavated slab that the Atomic Sifter is going through, as well as—"

"If we get that extra power, the serum will only need a week to develop instead of—"

"*Then you are just gonna have to wait six hundred ASC for all I care!*" Radien suddenly burst out in the hall. "That Atomic Sifter can't lose power or it gets compromised, Ellan's got Lab Six decrypting a server rack, and I don't even *know* what's got Lab Seven occupied, but I'm sure it's some other ridiculous bullshit that means you can't have the damn labs!"

Radien began to storm off when Veralis suddenly spoke up in response. "*Stop. Right. There. Tactician.*"

Radien froze in place at the sudden authoritativeness of her tone. "Process is only going to be a month instead, and *clearly* it can wait."

"Good to know—"

"*I'm not finished yet,*" Veralis sternly continued. "You're relieved of duty and ordered to take some time off."

Radien burst out laughing. "You can't do that!"

"As it turns out, I can," Veralis said. "As head of the Sciences division here at the Fortress, that gives me the rights and privileges of its Chief Medical Officer until a specific person is appointed to it! And as acting Chief Medical Officer of this fortress, I *do* outrank you on matters of medicine! And in the interest of the Raon-Arashal Defensive Militarium's policy regarding medical leave, *you are relieved of duty, and ordered to take time off!*"

"Hang on, what kind of ridiculous—"

"D-o-S-two Jorvask?" Veralis spoke into a comm-link.

"Micah here," came the reply.

"Escort Tactician Radien to the Kianar's Folly tavern."

"Acknowledged."

One of the six food-providing establishments at Torvaltyne Bastion. Micah soon arrived to show Radien the way to the place, though Radien was well aware of its location.

"Micah, I'm assigning you to ensure that Radien has a minimum of either five ales, two mixed drinks or three pints of mead before exiting the premises at Kianar's Folly."

"Understood. Anything else I should know?"

"What in all the realms—" Radien protested.

"You are also free to offer him any necessary incentive to fulfill all three conditions simultaneously."

"I can do that. Come on, Tactician. The universe won't fall in a day."

"Don't poke my ass with your parrying dagger, Micah!"

"Shut up, it's not even going through your pants! It's stopping just before it hits..."

"It's hitting the Passive Psi-Shield and poking up against me anyway!"

"You're *still* training that?!" Veralis exclaimed. "I told you, the process only pauses when it's not being progressed, not backtrack! Micah, orders have changed, his minimum intake requirements have doubled!"

"Works for me!" Micah agreed as she continued to push Radien along towards the bar.

"I'm about to kill something..." Radien grumbled.

"That's what we're trying to avoid, genius," Micah assured.

Once they had arrived at the titular tavern, Micah briefed the bartender, a Sandscale Dragon by the name of Asynter on the situation. He nodded, agreeing to make sure Radien got his fill of drink.

"Which one, Mead, Ale, or Mixed?" Asynter asked.

"Surprise me," Radien replied, his chin resting on the counter.

Asynter decided to mix an experimental cocktail, a glowing green one he called the Battery Acid. Gin-based, with a healthy amount of citrus to kick the senses in the teeth.

"They are incomprehensible, those two," Radien gruffed as he saw Micah nearby with a stein of her own, watching him to make sure he imbibed his minimum amount, and glaring mischievously. She was very good at that mischievous glare.

"Is it they who are incomprehensible, or their actions?" Asynter asked.

"Actions."

"The actions themselves, or the fact they are taken upon you?"

Radien thought for a moment. "The latter."

"I see. You didn't live well before you came to Raon-Arashal, did you, Tactician?"

Radien raised an eyebrow, simultaneously relieved that it was not common knowledge his 'true' planet of origin. "No," he simply replied.

"How many liars and traitors on your home world?"

"About… nine billion by the time I left? Give or take a few hundred mil? Something along those lines."

Asynter started preparing another drink, a deep blue cocktail he ended up delivering to a similarly blue-scaled Dragon at a nearby table. The Dragon then spoke briefly to Asynter, after which he nodded.

"Arcturus wants me to tell you that the Archonium will be his. Apparently he loafed on the shipping crate when it came in, so that means he's claimed it."

"Yeah, I'd like to see him try to collect on that. If he wanted to go by *that* system, he'd've had to loaf *directly* on the plates themselves, so the claim is moot. Inform him that he can have the box after it's unloaded when you give him his next drink."

"Will do."

Radien continued to ponder over his drinks for a bit, before deciding what he was going to do to satisfy

Veralis's order to take some time off. Veralis never specified *what* he had to do during that time, other than have these drinks while fending off Micah's teasing incentives for, as Veralis had put it previously, 'fulfilling all three conditions simultaneously'.

The following day, Radien made his way towards Tenbork Station, one of the staging grounds for entering the Kaladorum Black Zone with intent to train one's survival skills by subjecting themselves to the zone itself. The other station was actually Torvaltyne Bastion itself.

"Freestyle or Doombringer's Rules?" the administrator asked Radien when he requested a drop into the zone.

"Gauntlet of Doom," Radien replied, to the inquisitive raise of an eyebrow. Not in a dismissive way, but in the '*ooh, exciting*' way.

Miles Radien had just made his intentions clear: He was going to spend a month in each of Raon-Arashal's twenty-two Black Zones, with no more than seven days rest between each, until he had done them all. The Doombringer's Rules, which the Gauntlet is done under, has the survivalist entering each zone with no more than a bladed weapon of their choice, and a backpack containing a flint and steel, and three days' worth of food and water to start. Other than that, he was going to be on his own with his wits and his skill. It was a traditional coming of age-type endeavor in Death Worlder culture, and the trial had always been considered a paramount honor to conquer, the Gauntlet of Doom.

"Gonna start with Kaladorum?" the administrator asked as he entered into the computer that Radien was about to begin this ultimate test of survival ability. He thought for a moment, then shook his head.

"No, Jaltai-Vuul first. After that, I'll just go down the line from Azhenar to Zralanan, but save Relanon specifically for last."

The administrator nodded. That was the clever choice, and the usual one. Jaltai-Vuul was the single least popular of the Black Zones, and Relanon was considered the least stressful. A good one to do last.

"All right, Tactician. I've got you logged as beginning the Gauntlet of Doom, and Sraivenurel Station will be ready to drop you in once you get there."

Sraivenurel, literally translated as 'Fuck this area' from the Death Worlder language, was the name of the singular Survival Station within Jaltai-Vuul itself. Radien nodded and thanked the administrator before boarding a local transport vessel to Sraivenurel Station itself. There was no need to grab the Aura Runner for intraplanetary trips.

# 2

# Jaltai-Vuul Black Zone

The transport's turbines were loud as hell, but Radien and the local Jumpmaster were still able to communicate with each other.

"All right! We're coming near where we're gonna put you, Tactician!" he explained after the aircraft depressurized. "You clearly know what's up here with the rules, but regulation says I gotta tell you some of the finer points before we leave you to it since this is the first zone you're doing in the Gauntlet!"

Radien nodded as the ship lowered itself towards the desert sands. As soon as the cargo door began to open, the heat from outside flooded into the cabin, and might have floored a more unprepared person on the spot. Jaltai-Vuul's name was an earned one, translating as 'Swords are useless'. After all, one does not simply stab the desert, that would make it too easy.

"If you find civilization, such as occupied structures or a small town, you gotta turn around and walk away! However, abandoned structures are fair game! Though I don't think you're gonna have that problem in this zone, since everybody hates it!"

"It's a damn desert, no wonder!" Radien replied. "We're better at colder climates!" He was referring to the Death World Vulpians species themselves, of which both he and the Jumpmaster were, thanks to Radien's recent transformation in the wake of his victory against The Unmaker.

"No kidding! It's why Jumpmaster for Jaltai-Vuul is the most secure job on the whole planet!"

Both men shared a laugh at the comment.

"If you happen to find another person, nothing says you can't trade with them or help each other out!" the Jumpmaster continued explaining. "Once you hit day twenty-nine, that beacon on your backpack will light up red, so that you know we're coming to get you on day thirty for the next one, *so don't lose your backpack!* Soon as that light turns green, hop on out!"

Radien nodded, and the light then proceeded to turn green. Immediately afterwards, he ran at a brisk but not urgent pace towards the open cargo bay doors and jumped out, hitting the burning sands of the Jaltai-Vuul Black Zone ten feet later.

Normal rubber boots would have started melting immediately, but Radien was not wearing boots of ordinary rubber. In fact, when the Gauntlet of Doom's rules stated that one may take a bladed weapon, and a backpack with a flint and steel and three days of food and water *and nothing else*, it was quite literal.

The calluses on Radien's feet would protect him only for a few hours before they'd start to hurt from the heat of the desert sands. Within ten minutes of saluting the transport as it lifted off and left, he was already having to keep his tail from hitting the ground, lest he risk singing the fur on it. Despite his transformation or regeneration—whichever you prefer to call it—being only a few months ago, he was already in full kinesthetic control of both his tail and his ears. He had adjusted to the form quite quickly, a testament to how well it fit him.

The first thing to do was to get the hell out of the heat. He had about fifty minutes left to do so before his feetpaws would start to sting from the burning sand, and another five after that before proper burns were risked. Looking around, Radien's eyes switched in color to an amber glow as he used his Second Sight ability to see where the nearest shelter was.

Unfortunately, with the harsh winds of Jaltai-Vuul, Radien was finding out quickly that there was something in the sand that was screwing with his Psionic powers. He was going to have to either learn to pierce the veil, or find shelter the old-fashioned way.

Taking what cover could be had from the downwind side of a nearby dune, he focused his power harder in his mind, breathing steadily and summoning the mental fortitude to see what needed to be seen.

Two kilometers away, the dunes gave way to rocky cliffs, where shade could be found, even if not proper shelter. It'd be a start.

Radien started running towards the cliffs, but made sure to pace himself. As hardy as his Death Worlder body was, there was still a lot of room for further conditioning. With the sweltering heat threatening to drain his energy far faster than average, he made sure that he would get to the cliffside shade before the sands started stinging his feet, whilst also not expending more energy than he had to, let alone could afford to.

Taking it one problem at a time was Radien's main plan for each of the thirty-day segments of the Gauntlet of Doom. After all, that's how long a month was on Raon-Arashal, and the solar year contained eighteen of them, each with distinct quarterly seasons of *Fjaranan*, *Kaisenar*, *Vergeil* and *Kalotressanan*. It was a reliably simple The current season on Raon-Arashal was *Vergeil*, or 'almost', roughly translated. As in, 'almost winter'. *Kalotressanan*, respectively, translated as 'Finally, coat time', where eager Death Worlders would finally have an excuse to don their *Destiltress*, or 'Signature coats'.

Regardless, Radien had finally made it to the shade of the cliffside, and was no longer in danger of burning his feet on the scorching desert terrain. Now he just had to see if he could find shelter within a canyon that hopefully existed among these rocks. To his fortune and relief, there was one to be found.

Once he reached the bottom of the canyon, scaling with great caution down natural paths and rock faces for the entire two-kilometer drop in elevation, Radien sighed with relief. One of the hardest parts of Jaltai-Vuul was out of the way, now he just had to last thirty days in this canyon's valley.

The single most common critiques of Jaltai-Vuul as part of the Gauntlet of Doom, is that its nature as a burning desert dotted with deep canyons and rift valleys within the dunes, the actual *Volarthir-Ruuk*, or 'survival loop' was quite boring compared to others. Constantly watching one's hydration level in the scorching climate lest risking abrupt complications made for an experience that it was not easy to pass the time within, among other factors that earn this place its name.

There wasn't much hostile fauna within Jaltai-Vuul, most animals simply couldn't afford to have large surface areas in such a blazing climate. Most.

As soon as Radien knelt down to meditate and pass some time, he suddenly felt tremors in the ground. Something was coming, towards him, and fast. The rhythm of the steps was unmistakable: An Akraknahal was inbound, a massive scorpion-like creature that seemed to defy biology and evolution with its size, and the potency of its venom. Normally, larger scorpions have weaker venom and vice versa, but then again, Akraknahals were native to Raon-Arashal and not Earth, and the rules were different here.

Radien quickly drew the Borfblade to meet this creature, but as soon as he swung the hundred-folded Novasteel blade, the creature blocked it with its chitinous claw with seemingly unnatural reflexes. The zone was called Jaltai-Vuul for a *reason*.

"*Djalsej!* Fuck that!" Radien exclaimed as he ran towards the nearby rock wall to begin climbing up it, then remembering his Telekinetic Platform technique and deciding to use that instead. However, the platforms were fizzling in and out of the air they were suspended within. Whatever it was in these sands that made using Second Sight a chore, it was wreaking havoc on his power of the Aura as a whole.

*"Torrit Djalsej! Double fuck that!"*

The Akraknahal's stinger slammed into the rock face, barely missing Radien and throwing a fair amount of boulders and dust about.

*"Ja-jahada Djalsej! Extremely fuck that!"* Radien finally cursed as the venomous point barely was evaded, as well as the boulders that were thrown by the impact. The creature poised for another strike, the time was now or never.

Leaping from his perch on the rocks with a yell, the Borfblade was driven down and through the Akraknahal's hardened carapace, skewering the massive scorpion and pinning it to the ground by the blade that had just impaled it.

*"Duul valarin deyl. You annoy me,"* Radien sent off as the creature twitched in its deathrattle. He then grabbed the cutlass and pulled it out from the Akraknahal's corpse. "Maybe swords aren't entirely useless here."

As the sun began to set over Jaltai-Vuul, Radien realized that there wasn't going to be much in the way of starting a fire, as a desert is rather devoid of trees, generally.

Though he was able to get a fire going with the Aura after a brief struggle with the psionically-dampening winds of Jaltai-Vuul, what he was going to cook over it was still up for debate. There was, however, a very large and very dead Akraknahal next to the fire, and with the Gauntlet being mainly a training regimen, he figured he might as well train his stomach while we was at it. He hadn't been a Death World Vulpian for too long, and still had a fair bit to understand about his own physiology. That being said, it was still taking some getting used to. But since he had a moment under the dark skies of nighttime Jaltai-Vuul, he could start to figure that out.

Radien walked up to one of the sandstone walls of the canyon, and swiped his claws at it. They made marks in the rock, but the claws themselves had been scratched up a fair bit themselves. The dust of the rock floated to the canyon floor.

"It's a start."

Radien then began to train his claws, bringing himself just up to his limit before stopping to heal himself with The Aura, simultaneously training his ability to do so, and the reliability of his ability to use Psionic powers in general. Something about Jaltai-Vuul was causing the Aura to have a sort of dampened effect, like radio static cutting through the lifeblood of the universe. This equilibrium of training that he had achieved, it brought a strange sense of zen to Radien's mind, so much so that he didn't even notice the passage of time as he trained himself here, and on the twenty-ninth day, the silence was seemingly suddenly broken by the beeping of the locator beacon. Just as Radien realized that the beacon was active, he swiped one last time at the sandstone walls he had been training upon, causing sparks to fly onto the ground, and set the pile of dry twigs they landed on aflame.

"Oh. I uh… I guess I'm almost done with this one."

His voice echoed throughout the canyon he had found himself in, and a piece of the almost thirty day-old carcass of the Akraknahal rolled away and thudded against the canyon wall. Radien looked to his feet, and noticed that there was something strange about these rocks—he was on a path. A walkway within the canyon, leading to a small stone monument tucked away in an alcove. A slab of solid granite embedded within the wall, and scripture in the Death Worlder language, that Radien was seeing through his eyes as Latin characters, arranged in a way he knew instinctively how to pronounce. A most helpful trait of the Aura indeed, teaching him these languages on the fly so that in case he lost his powers, he could still instinctively speak it. This was the nature of the Equilibrium Cantrip Radien had planned out all that time ago when he was a Human, to assist in training, and gradually remove the training wheels entirely.

*Vel duul'e Jaltai-Vuul, duul'e Nexul duul'e Jaltai.*

*When your sword is useless, your body is your sword.*

Radien then looked at his claws, sharpened by the stone he had been clawing upon for the past twenty-nine days, using the Aura to heal and sustain himself during that time, not even needed to take a bite out of the Akraknahal carcass like he had first planned to, in order to train his stomach. He could do that in one of the next zones, he figured.

During the night that came, Radien continued to study the tablet in the sandstone wall. Out of curiosity, he reached out with a hand and touched the granite slab. The scripture suddenly glowed red as he placed his hand on it, illuminating the phrase carved into the granite with a bright crimson glow, and he could swear that he heard some kind of resonance, like some kind of Psionic bell that was gonged by his touch. By morning, Radien had climbed his way out of the canyon to meet the hovercraft that had come out to retrieve him. With his hardened and sharpened claws, he used them to jab handholds into the rock, so that he could climb the sheer cliff.

"Gentlemen, your timing is impeccable!" Radien greeted as he hopped aboard the hovercraft. "I certainly understand why everyone hates this zone now!"

The two Death Worlders with him aboard the speeding hovercraft had a good laugh at that as they headed back towards Sraivenurel Station. When they had gotten there, Radien was greeted by both Veralis and Micah, and he wasn't sure what to think of that.

"I said you were to take time *off!*" Veralis said in a bit of an exaggerated voice. Radien was startled at first, but he seemed to catch that it was a bit *too* vigorous, that delivery. "What could possibly make you think that this *counts?!*"

The three stood still before Micah let out a giggle, and then Veralis burst out laughing with her. Radien let out a huge sigh of relief, and did start to chuckle once his breath had resumed.

"Oh yeah, of *course* this is how Radien spends his time off! A train-cation like this *is* time off for him!" Micah manage to word out through her giggle fit. "That means I've won in the betting pool over at Kianar's Folly."

"What?" Radien asked, confused beyond imagining.

"Jarrek set up a betting pool for to what you'd get up to on your mandated break. Almost the entire

Fortress had a stake in it," Veralis explained.

"I'm almost afraid to ask what the other entries on the board were, but I've got to ask now..." Radien responded.

"It was between 'bar crawling in Kendradeyne', versus 'Training', which doing the Gauntlet of Doom falls under, I should think," Micah answered. "Dorg also bet on training."

"What of Miirkae?"

"He bet training, on the idea you were going specifically to Orvitaire."

Radien nodded. "I do need to visit Orvitaire, you're right..."

Micah and Veralis immediately burst out laughing again.

"What?!"

"Miirkae placed a second bet on that you'd at least *mention* Orvitaire!" Micah managed to cough out between laughing fits.

"*What did he bet?!*" Radien demanded.

"A Carved Brick he made in the Craftsman's Wing a few days ago," the Redarian answered.

"By the gods, that shark just made himself able to retire. He's *good* at Carved Bricks."

Carved Bricks, being a traditional Hykentiu form of art, where simple fist-sized cubes of granite would have intricate designs engraved into their faces, which ranged from simple designs and symbols to entire mythological fables told in pictogram form.

"Well, I've got seven days between this one and heading into Azhenar..," Radien said. "I'm gonna head to

Karnyne Station now and find a good bar to brood mysteriously in between now and then.”

"I've heard that the Warrior's Gate in Kendradeyne has a specific section of their Mysterious Brooding Corner unofficially *dedicated* to Radien now.” Micah commented.

"What?!”

"Have fun in Karnyne!” Veralis sent off as the two headed back towards the transit bay, leaving Radien to his own devices.

"Well... that was the reaction I *wasn't* expecting, let alone prepared for.”

# 7

# AZHENAR BLACK ZONE

zhenar's general climate was that of a tundra forest, or more like pre-tundra. The sort of generally evergreen landscape that gets a disappointingly low amount of snow per year, but no shortage of precipitation, thus rain. Which was Radien's least favorite weather of all. His disdain for rainfall was so great, in fact, that he had created another 'Autopsionic' Cantrip, as he had figured that 'Autotelekinetic' was not as appropriate of a term, hence his decision to switch the technical name of a passive use of Psionic power thusly,

The Autopsionic Cantrip of course, being one he called *Hostile Environment Shield*, which was a projected shield around his body that could act as his way of breathing underwater, in space, or ensuring stray shrapnel from an explosion wouldn't tag his leg. In the case of surviving Azhenar, the Hostile Environment Shield was being used to stop the rain from hitting his fur, because fuck rain. Rain is stupid and boring and dull and also stupid.

Finding a clearing in the old forest, Radien began

gathering some fallen sticks and logs, and jamming them into the dirt. By the time the first night over Azhenar fell, he had constructed himself an improvised training circle in the clearing. The first stick, he hit with the first two knuckles of his closed left fist. He then moved to the next one along the course, hitting it with the first two knuckles of his closed right fist. The next two sticks were a left knife hand chop, and a right knife hand chop. The next two, left and right sword hand chops. After that, left and right ridge-hand strikes, followed by wooden poles for a set of elbow strikes on each side: roundhouse elbow, straight elbow, rear elbow, rising elbow, descending elbow, obscure elbow. The last one was the one where your elbow would shoot up behind you like you were bopping the nose of someone who put their hand on your shoulder. After that, the kicks. A pair of poles for left and right snapping front kick. A pair for left and right roundhouse, upon which he would do a three-kick combo of first performing a low, middle, then head-high kick separately, then all three kicks with one raise of his leg. This routine was done ten times per pole, per side. After that, a pair of poles for left and right side kicks, where he would alternate between ten thrusting kicks and ten defensive side kicks, like how he had been initially trained to do them in Savate, all that time ago on Old Earth. But with both legs doing both variations of the side kick, he was making sure he trained it all. A pair of poles at the end of the course for left and right rear kicks completed his regimen.

Radien would alternate between doing this entire routine, and gathering some food to eat between sessions. His physiology as a Death World Vulpian made his stomach much more efficient and durable, so he was naturally able to imbibe on species of berries that would otherwise make an ordinary mortal Human drop dead on the spot. Granted, he would end up retching up the half-digested Reaper's Bush Berries less than a minute later, but even with spots in his eyes, he figured he was getting off easy.

This incident, which took place about ten days in, gave him the idea for a new Autopsionic Cantrip: *Irongut*. Where the Aura would, in a time of need, break down anything Radien ingested into its base chemicals for more compatible digestion. Anything that could be safely ingested would be, and anything else would be filtered and diluted again and again by the Aura before hitting the walls of his throat and stomach.

Radien soon began to meditate in order to configure the Irongut Cantrip. In his mind, he used the Aura to create and flesh out the details of these new enhancements that would aid him in day-to-day life as much as they would him in battle, and he began to understand that there were great battles to come as the Dark Six's encroachment upon reality loomed.

*They are coming. They are returning to this universe to finish what they started, so long ago. The Second War for Reality... the final war for reality.*

Radien began to remember the conversation he had with Veralis after exiting the Field of Unreality, having just become his true Death World Vulpian form. The two were within Torvaltyne Bastion itself, after the revelry in Kendradeyne that celebrated The

Unmaker's defeat.

"I can't help but hope that this is what I've been preparing for, what I've been training for," he had told Veralis. "On Earth, I made a lot of plans, kept myself ready for many things, but I could never even imagine that I might find myself fighting on the front lines of the universe's war, in the name of life. And though I am eager to join the battle, I also feel hesitant..."

The Irongut Cantrip continued to configure itself as Radien recalled this memory in his meditation.

"So what is it that has zeal dampened by trepidation?" Micah had asked him at the mead hall within Torvaltyne Bastion when he had almost the exact same conversation with the Redarian after having it with Veralis.

"I know what the Radien I *want* to be is like," he admitted within the dark corner of the bar, which was part of its design. Almost, if not every seat at the Honor's Stand Mead Hall was set up as a dark corner to brood mysteriously over a drink within. It was a good place to drink, and ponder. "He knows what he's doing whenever he does it, he's clever, skilled, tactful, and he's eloquent, too... he always uses exactly the words he means to, and without hesitation or falter. But this isn't a matter of me questioning if I am that Radien, or whether or not I'm capable of being him."

When he had this conversation with Arakai at Kianar's Folly, one the more 'generally social' of the six taverns at the Fortress Borfus, Arakai certainly had a response to that doubt within him.

"The Effigy told you to claim your victory, Radien.

Not just victory against The Unmaker, but the victory that is *becoming* that Radien," the Cynofrax-Crimsonian Vulpian explained. Though Veralis's fur patterns were lighter yellows and oranges, Arakai had the distinct pattern of whites, deep reds, greys, and blacks that was the appearance of a cross fox, though as Vulpian, he stood on two legs. And talked. And was a pretty cool guy overall.

"You made yourself that Radien when you fried The Unmaker," Jarrek Wöllschlager reminded in his own conversation with Radien at another one of the Fortress's pubs, the Pulsar Club, which was more specifically tailored towards being a more lively club-like scene. At least the mixed drinks had effort put into making them compliment the atmosphere, rather than being offensively overpriced two-ingredient 'get buzzed quick' non-cocktails of liquor plus soda. It was a reason Radien never visited those kinds of places back on Earth, but the fact it wasn't the case here made this place infinitely more worthwhile. "The moment you turned that guy to dust, the universe heard your declaration that you *were* that Radien."

"And so the universe has begun to learn the name Miles Sorvenjar Radien. The time is *now* to be that Radien you've always wanted to be, more than ever," Miirkae had encouraged when the conversation took place between those two.

"Besides, if the universe doesn't find that Radien to its liking... then it can burn for all I care," Dorg added when he and Radien had their own conversation following the regeneration. "And I know you'd agree with that."

Radien had nodded as he and Dorg finished their steins of mead, before slamming them down on the wooden counter resolutely back at the Honor's Stand Mead Hall. Not only did this in-house brewery, meadery and distillery make it easier on the supply front by meaning that such drink needed not be imported, but it was also the case that Radien wanted those things on-site. Win-win overall.

Radien's eyes shot back open in the forest clearing within Azhenar. He looked at the locator beacon on his backpack. It was blinking. This was the last day, and the Irongut Cantrip had finished configuring to boot. He looked at the wooden poles he had placed within this circle, and took mental note of the course, so he could rebuild it in Torvaltyne Bastion's indoor courtyard. With The Aura's Eidetic Memory and Clairvoyant Recall capabilities, Radien wouldn't have to rely on raw memory alone. It was like storing the information his eyes had seen to the Cloud, though in this case, the 'cloud' was the lifeblood of the universe itself.

And not a moment too soon, as Radien's head whipped around to the sound of rushing water. A flash flood was inbound, and that's when he remembered that the area was prone to them. This one was big, too. No flash flood on Earth would ever be this size, it was like a tsunami on land, crashing through the woods.

"You must be joking!" he called out as he ran towards one of taller, old-growth trees and leaping onto it, jamming his claws into the wood to start climbing to see if he could get above the wave that was inbound.

Though admirable, it almost worked against him, as he suddenly realized that the wave was too tall for him to scale out of its way. He was about halfway up. The next best thing he could do was go down, and anchor himself to the trees with his claws, and try to tough it out on the bottom, where the waters, which would still be harsh and unforgiving, would be at their lowest levels of malice.

He took several deep breaths as the wall of water approached, then held out his right hand to conjure a shield with the Aura around him. The water slammed into the shield, pushing against it with tremendous force, and Radien quickly sharpened the 'edges' and center of the directional shield to cut through the water and make it barrage around him, instead of blocking it from going through him force-on-force. Still anchored to the tree, which remained strong as it likely had across thousands of floods like this over its lifetime. A log bounced off of the shield, one of the poles Radien had set for his training course. Good thing he had that Eidetic Memory, courtesy of The Aura, so that he couldn't forget what that course he built looked like.

The rush ended almost as quickly as it had started. Within a few minutes, the water had passed, and it had only left behind its traces in the form of soaked ground and displaced mounds of dirt and rock. The clearing was washed away almost completely, revealing that the dirt had simply been lying atop a sheet of bedrock, with a granite tablet embedded within. Just like in Jaltai-Vuul, it bore an inscription in the Death Worlder language, *Zhernreli-Orul.*

*Pir Strell-ald pir Jasaln, Nejtarn ka'Nejtarn.*

*Whether by a hair or a mountain, a missed strike misses all the same.*

Though the more literal translation was '*a miss is a miss*', the message was clear.

"What even are these things?" Radien wondered aloud. "And how exactly is it that I'm finding them out here? I wasn't even looking for either this, or the one in Jaltai-Vuul..." He placed his hand on this slab like he did the one before, and the scripture glowed with bright red with a *bong* sound, just like the last one did. "I get the feeling there's one in each zone, and I should find them all."

Finding one of the wooden poles of his improvised training course, Radien stuck it back in the ground, and over the rest of the day, rebuilt the course. During that night, he ran it one more time. The first pole, ten left straight punches. On the tenth strike, he threw it full-force, full-power, and the pole snapped in half at the impact site. Seemingly inspired, Radien then performed one strike to each of the poles, the strike that he had been practicing on them. They broke each time, to the punches, the knife hands, the sword hands, the ridge hands, the elbows, and the kicks. The last pole was met with a wheel kick that tore straight through, the chunk of wood flying off into the woods, and the rest of the top half simply falling onto the dirt with a *thud*.

The buzzing of the retrieval craft's turbines signaled to him that this second segment of the Gauntlet of Doom, in Azhenar, was at its close. Next up was Bassoron.

# 4

# BASSORON BLACK ZONE

**S**pitemonger Station was the name of the main settlement within Bassoron, called such for the more infamous trait of the zone, the fact that it often takes a lot of spite to get through all thirty days. The mountains of this zone were of Radien's least favorite type; less 'mountain' as much as 'glorified piles of dirt and root', that always made them such a contemptuous hassle to climb. Footholds nearly fiction, these annoying excuses for actual proper mountains were easily the least fun kind of them all. Indeed, the *wrong* kind of mountains, to put it bluntly.

"Hill or valley?!" the Jumpmaster yelled as the back doors prepared to open, and let him out into the Bassoron Black Zone.

"Hill!" Radien responded. With three one-day ration packs as one of the allowed pieces of equipment under the Doombringer's Rules, Radien wouldn't need to worry about food while finding a shelter, for at least the first three days of the search.

The turbines stabilized the aircraft as it hovered over the ground.

"Looks good?!"

"Aye! I'm heading out!"

Radien's feet landed on the twigs and leaves that was this glorified hill's surface terrain, before he turned around and saluted the pilot looking down at him with the traditional Death World Vulpian salute, hand across chest, into diagonally pointing at the ground, little finger curled in while the other four remained straight. There was actually a surprising amount of nuance to that salute on Raon-Arashal, it served as both a bow for martial artists before a match, and the defensive army's salute. Little finger always curled in by default, and you're *supposed* to have the remaining four straight, but you could also choose to curl one in to express disdain for your opponent, typically as a 'counter-dishonor' sort of thing, like why someone might just dodge during a Sumo match. Only because your enemy did it first. The more fingers curled in, the more clear your dissent. Saluting someone with a closed fist the whole way through was effectively a challenge to a fight to the death.

Regardless, Radien did manage to find a dug-out cavern within the hills, and it looked pretty unclaimed. The twig layers hadn't been disturbed, nobody had been here for a while, from the looks of things. The wind blew mysteriously as if on-cue, and some of the twigs were brushed away by the breeze to reveal a flat stone surface beneath them. This was a *cave* he was about to walk into. Weapons-grade cave, like the one on Aldin Moon where the Spirit of Scorn he had released lived within.

"No symbols on the ground, that's a good start," Radien muttered to himself as he held the Borfblade at his hip, and stepped forward, into the cavern, sword at the ready. Whatever this was, it was old and powerful, and was not a living conscious system.

Radien began to hear a whooshing sound in his ears as he approached, that transitioned into drumbeats, like a line of timpani. His eyes locked onto an amber orb with streaks of black running through it like the atmosphere of a gas giant planet.

"What are you?" he asked aloud, though this was a raw manifestation of Psionic power he was dealing with. It was like a Font, but a traveling one.

"Wait… I know what you are," he then corrected himself. "I encountered something like you on Earth once, back when I was there, a Human… and it looked like I had clipped outside the fucking map…"

He continued to stare at the orb as it pulsated in place, within this cavern.

"But you're not *that*, are you?" Radien continued. "Same idea, though. A ripple in space, and you're the droplet of rain."

The orb continued to pulse, though it remained still. Radien could hear the timpani again.

"Name yourself," he asked the orb, and all suddenly fell dead silent. It was as if the world around him had suddenly escaped to the void between realities, and he had entered a pocket dimension of some kind, where only he and the orb existed. First, he heard a spark in his mind. It was trying to communicate telepathically with him, so he allowed his mind to receive the words:

*Nel Jalfjaa.*

"Radien," he introduced himself.

The orb, this *Nel Jalfjaa* suddenly vanished into thin air, seemingly poofing out of existence with a shower of golden dust. But the dust seemed to be laced with raw power, like this dust was power itself.

Radien let it hit his hands, but kept them still, holding completely still, until the dust had settled entirely, and vanished on the floor once it made contact. The particulates that landed on his hands, or handpaws, rather, similarly vanished. The rest of reality seemed to reconstruct itself around him, flushing out from the cave's entrance. The locator beacon on Radien's backpack beeped. Time must have been distorted, somehow all thirty days he was to spend in Bassoron had passed. Radien looked at the cavern wall where the *Nel Jalfjaa* once rested. Another granite plaque, with red runes in the Zhernrel-Vuljar script, transposed into Latin characters so that Radien could instinctively pronounce the way they were arranged.

*Anan akar alt, dokja sehljalv-ald ja-sliin. Jagikall fjure Ananagjeir.*

*Time does all things, whether heal a wound or cut it deeper. Progress is made all the same.*

Radien placed his hand on the stone slab and the runes glowed their bright red, before he turned around to leave the cave. But he turned back as he heard stone grinding against stone. The granite slab with that Death World Vulpian phrase vanished into the stone, like it was becoming part of the wall, to Radien's immense confusion.

"It's because something's about to burst through that wall, that's why," a voice said from behind him, and his head whipped around to see a hooded Laksorian charging a blast of power, hurtling it at the wall and blowing a sizable hole through it. Radien speedily drew the Borfblade and set himself in guard, his empty right hand crackling with azure power.

"As in, I'm about to blow the wall," the Laksorian said, and Radien responded with an '*ah*' as he sheathed the cutlass. The two looked through the hole that had just indeed been blown in the wall, and there was something on the other side, a chamber of some sort.

Radien's new companion motioned in an 'after you' manner, and Radien went in first.

"Why me first?" he asked.

"You're better with the sword than I am at powers. If something requires swords, you should be at the front, obviously. Kaltir, by the way."

"Radien."

"Gauntlet of Doom?"

"That's the one."

"That's a good one."

Radien and Kaltir explored the chamber. The air hadn't been breathed by any living creature for centuries, except maybe local moss and insects. Other than that, it was staggeringly well-preserved.

"Nobody's breathed this air for centuries," Radien commented. "What is this place?"

"A ruin, obviously," Kaltir responded.

"Right, I can tell that much, but what *kind* of ruin? Who built it? What was it? What flavor of ruins are we dealing with here?"

"Hmmm... ruined."

"Fuck you."

Kaltir burst out cackling, and Radien soon chuckled to himself in response. "Okay, that was funny," the Laksorian finally said eventually. Radien nodded as he examined and rummaged through the ruins, though being careful enough to not actually break anything.

"Oooh, bottle!" Radien exclaimed from behind a counter. Whatever this ruin was, they had found the bar. "This looks like fun stuff."

Kaltir's eyes flashed green as he examined the bottle, its liquid still inside. "You're right. Elurian Power Brandy."

"Holy shit," Radien said. "This might be the last bottle in the universe, then."

Radien's eyes flashed amber as he examined the bottle's liquid this time.

"What are you doing?" Kaltir asked.

"I'm looking through the chemical bondings and distributions, trying to reverse-engineer this stuff so that the recipe can be recorded and re-introduced to the universe. If this is the last bottle, we've got to know what it's made of."

"Here, let me help." Kaltir began to move his arms as emerald-green power surged through his body, collecting it into an orb that he held with both hands. The two began to see the place rebuild itself, like they were opening a window into time itself, placing themselves back at the memory point. of when this place was alive and bustling. And it was. Despite being on Raon-Arashal, despite being in one of the Black Zones, there was an entire community of Elurians within Bassoron. Lysanarr, too. Radien could see the two species mingling with each other as the place rebuilt itself around them.

"A Distillery-Chapel," Kaltir said. "A hidden Distillery-Chapel within Bassoron Black Zone!"

"The crafting of libations is a sacred practice on Gelvetori," Radien noted. "That's probably why it's a Distillery-Chapel. The Lysanarr factor."

"And the Elurians, their architectural capabilities were on par with the Talvas Vulpians. They probably built this place."

"There! I see it!"

Radien and Kaltir rushed over to where Radien was running towards, the Power Brandy being prepared and bottled. "Focus here, Kaltir!"

Kaltir pushed his hands, coursing with the smaragdine flow, focusing on finding out the process that made the liquid about to enter this glass bottle that had just been finished being hand-crafted and cooled only a few days before, likely by the resident Bottlesmith or Glassblower. The terms were synonymous in the Lysanarr language.

Radien and Kaltir watched as the process first was rewound in time, then played forward, and Radien made sure to pay absolute attention to what was happening, making sure his eyes grabbed every detail so that he could reconstruct what he was seeing, thanks to The Aura's eidetic memory capabilities.

"I've got it! You can let go now!" Radien instructed, and Kaltir nodded, relaxing his arms and letting the crackling green sphere fall from his hands and hit the floor, disintegrating as the room reformed itself back into its present-day manner.

"They may have been the last ones," Radien said. "After Caltoran happened, maybe even after he died, they might've still been alive."

"Probably just stopped having descendants," Kaltir added, to which Radien agreed.

"Who the hell would want to bring someone into the universe at a time like that, anyway? Anyone having kids in a time like Caltoran's fallout would've clearly *despised* children," Radien added.

"Thus, it seems abandoned. But where are the residents?"

"Buried here."

Radien held his hand out, letting it swirl with a golden yellow trail of power, as he used the Aura to find out the answer to Kaltir's question. "They lived their lives, died and were buried."

The Laksorian nodded somberly, and the two looked back at the bottle of glowing green drink, with a heavy sigh, as Radien realized who he was in the company of.

"That's not possible. Is it?" Radien asked.

"It is, though I wish it were not." Caltoran sighed once more. "Can't even seem to get dying right, huh?"

"I would consider that a positive trait."

"I did too, until it happened."

Radien allowed a vision of the past to enter his mind, that Caltoran began showing him.

*The battle was long and hard,* Caltoran narrated in

that shared headspace. *But it had been won. My presence assured it. But in the aftermath, as everyone caught their breath, counted their limbs and how many Demons they killed, one of the enemy soldiers, a Converted, used its vessel's last breath to leap from it... to me.*

*It had won before I was even finished screaming as blackness filled my vision, and it was as though I was locked in a great void within my own mind, like my brain had been removed from my skull, and I was stranded in the void it left in my head.*

Radien's vision returned to the mortal universe, back in the old ruins of a Distillery-Chapel.

"By the time I clawed my way out, it had all already happened," Caltoran despaired, before using his power to project a massive starmap, planets teeming with life and technology. "All this... was gone."

Radien looked at the ruins that were what those planets and stars looked like today. Some were utterly bombed-out cities, others where oceans had become desert, and some entire solar systems that no longer existed, that had been destroyed entirely, even the star at its center of mass itself.

"You've walked out of the frying pan and into the fire of the universe, Radien," Caltoran said with an apologetic tone. "I know you are a Death Worlder, but I can sense you didn't... start as one."

"That's true," Radien said with a sigh of his own. "Caltoran... I know these look like ashes to you, and by any other measure, they are. But even these ashes and embers glow brighter as a beacon than any I've known before!"

Radien reached his arm out and placed it on Caltoran's head, now he was the one sharing a memory.

*The cage you speak of, Caltoran. That cage the Demon coward put you within, in your own mind, too small to stand up in and not large enough to lie down in, that's what life was on that backwater planet, with an uncompromisingly corrupt species that was called Earth. It was appropriate, honestly, since its translation was 'dirt', and that planet was fucking dirt.*

*Not even the kind you can make something out of, not even something to just pass the damn time with, no, it had to be the dullest and most useless dirt in all creation, just to make it sting more!*

*My wanderlust, my thirst to partake in life itself, was squandered and crushed, decided long before I had even fucking got there that all roads led only to disappointment, and a death without the decency to be swift!*

The vision ended, Radien stopped showing Caltoran Earth. He took a few steps back, shocked at what he saw, and what it turned him into.

"Stars and void..." Caltoran couldn't help but utter an old slang term, akin to 'by the gods'. "Radien... when the student is ready, the master will appear."

"There's something to be said about the search for the master, too."

"Agreed. I will endeavor to find you in the next Black Zone you enter. Which one?"

"Denrenath is next."

Caltoran nodded as he exited the cave.

"Caltoran!" Radien called out, holding up the

bottle of glowing green liquid. "Did you want to at least try it?"

Caltoran scoffed as he realized the answer was yes, strutting over to the bar counter that Radien was standing behind, two glasses had already been poured. "It's funny, you know," the Laksorian commented. "Here I thought *I* would be the one where you stand."

"And I thought I'd be the one where you stand."

Caltoran sat down at the barstool, Radien standing behind the counter, the both of them soon putting their hands around the glasses with measures of the Elurian Power Brandy. "I think we both stand at the same place, in a strange way."

"Aye, I get it."

The glasses clinked together, and both sipped, before downing the contents, and exchanging comments.

"Oh, shit, that is *good.*"

"Fuck, that's powerful stuff. The universe needs more of this."

Radien poured himself and Caltoran another glass. "I've got the recipe stored in my head, now. During that little past-memory thing, I found the recipe book and got a good look at it. Once things are a little calmer for the universe, I'll write it down and recreate it."

"Oh, good. Elurian Power Brandy is one thing I miss from... back when they were still around."

"Caltoran, no one blames you for what happened, only that coward Demon who—"

"*Do you think that matters to me?!*"

The empty glass was flung across the room by

Caltoran swiping at it with his hands, and the shatter punctuated the air louder than anything that had been in this hall for centuries. "This hall is empty, because of me! That brandy, and the people who made it, they're not here anymore, *because of me!* It is on *my* hands that the blood of so many entire species and worlds are stained!"

Caltoran just breathed heavily, having stood up from the stool he was sitting on seconds ago. Breathing slowly and heavily, and physically forcing back the very idea of even a single tear.

"No, I don't," Radien admitted. "And I know that because if it were me, I'd be exactly where you are now."

"We're one and the same, you and I." Caltoran chuckled. "We've just... we've walked different paths, but we're the same kind of person, the same soul... aren't we?"

"I suppose so," Radien said, placing the glass on the table. "The stars themselves may be ashes, but these are the kinds of ashes I couldn't even dream of having."

Caltoran looked over to Radien, visibly surprised.

"It may be you, then."

"What?"

"My successor. The Tenth Defender."

"Caltoran, the last breath of a Defender is the first breath of their successor. And you're here, talking to me! I think that somewhat disqualifies me from the position."

"My last breath took place when that coward Demon wormed its way into my mind."

"Bugger. You're right, that would be a way to interpret those words, *Djal. Fuck.*"

"It seems we're both at the frontiers of our

knowledge.”

"Maybe we can both teach each other something. I hope I'll either see you in Denrenath, or any of the ones after that."

Radien began to walk out, leaving the bottle behind for Caltoran. He then spun around and walked back to the Laksorian staring at the bottle of glowing green Power Brandy, and placed two fingers on the side of his head, that glowed with The Aura's power.

"The recipe," Radien said. "You look and sound like you need it."

Caltoran simply nodded as Radien headed out of the cave to meet the hovercraft that would take him to Cannonade Station, the station within Denrenath Black Zone.

# 5

# DENRENATH BLACK ZONE

adien practically hit the ground running on his exit. He was starting to get the hang of things. Between the tornado-stricken plains and the Red Inlet, a beach crawling with siren-like creatures that honestly may as well just be called Sirens, Radien decided he was confident enough to try the beach.

Once he got to the cliffs that overlooked the rocky beach, Radien could see the buggers sitting on some of the rocks, that soon scattered at the sight of a Death Worlder, here to survive and train himself to never succumb.

With many of the caves themselves that lined the Dover-resemblant cliffs themselves being Sirens in their own right with how good of caves they looked like, Radien's eyes switched to the amber glow of Second Sight. He scanned the cliffs and the caves, looking for one that wasn't planning to swallow him within its stone walls. There had to be at least *one*.

But because he wasn't paying attention to what

was behind him, one such gust of wind that would form a tornado that Denrenath's fields were known for, Radien was flung over the cliffside, to meet the rocks below. Though blasting raw power through his hands like stabilizers, trying to slow his fall with his powers, channeling it through hands and feet both, trying to see if he could make *something* work.

The fall began to slow down, he was no longer at terminal velocity.

Soon, the effect was visible.

Soon, he was simply hovering in the air, twenty feet away from what would've been a painful landing otherwise. He held himself there, chuckling as he caught his balance, in midair. He was hovering, and there was an extra step that could be taken off of that.

He chose to set himself on the ground. "Soon," he commented. "But holy shit, I can *definitely* do that, and I've totally got to."

Suddenly, a voice spoke up. Radien's head whipped around to meet it, because it was not possible, that voice. He knew that voice. "Effigy?!"

Radien stood, frozen. He suddenly felt the touch of a stone grey canvas jacket on his shoulders, a black t-shirt on top of it, and olive green pants on his legs. His shoes were Wolverine-branded steel-toed boots. Had to have the actual steel toe. Anything short of real metal felt... inadequate. He felt and knew that suddenly, he was a Human of Earth again.

"I... no, you can't be real," he said. "I can't be seeing you! You're gone from my life! I've moved on from being *you!*"

Radien threw out his hand and blasted the air before him. Both souls suddenly existed in the same place, past and present had become one, and two. Two separate bodies, whose consciousnesses were one and the same, just at different points in time.

"What the hell, what is this?" Radien asked.

"You're not the Effigy. The Effigy doesn't talk!" Miles said. "You can't be real!"

Radien dropped back into a horse stance, facing Miles, holding his palm out, though his sword was still at his hip. Having deliberately chosen not to grab the sword, he signaled to the Human that he had no intent to fight this day. A blue spark bapped in and out of existence in Radien's outstretched palm.

"We are one, at different points in time!" Radien exclaimed. "Protocol of Vigilance! ETF Delta-one!"

The Human, having entered a guarded stance, ready to fight, tilted his head slightly. "The prompt is Kierkegaard!"

"The response is *do you think me the kind of fool who thinks that the world gets better simply because it praises him?!*"

Miles lowered his hands to his hips, and nodded to Radien. "Speak. You've earned the chance."

Radien nodded, left hand upon the Borfblade, but tapping his fingers across it, as if to symbolize that Miles wasn't who it was meant for. "This is a test, for both of us. I'm being tested right now, and so are you, I think."

Miles nodded. "Accepted."

"I'm on another planet, another galaxy, undergoing a rite of passage-style trial, I'm in month three of twenty-two.”

“Fuck, that sounds awesome.”

“Oh, it’s a fucking *blast*. I’ve found like what, three different locations to build a mysterious lair within!”

“Oooh, that *is* good. We’re the same consciousness?”

“Aye.”

“Okay, accepted. Everything’s checking out for me right now. What do you need?”

“I’m not sure... I think I need to survive this.”

“Well, so do I.”

Radien took a step back. He knew what that meant. He knew where Miles was in the timeline.

“Shit.” Miles grunted. “I know myself well enough to know *that* look, even if it’s on a vulpine face. How bad is what awaits me?”

“It resolves.”

“Resolves...”

“Retribution is unnecessary, due to the event’s nature. But in the end, loose ends are gone. Nothing will bind you, soon enough.”

Miles nodded. “I’ll consider that fortunate.”

“You will. I still do.”

“Don’t name it to me, knowing the future can change it.”

“Oh, believe me, I wasn’t planning to.”

Within the vision, Radien stood across from the reflection of the person he used to be. Death World Vulpian stood across from Human, an echo of the past.

The two finally relaxed their shoulders, breathing

a simultaneous sigh of relief.

"So, what's called me here?" Miles asked. "What's managed to rip me all the way to this point in time, out of my own?"

"The *Nel Jalfjaa,* I'd imagine."

"What does that mean?"

"Heart of the Flaming Sword."

Miles threw up his eyebrows and shifted his head, indicating he wanted to hear more.

"On this planet, it's... a good omen. To all involved, whether they see it, or feel the effects of it. Wait... how the hell do *I* know this now?"

"It's funneling you information, isn't it?"

"Fuck, you're right! I can feel the flow of its power boring into my mind! It's filling my head with... raw history! Like my mind is becoming the archive of Raon-Arashal itself!"

Radien's eyes shot open, and the pulsing orb that he saw not long ago, that named itself the *Nel Jalfjaa.*

"What are you doing here?" Radien asked aloud as his head pounded to the beat of the timpani that was the orchestra of the amber-black orb's violent spinning in place. "What do you want?!"

*<When the student is ready, the master will appear.>*

"Shit... uh... but there's something to be said about the search for the master! When they can't show themselves, the student must seek them out!"

*<Indeed. You shall prove to be a worthy challenge.>*

The vision suddenly ended, and Radien's locator beacon was beeping. He had suddenly passed the days once again.

"Time-slip? Okay, *that* feels like cheating, but whatever."

He stood within a cavern within Denrenath, and after a quick check from The Aura, learned that he had been the only one inside or out in the last thirty days.

The *Nel Jalfjaa* hovered before him, before shooting off once again like it had before. Behind it, a granite tablet, with runes glowing red, that Radien's hand had already touched before he realized it, to make the runic text glow red

*Sjelliarae-zesh. Arkeir flowval kyrald-ald duul, il Koulhaanth tlelgi zukiir.*

*The wheel turns now. Ride alongside it until you are ready to face it alone, or be crushed by its gears.*

"I am no child of destiny," Miles said to himself as he stood beside Radien once again. "How the hell am I supposed to accept this?"

"Fuck, I don't know either. I don't like the idea of being some everchosen champion, myself."

"Shit... well, you said you were on month three of twenty-two?"

"Aye, that's the number."

"Okay, what's the pattern here?"

"So far, the sequence has been spent training, standing before a possible mentor, and debating with a reflection from my past."

"See if the pattern holds, that's my advice. I will, too. We'll have an answer in three months, it seems."

Radien nodded to Miles. "Well, if nothing else, I'm glad to at least know I've always been me."

Miles shrugged his shoulders as he started to flicker out of existence, the vision was ending. "I'm similarly glad to know I'm never gonna stop being me, if nothing else."

The turbines were heard outside the cave, and one of the crewmembers was shouting to get on board. Apparently, the tide was about to come in, the high tide that would submerge this cave in water.

"Save the water-breathing Cantrips for Ilkai, Tactician! You're good in this zone, let's go!"

Radien nodded, running towards the turbine and jumping aboard, his arm wrapping around the Death Worlder crewman helping him aboard as the craft lifted off.

"You found a good cave right there!" Jarrek said over the comms, piloting the craft. "It looks like you're having a great time so far!"

"Jarrek?!" Radien yelled into the comm-piece once he got a headset on. "What in all the realms are you doing here?!"

"Come on, you're doing the Gauntlet of Doom?! How could I miss out on this?! I've *gotta* see how much grime is gonna be on your fur once you're done with Melketh-Iklar!"

"Shit, is that the fucking swamp zone?"

The crewman nodded to Radien. Melketh-Iklar was indeed the swamp zone.

# 6

# Dromos-Balth Black Zone

It was called that, because this was the place that the previous Haji-Son Exemplar had died in, unfit to survive the tundra of Dromos-Balth. Of course, Dromos-Kaledrion himself was easily the least popular Exemplar in modern Haji-Son history, so nobody really minded. In fact, the three survival stations in the zone had names translating as *"Dromos the fool,"* *"Dromos the wimp,"* and *"Hell yeah, Dromos died here,"* in one of the four Haji-Son languages.

It wasn't bad, this tundra. But Radien could sense that there was some weird Psionic fluctuations in this area, that seemed dead set on more quickly draining one's energy than your average tundra. This sort of 'boost' that the tundra itself was under was likely the cause of Dromos-Kaledrion's death, succumbing to unnatural tiredness and falling asleep, never to wake up again, to the relief of a universe that was quite frankly, done with his bullshit.

The tundra was alarmingly flat, enough to vanish

beyond the horizon. Featureless ground, dotted with patches of dark green grass, though mostly just permanently frozen dirt, that didn't even crunch beneath Radien's footsteps.

"Something's not right here..," Radien said to himself. "This place is dead."

There wasn't even a gust of wind to blow ominously. Everything was just so still and silent. Darkness seemed to bleed from the ground, as the wisps of black smoke bled from the earth and caused the hairs on Radien's legs to stand on end. He looked down and saw the blackening ground before him, stepping back and placing his hand on the Borfblade in its sheath.

The blackness seeping from the ground suddenly pulled away and lifted into the air, a dark cloud of doom that hovered before the Death World Vulpian, his sword already in his hand, ready to fight.

The dark cloud slammed onto the ground and coalesced into a physical form. A Voidspawn. But it looked... different, somehow. Unlike the Voidspawns Radien had encountered and slew before.

"What's different about you?" Radien asked. "You're not like other Voidspawns I've seen."

The manifestation of the dark power between realities finally spoke. "I am older and far more powerful than any of my kinsmen you have met in battle!"

It conjured a sword, adding the blade to its form. Radien stood ready, and the two clashed. The strikes each fighter threw were swift, as were their parries. Radien kept blocking and evading the Voidblade that kept clashing with the Borfblade, and it couldn't be sure which one threatened to shatter at the sheer vicious force the two imparted against each other, and the speed at which the blows were being deflected.

The Voidspawn shifted out of existence, warping behind Radien, who anticipated the move and simply held the Borfblade still in the air where the Voidspawn soon landed.

"Come on, man," Radien said once it had impaled itself on his sword. "Teleporting behind your enemies? That's rookie shit."

Radien yanked the sword out of the Voidspawn and spun around with a side kick to knock it away. The creature, unable to heal itself from the sheer bite of the Hunderfold Novasteel Cutlass, convulsed on the ground as darkness seemed to spill away from it, like it was bleeding out.

"What... are you?" it asked.

"I am Radien."

"You have told me who, but not *what*," it sputtered. "You don't even know whom you have defeated... don't you?"

"Feel free to enlighten me."

The creature simply cackled as its dark form sank into the ground, dispersing in its death throes.

"All right then..." Radien muttered as he pressed forth. He wasn't entirely sure where he'd be pressing forth too, Dromos-Balth Black Zone being a flat tundra that the curvature of Raon-Arashal could be observed within. A quick calculation assisted by the Aura later, and Radien actually figured Raon-Arashal to be about double and a half the surface area of Earth in size.

Radien continued to wander the tundra plains of Dromos-Balth for three days, not bothering to sleep, allowing what food was already in his system from his stay at the station to sustain him. With his Death Worlder physiology and the efficiency thereof, he never had to use one of the three ration packs until about a week in, on average.

The silence of the Dromos-Balth Black Zone was almost deafening in and of its own self. Night soon came, and Radien sat on his knees at a fire he had placed on the ground with The Aura. No firewood to be found in this place, it was just a ball of flame, flickering as it hovered above the ground.

Radien's head whipped around as he heard footsteps behind him. Caltoran then sat down in front of the fire.

"Not exactly hard to find things here," Caltoran said. "Especially a fire at night."

There was another Death Worlder next to Caltoran, who joined in. "Gauntlet?" he asked Radien, and Radien nodded in response. "Nice."

The three sat at the fire, and Radien funneled some power into it to make it large enough for all of them.

Agranz, the third member of this little bonfire gathering, reached into his backpack and grabbed some things for Radien.

"Here, these'll fit you better than they do me," Agranz said, tossing the solid black t-shirt and olive green cargo pants to Radien. "Picked 'em up in Jessel-Tarn. That's the fun one."

"Is it?" Radien asked, and Caltoran nodded as the Laksorian used some of his own power to conjure something to roast over the fire, hovering it over the flame and letting telekinesis turn it slowly and steadily. "Well, clearly I'll be finding out soon enough."

"Saving Relanon for last?" Agranz asked, and Radien nodded again. "Smart, that's the one you just kinda turn your brain off for a while in."

Agranz grabbed a book from his pack, and handed it to Radien. "Here. This'll tell you which plants are the fun ones."

"Thanks, Agranz. You don't need this?"

"Bah, I've memorized it cover-to-cover. It's better off in someone else's hands, someone who's still learning."

"I've a lot to learn."

"Even so, you've done well so far," Caltoran commented. "What you know has gotten you this far already."

Radien breathed in and out. "I guess I can't argue with that."

That familiar amber-black orb, the Nel Jalfjaa, rippled itself into existence, as if to join the bonfire as its fourth participant. Caltoran was calm, Agranz was intrigued.

"Nel Jalfjaa," Agranz greeted. "You honor us."

"And confuse the hell out of me," Radien added.

<I'm sure it's not exactly fond, my response that my means and purposes are difficult to explain... but it is true.>

"Well, even Grand Psionic Entities have to pass

the time somehow." Caltoran admitted, to which Agranz nodded.

"So that's the term for them?" Radien said. "Beings like the Aura Prism, the Emerald of Quast, and what have you?"

"Emerald of Quast is a Keystone Gem, not a GPE," Agranz corrected. "But yeah, the Aura Prism's one."

*<How fares that grumpy old gem, anyway?>*

Radien burst out laughing. "I've never heard anyone call the Prism *that!*"

"Oh, he totally is, though!" Caltoran said, chuckling as well. "This one time, I had just cleaned out an entire marauder citadel, right? Even did a hell of a one-liner at their warlord, too! Tossed him a sack of his bodyguards' heads, and just said 'don't worry, not like they were using them anyway'."

Radien spat out the water he was sipping on, bursting out laughing again as Agranz let out a hearty one as well.

"When I told the Prism, you know what he said? 'A high level of brutality indeed'."

The Nel Jalfjaa's amber pulses flashed as if it were somehow laughing, too.

*<That... is indeed something the Prism would say. I think he's forgotten how to have fun in his old age.>*

"Probably just bitter about having to stay on Cynofrax all day, keeping strong the barriers between realities," Caltoran commented. "I'd say he needs to get out more, but I'm not sure how he even would."

"I mean, Grand Psionic Entity and all, surely he can summon a projection his consciousness can inhabit?"

Radien asked.

"Dunno, never asked."

*<I don't think he's ever thought of that, come to think of it. Radien, you should bring that up next time you see the Aura Prism.>*

Radien paused for a moment as he thought.

*<He doesn't like to ask for help. It's a trait you and the Prism both bear. Trust a Grand Psionic Entity, if nothing else. The Prism does sense kinship in you. Suddenly brought into a universe you barely understand, knowing only that it needs help and defense, and hardly knowing how, though help is the only thing you want to give. Flying by the skin of your teeth for gods only know how many years... just scrambling for a chance for things to calm down for a moment, so you can at least take a breath and gather your thoughts...>*

"Familiar story," Radien commented. Caltoran nodded. Agranz was preparing to take his leave.

"I'm sure we'll be seeing more of each other, Radien. You just don't need me for this bit," Agranz said, and Radien nodded. Caltoran and the Nel Jalfjaa remained at the fire.

"Here I was, prepared to live a long and angry life on Earth, and die an unfulfilled old man, when I hardly want to grow old at all."

Caltoran was next to take his leave, nodding to Radien and the Nel Jalfjaa before departing. Soon, it was just the two. One Death World Vulpian, one Grand Psionic Entity.

"I'm so damned confused," Radien finally admitted once Caltoran was out of earshot. "I'm still learning new things even about that first day on Earth, when it all started. I keep finding out new things about just how many hands had cards to play there, on Earth, of all fucking places…"

The Nel Jalfjaa simply hovered.

"Confused as hell, too, about seeing you here. Caltoran, too. So many names that mean so many things, and… and then there's me. Just… still flying by the seat of my pants in all this."

<Answers will come, Miles Sorvenjar Radien. They will not elude you forever. And you will have those answers before they are needed in the days to come.>

"The days to come… the Final War for Reality. I cant hardly even bother to call it the second now, because I know that's what it is, the fight against the Dark Six that's coming."

<Even the lords of evil cannot bring to fall the universe in a single day,> the Nel Jalfjaa assured. <The Unmaker could not. The Opponent Unbeatable could not. There is no reality in which it all can come crashing down in an instant, just because one person, even if the Defender, decided to take a breather.>

"This *is* my breather, you know," Radien said. "Veralis managed to obnoxious-technicality her way into being able to order me to take a vacation. And of course, Micah was there to make sure I got started."

More footsteps were heard approaching. Radien looked up, and saw something else impossible.

"Arakai?!"

"Good to see you too, Radien. Nel Jalfjaa."

The Nel Jalfjaa let out a single pulse of amber light

as its greeting.

"Well, what are you doing here?!"

"Jessel-Tarn shares a land border with Dromos-Balth," Arakai explained. "I was running one of the spots there and heard you were in the area."

"Jessel-Tarn again... I can't recall what's so special about it."

"Well, to put it in Old Earth terms... the whole place is like a bunch of procedurally-generated dungeon crawler levels. Some artifact powers it, keeps it running with loot chests and enemies to fight, too."

*<I did not create the artifact itself, I just put it there when I found it,>* the Nel Jalfjaa commented. *<Seemed like a good idea at the time.>*

"I'm personally glad you did," Arakai commented, reaching into his backpack. "I found this on my most recent run."

Arakai tossed a glowing blue ingot of metal to Radien, who caught it. "Rerorium. Some call it the Dragon Element. It's excellent for making commemorative coins and medallions."

"Don't let the shipyard maintenance chief at Torvaltyne see this." Radien chuckled. "That blue bugger's a menace whenever something shiny rolls in. Keeps trying to impose a 'horde tax' whenever the Reclamation Refinery puts out a shipment of bars."

Radien, Arakai, and the Nel Jalfjaa continued chatting through most of the night before Arakai took his leave. Once again, it was just Radien and the Nel Jalfjaa.

*<Speak your mind, Radien.>*

"I took down a Voidspawn not far from here, but

it was clearly a more powerful one than the most that I've seen."

<Ah, yes. The vengeful soul of Dromos-Kaledrion himself, reborn as a void-amalgamation of his greed and contempt. What did you slay him with?>

Radien showed the Nel Jalfjaa the Borfblade.

<Hunderfold Novasteel... carbon-plated for color, red dust for the glowing accents. Belariq Ironwood handle...>

Things fell silent as the Nel Jalfjaa realized something.

<He won't come back this time.>

"This time?"

<As a Voidspawn, the spectre of Dromos-Kaledrion is not bound by the typical rules of life within Cynar. Only a weapon whose material has been folded one hundred times exactly is capable of permanently destroying Voidspawns. The same goes for Demons, too.>

"So I've heard..." Radien said.

<Radien, I don't know who got ahold of Hunderfold Novasteel for you, but whoever they are, they truly are friend to you.>

"What?!"

Radien couldn't believe what he had just heard. Veralis had gotten him this weapon, she made sure that the Orvitarian Armsmaster got him Hunderfold Novasteel. To say that he was confused was an understatement. "I... I'm speechless, honestly."

<That someone would give you such a mighty weapon?>

"That someone would even care to bother to..."

The Nel Jalfjaa's amber pulses resumed, like it was laughing.

*<All the eons I've traveled this world, all the people I've spoken to, warriors, survivors, thinkers and doers alike... And still I find myself surprised every time I see someone like you, Radien.>*

"And what's that supposed to mean?"

*<It never stops being one of my favorite things to discover.>*

The Nel Jalfjaa rippled and pulsed, and then vanished.

"Oh, you dick."

As Radien scoffed with slight annoyance at the Nel Jalfjaa playing the pronoun game with him, he noticed another granite slab on the ground they had been hovering above.

*Deliis Unzhernreli hol kyr-nah fuur Valzhi.*

*To be a Death Worlder is to stand alone, and to make it strength.*

The rest of Dromos-Balth Black Zone remained uneventful, considering its major threat had just been killed by Radien, who wondered if Dromos-Balth might lose its status as such a survival test for that fact, that he had just removed the ghost of the zone's namesake. Time would tell, he figured.

# 7
# FIRENTHAL BLACK ZONE

Firenthal. The Jungle One. Specifically, the chunk of the Devouring Jungle that wasn't part of neighboring Kaladorum, The Mountain One. Surprisingly, Radien was quickly getting the hang of this zone, despite the fact that he figured desert and jungle would be his worst biomes for survival, and he had already finished Jaltai-Vuul.

More surprising to himself than anything else, he was quickly entering the *Volarthir-Ruuk, Survival Loop* of this place, swiftly picking up the routine that needed to be done to survive, and maybe even thrive within this zone. It was not unheard of for some Death Worlders, for whom an area really just clicked with, to build homes for themselves within a Black Zone. The Gauntlet of Doom's rules did not forbid from paying such persons a visit when their homes were encountered, as the Zhernreli word for them was *Ja-Anan Volarthir*, or 'Elder Survivor', translated. It was considered good fortune to visit or be visited by a *Ja-Anan Volarthir*, as they often would be happy to teach some trade secrets to whoever was good enough at a given zone to find them.

Regardless, Radien was quite adept at staying off of the ground level, considered to be the most dangerous part of the Devouring Jungle, as its name was derived from a species of moss that grows in patches on the jungle floor, and is also carnivorous.

Hopping from the branches that could support his weight onto others, using the Aura to catch himself if he was about to slip, he was definitely navigating this jungle well. Maybe not in the most stealthy or least traceable way, but he was moving swiftly, and with purpose. That purpose? To get better at moving, obviously. Firenthal was doing wonders for honing Radien's kinesthetic awareness, his control over his own body, and his ability to quickly react to new stimuli, in the zen-like state he first felt in Jaltai-Vuul, where he had trained his claws into the razor-sharp and stone-hard grippers and rippers they were now, and it was certainly paying dividends in the form of letting him grab onto the trees and branches he was moving between and throughout.

A landmark suddenly caught his eyes. He could see it pass through his vision just before he would've missed it, then halted in place to look back at whatever it was that just made itself known. It was a clearing within the jungle. Well, less of a clearing, more of an entire area within the jungle with vastly different terrain, a savanna surrounded by the Devouring Jungle itself. Still within Firenthal, so it sure as hell wouldn't violate the Gauntlet of Doom's rules on fleeing a zone to check it out.

Generally, the rule was that if you accidentally exit a Black Zone and enter another, you're supposed to head back in once you realize the mistake. But this was not a common problem, since this rule was specific to the Gauntlet of Doom, which is only ever partaken by those intending to complete it for its intended purpose; that being simultaneously training and rite of passage.

Regardless, Radien was in no danger of exiting Firenthal when he entered this mini-savanna. He could see in the distance, a very large red rock, redder than Uluru of Old Earth, and almost polished-looking, honestly. On one side, a gradual slope that led up to its sheer vertical drop, upon which Radien could see hundreds of thousands of carvings and pictograms. The sun that Raon-Arashal orbited was shining directly on this cliff face, and striking it just right to make this wall of stone look like an enormous ruby, upon which countless stories and fables and myths were carved upon.

This was one of Raon-Arashal's wonders, the Red Cliff of Stories. It was a popular pilgrimage spot for many types of people, from historians to artists among others, this massive stone face upon which many had told either their own stories, or legends of old.

Radien studied the great wall of fables and tales, many of them depicting battles fought and won by one of the nine people who once bore the title of Universal Defender. Oftentimes, this was simply shortened to just being 'The Defender'.

Stories of children of destiny never appealed to Radien, however. They seemed to defeat the point of inspiration. Why bother to be inspired by a perfect hero? If this creature so brilliant at everything exists, then why bother to be inspired by something that for its existence, promises always to be someone else?

The essence of stagnation, the allowance of complacency, when the hero is just too damn perfect and destined.

But Radien seemed somehow to understand that the Defenders never were everchosen champions of some breathless god. It simply was the case that their purpose, what they found purpose in doing, was what they did. To partake in the universe, and remaining true to themselves. It seemed that in doing that, they just... happened to become known as the Defenders.

But if the last breath of a Defender is the first of their successor, then that would somewhat signify some unseen hand ensuring it? Fate was not a concept Radien was fond of, he preferred to make his own.

But that's what the Defenders did. They made their own. It looked like that.

"Fuck, I'm gonna have to ponder that one," he said aloud to himself.

"It's a good thing to ponder," a voice said from behind him. Radien turned around, and saw someone who was undoubtedly one of the *Ja-Anan Volarthir* he had heard about. A Death World Vulpian, who sure as hell didn't look his age.

"How do you even know what I'm pondering?" Radien asked.

"There's a lot of things anyone could ponder at this wall, all of them good. All I heard was that you're pondering."

Radien nodded. That was fair.

"Care to enlighten me?" the Death Worlder asked.

Radien sighed and rolled his shoulders. "Honestly?

Take your pick. There's a *lot* of them happening right now."

"Hmmm... We'll go with what I was pondering at the time. Who is it?"

Radien laughed. "Who is what? I do hope you haven't mistaken me for someone else. The Oldest Truth is that I stand alone, but this is not a bad thing."

"Indeed, indeed. Kennan, by the way."

"Kennan?" Radien said. "As in, Kennan Ironbork?"

"The very same."

"I read of your achievements during some downtime at Torvaltyne Bastion, your skills are legendary."

"I know, I wrote those legends myself."

"I suppose so, yeah."

The two stood at the cliff face, eyeing one of the carved pictograms showing a character from a fable. This was very much the 'fables' section of the cliff.

"Speak your mind, Radien," Kennan encouraged.

"You know me?"

"I only *live* in Firenthal, I don't *stay* there under a rock. I still partake in this universe," Kennan explained.

"That doesn't exactly explain how you know my name already," Radien pointed out.

"You do not realize what deeds you've already done?" Kennan scoffed, and then chuckled. "Radien, in so short a time you've answered so many questions that seemed eons beyond you, and you thought *nobody in all the stars could take notice?* You destroyed the Demon Avanchenvaldr, who would've become one of the Dark Six's most trusted and revered generals had she successfully delivered your birth species to them as thralls. The Conclave of Sentience noticed your actions, your race, and you spoke for them in a time when they were by and large, not ready. And you demonstrated the honor and morality that your species, that all sentient life is capable of choosing, and remaining true to. It may be that your race is full of inherent evil, and you're not wrong. Yes, evil is a choice. It has to be chosen, and in order for it to be chosen, it must be preferred. And anyone who would make that choice must be inherently evil. It is known."

Radien turned to Kennan, unsure whether to be shocked by the pretense and the gall of what he was saying, or utterly impressed by the fact he had this level of wisdom to spare.

"Despite that, you've remained true to yourself, because you've chosen to, and prefer to. Someone who chooses that, in spite of everything else that would encourage and reward not to, is not something that is even *possible* to ignore among the stars. Even if that planet of yours was in a true void within the lifeblood of Cynar."

"Cynar... I heard the *Nel Jalfjaa* mention that name, too," Radien remembered.

"Cynar is the given name of the mortal universe, this one you call reality. It is the dominion of what you observe and experience, what you understand to be physical, mortal reality."

"Ah, okay."

"What is known of the expanse of Creation contains Cynar within Auros, The Aura, the blood of

Cynar."

Radien suddenly found himself flung into a vision. He could see the universe zooming out and away from him, until the border of mortality itself gave way to a grander expanse, a plane of raw power, blue lightning flashing and crackling in his vision, and galactic filaments being left behind in their wake as they faded into the void.

*The Void, the Space Between Them. Where space itself does not exist, and instead a dominion of darkness that sometimes makes intent to bleed into Cynar.* Kennan's voice echoed in Radien's mind as he traversed this landscape in his own head.

*The other realms, of Burning Hells and of Non-Knowledge, one from where comes the Dark Six and their armies, the other, where new knowledge, new information constantly creates itself, to ensure that it is impossible to know all. A realm whose very existence ensures eternally the denial of omniscience, thus always giving purpose to exploration and reason to learning, and always ensures learning can take place.*

*Beyond Ulguluth's Road lies Greywatch, the Nexus of Torment. It is unknown what is imprisoned within that terrible realm, though all who pray and hope, do so that no creature of any other realm must one day find out.*

Radien snapped out of the vision.

"There are of course, bridges between these realms that allow one to cross into another. The Nel Jalfjaa, for example, acts as the keymaster for one such bridge from Cynar to Auros, the Realm of Reality and the Realm of Power," Kennan explained. "A bridge between

Cynar and the Realm of Non-Knowledge actually exists on Cynofrax, the Secret Fire of the Aldzul Rayd."

"*Aldzul Rayd?*" Radien asked. "That can't be good."

"It's a misnomer, admittedly," Kennan further explained, as to why the name of this bridge translated as *Dark Defense.* "Someone thought it would be cool to call it that, and now we've called it that for too long to bother changing it. Besides, it's far from derogatory, so we at least have that."

"Fair, fair."

"But you have yet to answer my question, Radien," Kennan reminded. "I asked you a question that you have not answered, because you told me to pick one. So I will ask a different question of the same nature... What is it about them?"

Radien shrugged. "I'm sorry, Kennan. I don't know what you're talking about."

Kennan looked to Radien, and saw that there was no lie in his eyes.

"Intriguing," Kennan noted, before heading off.

"Wha—Oh, whatever."

Radien continued to ponder the wall, before the Nel Jalfjaa rippled into existence next to him.

"Ah, you again."

<*I'm not sure whether you're pleased or annoyed to see me.*>

"Me neither, to be fair. Wonder where I'm gonna find your next tablet..."

<*Tablet?*>

"What, you mean to tell me you haven't been the

one sticking granite slabs with Zhernreli scripture in the ground? That glow red and go 'bong' when I touch them?"

*<No, but I know of what you speak. I will have more information in the next zone.>*

"Sounds good."

The Nel Jalfjaa rippled out of existence just as quickly as it rippled in once again. Radien continued to ponder the wall. He decided to pick a random pictogram, a random fable, and study it a little further. To this end, he closed his eyes, and moved them underneath his eyelids for a bit. Whichever one was the first he saw, that was his choice.

The one his eyes landed on when he opened them was the text that described a fable from Death World Vulpian folklore, The Tale of Nulran the Haunted. The scripture translated itself in front of his eyes. Since he was still learning the Zhernreli-Orul tongue, he really didn't feel like doing the hard work at the moment, so the Aura picked up the slack for him on this one.

*Nulran, Haunted. Is his past shameful?*

*He does not know.*

*He only knows the shame itself.*

*His name, ceased to exist.*

*Known only as his forefathers, legends of evil.*

*He wishes only to be his own honorable self.*

*Though he knows the shame, he feels no shame.*

*All he knows, is that all around him demand he weep tears undue, for a past that is not his.*

*What will he do in his refusal?*

*Will it galvanize his honor, or fuel his corruption?*

*We are glad it was the first.*

*For Nulran halted fast his foes when they came, and for it, Firatyne was not conquered when the Rogues of Cynofrax came despite the tenants of reason, and the wishes of their kin.*

*Nulran stood strong against the Rogues, though he was of Cynofrax. He stood beside Zhernrel-Vuljar, for he was Vuljar, and Torvalien.*

'Torvalien', translating as *One of Honor.* Zhernrel-Vuljar was the proper name of the Death World Vulpians in their native tongue.

*And so, because Nulran was not his forefathers, he brought honor to the name of Cynofrax, he brought honor to the name of Vuljar, the blood we all share when traced far back enough.*

*Nulran, Haunted. Does he know what he has done?*

*Nulran, Haunted. Does he know his honor?*

*Nulran, Haunted. Does he even believe his honor exists?*

Radien fell to his knees as the tale resonated with him. He barely even registered the last line of Nulran's tale. The Rogues of Cynofrax placed the origin of this fable during the Purification Campaign, an ill-fated attempt at an ethnic cleansing from a splinter group of Cynofrax Vulpians who already were known to be radical isolationists. The campaign fell flat on its face when the rogues who numbered over two hundred thousand were utterly crushed, having made corpses of less than a thousand Death Worlders in proper combat. The majority of the fatalities were in the initial surprise attack, and once the Death Worlders figured out what was up, the game was on.

The 'proper' loss tally was six hundred eleven Zhernreli, to that end. None of the nearly three hundred thousand Cynofrax Rogues survived. Needless to say, it was a downright hilarious failure of an ethnic cleansing attempt.

Nulran survived the campaign, having slew almost a hundred Cynofrax Rogues on his own, many of them the most elite fighters of the extremist group. Similarly by all accounts, Nulran lived the rest of his life in seclusion upon Raon-Arashal, granted a home within Firatyne by the parliament of the city itself, where he lived a hermitic life, sure that he was shunned by all around him for being part of the same species that had just attempted genocide on this planet, in this city, even. Though he had fought them and though the enemies had failed, Nulran never could shake the intense dread of stigma that followed his visage, that followed his ancestors' names.

Nulran wasn't even descendant of any particularly evil ancestors. In fact, by all accounts, Nulran's predecessors shared his sense of honor and justice. It simply was the case that 'everyone else' seemed to be ruining it all by association.

Just like Nulran, Radien didn't believe in 'guilty by association'. But like Nulran, Radien also knew that far too many than could be counted did. And maybe it wouldn't matter overall, but maybe Radien would just be unlucky enough to only find enemies.

Nulran sure didn't want to take the chance, and Radien didn't blame him. He couldn't. He knew all too well how Nulran felt all that time ago, for all those reasons.

"My only comfort now," Radien said to himself, "is that my world and where I can go, is the size of this universe instead of the cage of Earth. And if I can't find allies, then I can find somewhere where my enemies cannot. And if the universe chooses to be enemies with me, it can burn in Demonic fire for all I care."

Radien stood back up, adjusting the sword on his hip. "And at least I've got the time to wait and find out. At least I'm not mortal anymore, watching time tick away, ushering *torschlusspanik* through the door like a welcome and familiar guest."

His hand wrapped around the Borfblade's hardwood hilt, the two-piece segment with the tang going through its middle to show that the Novasteel blade was that single, long, sturdy piece. "I'm not on Earth anymore, and that's all that's gonna matter to me when nothing else does."

Looking once again upon the pictograms and poems upon the Red Cliff of Stories, Radien's eyes soon found the granite tablet he wondered if he was going to see here. The scripture glowed red to the touch once again.

*Jazukiir aldir nejtarn. Tais deliis pir Jazukiir-nah hath nejpiril toulth.*

*Vigilance is never wrong. But there is a difference between vigilance, and merely seeking reasons to be enemies.*

Eventually, the locator beeped again, and soon came the lift out of Firenthal. Next up was Ilkai.

# 8

# Ilkai Black Zone

Ilkai Black Zone was among the three in which an additional piece of equipment was provided, even when doing the Gauntlet of Doom. In this case, a high-tech diving mask to allow for breathing underwater. It had an internal reserve that would allow for up to five hours of regular breathing, which would itself 'recharge' off of native oxygen present in whatever environment it was within. In Ilkai's waters, this actually meant an overall 'stretch amount' of an additional hour of controlled breathing, as long as the user wasn't panicking.

However, with Ilkai Black Zone dotted with underwater caverns with pockets of surface to camp within, a decent enough swimmer could find such a cave in a perfectly healthy amount of time. In Radien's case, this took about an hour, that had been mostly spent using the Aura to find such a cave, and then navigate his way to it, whilst avoiding the larger and more hostile native fauna of Ilkai.

Backing at least twenty feet away from the pool of water he emerged from into the pocket of surface that was a hidden cavern within the waters of Ilkai, Radien allowed the Aura to course through him and immediately turn the water that soaked his fur into steam, conveniently drying off as he laid some lengths of the native kelp species across some nearby rock outcroppings to dry off. According to informational dossiers on the zone from Rimfalls Station, this particular species of kelp was 'comically nutritious when dried out and lightly cooked'. An interesting choice of words for sure, but these were the words of the data-boards from the station, and thus likely of one of the technicians being very bored. Granted, it wasn't an inappropriate choice of words. The Ilkai Monstrokelp indeed contained enough vitamins within its leaves and veins to sustain an adult human for an entire day in only a few square inches of its surface. Granted, it would need to be cooked first, in order to get rid of the toxic coating on top of the leaves. Radien wondered if he should try to test his Irongut Cantrip by forgoing the cooking, but decided against it after remembering the incident with the Reaper's Bush berries back in Azhenar. Making sure to remain at least twenty feet away from the water's entrance, Radien figured now was a good time to meditate for a bit in this cave. After all, it was a pretty good cave. Granted, it still almost felt like cheating, meditating for basically the entire period that he was supposed to be testing his survival skills.

The debate was interrupted by the reason he was keeping his distance from the water's entrance, as a loud whipping *thwack* slammed against the cavern floor. An Ilkai Whipsquid was checking the cavern to see if there was anything to be grabbed within it. Though their tentacles never measured more than twelve feet in length, twenty feet was still the minimum recommended distance for the reason of 'just in case' there was some ancient specimen that could make the Kraken look like a pushover. Granted, though Old Earth myths of the Kraken depicted far more than twenty-foot long tentacles, an Ilkai Whipsquid could still make it look like a pushover, because as far as Radien could recall, the Kraken's tentacles never had spear-like venomous talons protruding from them that could pierce straight through the rock, which is why the floor of the cavern was dotted with holes like someone had been drilling bore holes into the stone for dynamite to be put in them like it was a quarry or mine.

Radien raised an eyebrow at the tentacle that had just embedded itself into the stone, contemplating whether or not to slice it off for having a very annoying sound when it hit the floor and pierced the cavern floor. He was tempted, but decided not to this time. If it came back, however, his mercy for this one would end. Taking note of a distinct red vein that went along the length of the dark violet tentacle, he would remember this particular Whipsquid if it decided to come around again.

Within the cavern, Radien pondered. The Nel Jalfjaa rippled into existence again next to him.

*<I have information regarding the tablets.>*

"Go on, then," Radien said, though his voice sounded somewhat... not tired or exhausted, but winded. Like it was less his lungs that were out of breath, but his voice.

<Is it too presumptuous for me to say that you look like you'd rather wait for a bit before hearing it?>

Radien was about to instinctively respond with 'no', but then he remembered he was speaking to a Grand Psionic Entity, a being that there was no sense in lying to. He nodded as he leaned back against the cavern wall.

<It is understandable,> the Nel Jalfjaa concurred. <I am not ignorant to your tale, Miles Radien. Though you have lived eight times longer than your birth species typically does now, for all that time you have been in quite the rush to learn and be ready for as much as you can.>

"Yeah, that sounds about right."

<You know, with the Aura ensuring your agelessness, it's not like you're under a time crunch now.>

"Seems I've yet to really get that memo," Radien admitted. "But the rush keeps happening for different reasons. Before The Unmaker, it was the rush to get my feet back on the ground in this wider universe. During The Unmaker, it was... well, The Unmaker. Now, it's the imminent return of the Dark Six."

<You speak as though the Dark Six are not already waging the Second War for Reality against Cynar.>

"Then I suppose the rush is to get myself ready to fight them alongside Cynar's defenders."

The amber glow of the Nel Jalfjaa dimmed, as though they were sighing. <I can't imagine I'm the first one to tell you that the universe won't fall in a day.>

Radien chuckled and shook his head. "It is

regrettable that I can't seem to shake the fact that where I came from, if your guard was down for even one day, your universe absolutely could, and *would* fall."

<*That is no longer the universe you occupy.*>

Radien fell silent. He had no response to give. The Nel Jalfjaa was correct, and Radien knew it. But by the same token, Radien was also correct in what he had said, and the Nel Jalfjaa knew that as well.

Minutes that passed became hours, and then days as both Radien and the Nel Jalfjaa pondered in this hidden space within Ilkai.

"I wonder..." Radien eventually said to break the silence. Though the silence had been welcome, its breaking wasn't unwelcome. "What does a Grand Psionic Entity have to ponder about?"

<*Proto-Antiuniverse Metapsionic tendencies, for one,*> the Nel Jalfjaa spoke.

"That's not actually a thing, is it?"

<*Not really.*>

Radien burst out laughing, and the Nel Jalfjaa pulsed its amber glow that was their own way of doing the same.

<*And what does a Death Worlder of your caliber have to ponder?*>

"For one, I'm curious what you plan to do against the Dark Six," Radien said honestly. "Whether you're planning to help at all or not, how you would if you're going to, why you wouldn't if you're not."

<*That is what I am pondering as well.*>

Radien nodded. "To do nothing because you're a Grand Psionic Entity, and there's no way in all the realms the Dark Six could actually harm you, and risk untold suffering from your inaction? Or to aid, but to what end? If you just wiped them all from existence and chose the fate of the battle outright, the universe learns nothing of how to defend itself. So what balance can the Nel Jalfjaa achieve between the will to learn, refusal of ignorance, and the demands of reason and justice?

*<Between the will to learn, the refusal of ignorance, and the demands of reason and justice... indeed,>* the Nel Jalfjaa concurred. *<It is always good news to me, that I still can learn something from the peoples of Cynar.>*

"Glad to help."

The Nel Jalfjaa rippled out of existence, off to wherever they were heading next, leaving Radien to ponder once again. Blue sparks began to fizzle in his hands as the power of the Aura coursed through them, and he felt as though there was something he could do.

With a single swift motion, he stood from his place and sliced the air with the claws of his index and middle finger, tearing a rift into the fabric of space itself, a window of a view that gave a look into the past.

"Radien!" the Death Worlder yelled into the rift, as he saw a familiar-looking Human walking towards the woods.

"You again... or me, I suppose," Miles responded. "This is a bold fucking move, I'll tell you that, manifesting visually in my waking life."

"You sure you're awake?" Radien asked. "Furthermore, are you sure I'm in your visual cortex?"

"I see the rift, I hear your voice, I'm not dreaming."

"Does anyone else?"

Miles looked across the street to where a pair of Humans was walking along the sidewalk, not noticing the apparent tear in reality itself. "All right then, I suppose there's that explained."

"Where are you right now?" Radien asked.

"Dangerous question to be asking." Miles answered.

"Protocol of Vigilance, ETF Delta-Nine."

"Delta-Nine? The prompt is *castle.*"

"The response is *sunken.*"

"The last major event was Designation Prime-Fix."

"Shit," Radien realized, knowing what was awaiting Miles.

"Fuck, that bad, huh?"

"We both hate cliché cat-poster shit like 'you'll get through' and what have you, but I'm not sure what to say."

"It's not—is it?"

Radien shook his head. "No. It isn't *that,* at the very least."

Miles sighed with relief. "I won't ask what, then."

Radien nodded in response. "There's just one problem. I don't remember doing this as you."

"Erase my memory of this and the last conversation, then," Miles replied. "Clearly I'm going to remember, just the long way 'round."

Radien nodded, flicking his hand forward and firing a bolt of the Aura through the window in time, charged with a mind-scrubbing kick that would ensure whomever it hit would lose the last fifteen minutes of their memory. The window closed behind the bolt, hitting the Human Miles just after the last of what he would have called a vision faded away.

Radien then hit the floor of the cavern on his hands and knees, panting with confusion far more than exhaustion. Somehow, he couldn't help but figure he hadn't seen the last of his old self yet. At the very least, next time it probably wouldn't be under such risky temporal circumstances. Even though Radien wasn't even sure what the risks even were, some deep instinct warned him that they were all too existent.

He was swiftly snapped out of his pondering by the sound of the signal beacon beeping, telling him that this was the last day he needed to spend in Ilkai. He still wasn't sure whether or not meditative stasis was considered cheating. On the back wall of the cavern, another granite plaque.

*Klorn jaflow orvu-nah sok tsingtarn kasrah jasaln.*

*Water moves within its current, and yet can carve canyons from mountains.*

# 9

# KALADORUM BLACK ZONE

We're gonna drop you in the Blizzardblade Foothills section of the Devouring Jungle itself, so you gotta make your way into the mountains on your own!" the Jumpmaster informed Radien within the hovercraft.

"But I like being in the mountains!" Radien mentioned.

"That's why we're dropping you in the foothills! Earn those mountains, Tactician!"

"Works for me!"

Radien hopped out from the hovercraft and hit the ground, on the foothills of the Blizzardblade Mountains, where he had built Torvaltyne Bastion. Of course, his route wouldn't take him within a hundred leagues of the place, as he was immediately gunning for the mountains themselves, grabbing what edible berries and the occasional game species he could find along the way. Once the last trees were gone, and it was nothing but the snow and the rock, Radien definitely was finding himself feeling comfortable with it. The fur coat of the

Death World Vulpian was definitely helping, as was his prior fondness of being within the mountains. Not looking at the mountains, but being among them. That was fun. The former was annoying, especially when one must deal with insipid comments about the mountain's presence, only made more and more grinding by the desire to be among them instead of away from them, as though taunted by the call to attention to look at that damn mountain that you'll never find yourself upon, by someone whose sappy comments about the mountain is matched only by their dishonor, bringing you dangerously close to no longer being capable of appreciating mountains.

Regardless, Radien did manage to make his way to the mountains, since all it took this time was skill rather than luck. Radien found it very impressive, the amount he could get accomplished when skill would decide the outcome, rather than luck or lack thereof. It was without a doubt, an incredibly liberating change.

Within Blizzardblade, Radien also remembered that Kennan Ironbork lived in the Devouring Jungle of Firenthal. He had built a home in there, likely with far more to it on the inside than its outside would suggest. Radien wondered if he could find a spot for such a place here within the Blizzardblade Mountains. When night fell, the wind was cold and biting, the skies dark and the snow flying everywhere, but somehow, Radien didn't mind at all. Though his Death Worlder fur coat and other clothes on top of that protected him from the weather, he didn't *feel* as though he was in this weather. As in, not under this weather. As in, this weather was of the kind he would dare to enjoy being within. He then took a moment to look around the area, finding it to be a secluded area within the mountains, a cavern entrance visible in one of the solid rock walls. The entire area was surrounded by the frozen stone peaks of this area of the Blizzardblade Mountains, which gave this area the appearance of a large, circular clearing under the sky. It probably looked way better in the daylight. Radien, with his fondness for caves, went over to the one that was visible, figuring the same. Though the cavern itself was small, it was large enough for him to comfortably stand within, while being deep enough that the freezing winds outside could be sat well away from. More than enough space, as far as he was concerned. If he could fully stand up and fully lay down, there was only room for improvement, he figured. Suddenly, he started to figure this was where he'd build his hidden sanctuary, like how Kennan had his own in Firatyne. Kaladorum would play host to not only Torvaltyne Bastion, but the Lair of Radien as well, whatever title he figured he'd call it. When day came around, he had made his decision. Like how Torvaltyne Bastion was nicknamed the Fortress Borfus, Jernrev Sanctum would be known to him by other colloquialisms, such as the House of the Hecking Borf, or the Loaf Lair, or... other things along those lines. But he found where he'd build it, in Kaladorum Black Zone.

When the morning came, Radien walked out into the area that was at first nearly completely obscured by the blizzard of the prior night. To describe the scenery as the perfect mountaintop training ground would be an understatement. He froze in place, but not because it was as cold as it was. The cold was trivial to him, and the fur coat that his Death World Vulpian form granted him.

The first words that came to his mind were spoken as suddenly as they came.

"By the gods, this would make a *hell* of a training ground!"

No sooner said than realized, as Radien chose to commit the rest of his time here in the Blizzardblade Mountains towards utilizing the icy terrain to train his balance along with his raw ability. He just couldn't get enough of it, being able to freely fling his fists and feet in practice, flipping and jumping around the vista without fear of being observed, training on his own, and training *hard.* The very air itself seemed to ripple at the strength of his fists, and the claws on his feet made the air whistle as his kicks sliced through the cold winds of the Blizzardblade Mountains. He trained into the night with the Borfblade, soon allowing himself to return to the cavern to start a fire and cook some of the game he had caught while on his way up the mountain.

After setting the sticks and tinder pile, Radien swiped at the cavern wall with his claws, and the sparks that rained down set the dry twigs aflame. It was a pretty neat trick. Even though he could've easily done the same with a snap of his fingers and a pulse of The Aura, there was an undeniable catharsis to just doing things truly on one's own.

The Nel Jalfjaa rippled into existence once again as Radien sat by the fire, looking out onto the training ground he had just discovered, and was already planning the layout of the house he was going to build out of this cavern, and how much expansion of its space would need to happen.

"Y'know how Kennan Ironbork lives in the Firenthal Black Zone?" Radien commented. "I get the feeling this place is where I would like to live within Kaladorum."

*<I could hear you imagining the floorplan of the house's armory from the other side of the planet.>*

"Bullshit."

*<True, but it's a good metaphor.>*

"That is fair."

Radien breathed in and out again, before gruffing. He wasn't sure how, but somehow the Nel Jalfjaa seemed to be glaring at him as though to indicate that he should speak his mind.

"Instinct tells me you want me to speak my mind," Radien voiced aloud, just to make sure.

*<That you even must ask... you don't take much on faith, do you?>*

"Faith is a virtue that I do not possess. I can't allow myself to take anything on faith alone."

*<Well, you are speaking your mind now.>*

"That you say it, tells me my instincts were correct."

*<Good thing you trained, huh?>*

*"Exactly."*

Radien and the Nel Jalfjaa continued to ponder the fire.

*<What is it, then, that brings you such pause?>*

"I may be inept, but I'm not stupid. My hearing

was pretty good even *before* I became a Death World Vulpian. I've heard things, what people have thought of me when they believed I was not paying attention... I've heard them whisper of the Defender, and that they believe it is me."

<I've seen my share of Defenders pass through here, including your predecessor, if you are indeed the Tenth. Every single one that I have met has said almost the exact same thing, at one point or another.>

"Everything I would stand for goes *against* the idea of me being some child of destiny," Radien continued. "What does it mean for everyone else, if I'm some everchosen protector of the cosmos? I *fought* against what kind of person I would become, I *destroyed* The Unmaker!"

<That you did,> the Nel Jalfjaa recalled. <That was also the day you became Zhernrel-Vuljar.>

"And yet, somehow... they did not scorn me. They did not ask me how dare I defile their name by calling it my own! It is... baffling. It is nothing I have ever known before. What am I even to do about that? Even after The Planet of Traitors, they did not scorn me... even after the day I fell further than ever before."

<Nobody in their right mind blames you for what happened to the Planet of Traitors, Radien, only the coward Demons who—>

"Do you think that matters to me?!" Radien yelled, firing a bolt at the fire, and almost the entire mountaintop was illuminated by the newly-fanned flames. "I don't care that it could have happened to anyone else! I don't care that I had an impossible choice to make that day, and I *certainly* do not care that anyone else would've done the same! It is *I* who took that fall, *I alone* who was the one there that day! It is upon *my* hands, the blood of an entire species is stained!"

The side of the mountain Radien's bolt impacted smoldered in the aftermath of his remembrance of that dark day.

"And it had come so quickly, too..." Radien continued. "With no hesitation, I was the executioner of a world and all its people. I locked them into an arena with me, and I did not stop until every single traitor to the universe was dead by my hands."

Radien's hands sparked as he calmed the power within him down.

"My only solace is the truth of the matter, that the Exiled Chapter were no longer themselves, and they had chosen to renounce it all to the Dark Six."

*<Aren't you glad you trained to be this way?>* the Nel Jalfjaa asked with levity.

"I am..." Radien sighed. "I am. But I cannot help but know in my mind of minds, that Kalivan Tor was a choice *nobody* should have to make. If I can help it... no one will have to make that kind of choice again. Even if I must be the one to do so, It will only be my soul that must face the judgment of the gods."

*<The gods... those buggers.>*

"No kidding!" Radien snorted. "Right bunch of bastards, those guys."

*<What would you tell them if they stood before you?>*

"I would ask them, '*what's your excuse?*'... among

other choice words. What should it matter, anyway? The gods may be holy, but one should never rely on them for anything."

<In this wider and more civilized universe, it doesn't. You think as the rest does, a stance seen only as sensible.>

"I suppose it goes to show how completely fucked *they* are... the Humans, who I am nothing but glad to no longer be among. What the universe calls sense, the Humans call madness. What the reasonable people of the stars value, the Humans despise. To read their history is to read a manual on all the horrid things never to allow a species to become, and even after all these years I've spent beyond them, I can't seem to get over the first ones, where I had the misfortune of being among them."

Radien sat down in front of the fire again, letting himself stare at the patterns of flame in the air.

"I expect no veneration from the stars merely for suffering it, but I cannot ignore the countless hours I spent on Earth wishing I was anywhere else, and how the stars were so blind for so long."

<There are many secrets of this universe, Miles Sorvenjar Radien. Among them is why by all rights, you and the Humans would have never left Earth, and yet... here you stand, ready to turn the tide with your bare hands, if only it was asked of you.>

Radien sighed again at the fire, before looking back at the mountaintop he was to make his training ground. There he trained for the rest of the days in Kaladorum, save for the last two, where he wandered around the mountains to make sure that his locator beacon wouldn't start pinging where he was going to make his sanctuary. Thanks to The Aura's passive eidetic memory, he would not forget the place he found within Blizzardblade. The Nel Jalfjaa rippled out from existence, presumably to continue being a wandering mysterious and absurdly powerful Grand Psionic Entity. Radien then noticed that another of the strange stone tablets with Zhernrel-Vuljar script was behind where the Nel Jalfjaa had been.

*Valgitay jashal djalanan, Jagizhfuur ves deltins Valtai-Ej anantarn.*

*Glory is as eternal as suffering, training is what decides the warrior's fate.*

Funnily enough, the main hint that this was ancient script indeed was the use of the word *djalanan* to indicate suffering, where in the modern Zhernreli-Orul, it was more akin to 'bullshit' instead. Radien placed his hand on the stone like he had for every other plaque he had come across, and just like the rest, the runes glowed red, before the stone faded into the wall that it had just come from.

"These words seem to wander just as the Nel Jalfjaa does," Radien noticed aloud. "I envy them, just as I envy any wanderer. Perhaps one day, I will find myself in a calm enough universe to wander it."

# 10

# KIATARS' KALL BLACK ZONE

The zone's name translated as 'pathways into darkness', and was the only non-natural Black Zone on the planet. An irradiated industrial wasteland that historians believed to be an early attempt at a third major city on Raon-Arashal, after Kendradeyne and Firatyne had already been founded. The danger didn't come from the radiation, as a radiation shield was provided for anyone going in, much like how diving equipment was granted for those heading into Ilkai. The danger instead came from the creatures born of this irradiated city, its former name long lost to time. That, and the predatory mycelium colonies that migrated throughout the city, and were known to swallow even the largest creatures overnight, covering them in a ravenous fungi that would strip fauna to the bone, before turning even the bones into spores. Of course, these malignant mushrooms did not speed across the landscape, they moved at a little under half a kilometer per hour. One would be able to see them coming, and move away from the encroaching fungi. The main prey of these mushroom colonies were the skyscraper-sized terrors that wandered Klatars'Kall, and made traversing the streets a deadly game of hide and seek, and even considering the dangers that lurked within the buildings, indoors was still preferable if it could be helped.

The people of Raon-Arashal considered themselves lucky that the monstrosities that roam Klatars'Kall Black Zone were only capable of surviving in such a radiation-stricken environment. Then again, the cannons of Firatyne and Kendradeyne would prove more than a match for even these lumbering terrors.

Radien wandered the dark halls of another dilapidated and vaguely industrial-in-purpose building, wondering what kind of place required such a strange and labyrinthine bunch of walls with scattered computer terminals that barely seemed to make architectural sense. It was like this place had been designed deliberately to be confusing to its occupants.

Radien's footsteps suddenly seemed to echo loudly within the corridor, as though all sound other than his own movements were suddenly drained from the world. It felt as abnormal as it did sudden, and as sudden as it was unnerving. He couldn't help but become under the impression that something was about to happen.

Drawing his sword and slicing it upwards, Radien deflected an incoming projectile aimed for his throat with reflexes as honed as he was thankful to have them. After that, another swing and another deflection, followed by two more. Whatever was lurking within the shadows, it was trying to kill him.

Radien fired a bolt of the Aura into the shadows to illuminate them, but nothing was revealed. Another projectile hit its mark this time, right into his side. Radien cursed as he yanked the jet-black spike from him, and rapidly healed himself with his power. He then used his free hand to trace an arc into the air from his left to his right, going over his head and summoning a dome shield of The Aura, which the next few projectiles bounced off of. Second Sight couldn't find this hidden assailant, for reasons Radien did not know. But there wasn't time to speculate as to why this was, and he knew it.

The dome shield was dissipated in a flash of light as Radien vaulted into the shadows, and out of the lit corridor. The projectiles stopped being flung, and the hide-and-seek game began. But between Radien and his unknown foe, it couldn't be told for sure who needed to hide more, as both sought the other.

Moments felt like minutes as the silence wracked the air with anticipation of one decisive strike, neither combatant giving an inch to reveal their positions within the darkness. And in the darkness, Radien's eyes saw through everything like the room may as well have been lit. The vision of a Zhernrel-Vuljar knows no falter, and his now cut through the shadows as he made them his ally, and the shadows betrayed his foe, who looked like a Death Worlder himself, but... off. Something dark had seized the mind of the once-warrior Radien faced off against in this contest of shadow, and he was going to release his foe from this fate.

The Borfblade in his left hand as always, Radien readied himself for the movement, breathing silently as the Decayed One similarly searched. It was not clear if this was a feint, or if his opponent's senses truly had dulled to such a degree that it could no longer be told which. It also held a blade, but was blind to where Radien stood. Now he knew that it had to rely on sound alone to find him.

*Ves akar duul...* it spoke suddenly. It was an older dialect, but it translated as, *What are you...*

Not where, not who, but *what.* That was the part that intrigued Radien as he stood silently, wondering how to respond.

*Duul soof Zhernrel-Vuljar... Ald? You smell of a Death Worlder... but you also do not?*

Was this creature *smelling* the fact that Miles Radien was once a Human? It seemed impossible.

"*Ves akar Duul?*" Radien returned the question. The decayed form of a Death World Vulpian snapped it's head to where he stood in the darkness. Now it knew where he was.

The two squared off. Neither moved an inch. Radien could see him in the darkness with The Aura, but the Decayed One knew where he was standing, its hearing was that attuned to everything around it.

Moments became minutes as the two waited on the other to make their next move.

Both remained breathing, neither of them moving, both still knew where the other was standing.

"I don't want to wait for too long, now," Radien said aloud.

The Decayed One adjusted itself just slightly, its motions twitchy and jutting.

"We have bigger problems now," it replied.

"Name them," Radien instructed.

"Follow me."

His sword at the ready, Radien did just that, following the Decayed One up a spiral staircase, and to a vantage point that looked out upon Klatars'Kall, a great lumbering beast in the middle distance.

"Look upon that creature, do you see it?" the Decayed one asked.

"I do," Radien replied. "I just wonder how it is *you* can see it, and I mean no offense."

The Decayed one chuckled, though this did illicit a few coughs and sputters for the effort. "None taken. My eyes have been gone for longer than I possessed them, and though I miss the sight they gave me, I cannot deny what was gained in their absence. Regardless, what lies behind the great beast?"

"I can see one of the mycelium colonies trailing it," Radien observed. "They travel slowly relative to the great beast's speed, but if the beast were to stop moving, the colony would overtake it within... seven hours, I reckon."

"Six, actually," The Decayed One corrected. "They can sense when their enemy is resting. They pick up speed when they sense their quarry taking a shut-eye."

"Isn't that just like a *nejtoulth?*" Radien commented, deliberately not taking notice of the hacking of the Decayed One's lungs. Or at least, what was left of them.

"Are the colonies a *nejtoulth*, though? Or are they just doing what they were built to do?" the Decayed One proposed. "Does that make a difference? I've watched this cycle far too many times to even know anymore..."

*Nejtoulth*, the Death Worlder word for an Enemy. In the *Zhernreli-Orul*, there was a difference between an Enemy and a Foe. To the Death Worlders, an Foe was one who's strength and wits were pitted against your own, and who sought to defeat you at your own game to supplant you, and a *Jatoulth,* a Foe, fought with honor. A *Nejtoulth,* an Enemy, was one who simply sought your end, and had no care of honor, no doctrine of decency, and whose only goal was to see you dead, by any means necessary. In Death Worlder culture, *Nejtoulth* was an insult to one's Enemies, and *Jatoulth* was an acknowledgment to the skill and determination of one's Foes.

"So, what's the problem?" Radien asked.

"I can't tell which they are, that's it," the Decayed One responded.

Radien nodded, trying to test whether or not the Decayed One could detect it. Though it was true on a factual level that this Decayed One did have a bigger problem on his hands than a duel in the form of a philosophical question, it did annoy Radien slightly that he had been dragged all this way to find out only that. However, Radien also knew that this beat the alternative, which was to duel this honed creature to seemingly zero end. The only thing that stopped this was a preemptive strike, and Radien made sure to commit that to his memory. He had averted disaster, and invited diplomacy, only by awaiting the mistake of first strike by his foe. Had the Decayed One struck first, he would not have hesitated to unleash all of his skill.

"Please, do not dance around the point with me. I have grown hideously tired of it." Radien sighed.

But when he turned back around to look upon the Decayed one, he had vanished. Radien looked back upon the lumbering beast that it had referred to. It was consumed by the mycelium colony that had caught up to it in those past hours, while it had been resting.

"How long have I been waiting here?" Radien wondered aloud. "Too long to stop that which closes in upon me?

A group of the mushrooms jammed up from the very ground itself, tunneling through the building, the stalks beginning to tower beyond the ruined skyscrapers, as their heads prepared to rain down spores upon the streets, to cover them with sheer doom and destruction.

"What in all the realms?!"

*Look back to me, Defender!*

A glowing green orb of power slammed into the stalk of one of the enormous mushrooms, tearing the fibers to shreds, and causing the stalk to snap entirely, that it could not support its weight anymore after the blow that had been struck upon it.

Caltoran had begun to blast these mushrooms to shreds, rendering them as inert as was possible in Klatars'Kall. That was, that no longer posed a threat to the rest of Raon-Arashal.

After he was done dispatching the wayward mycelium, Caltoran, for the first time since he had begun battling them, landed on the ground.

"Those weren't the mycelium colonies of

Klatars'Kall I had been warned about..." Radien commented.

"No, it looks like a new spore breed," Caltoran informed. "But with the primary hive stalks on the ground now, it'll just be like a whalefall for the rest of Klatars'Kall's denizens. This new brood has been effectively eradicated."

"Brood is an interesting way to describe mushrooms," Radien admitted, to which Caltoran nodded in agreement.

"It does seem like the only one to describe this, however," Caltoran countered, and Radien now nodded in agreement. He then looked around, the Decayed One was nowhere to be seen.

"This encounter has been very odd indeed..." Radien processed aloud. "But I suppose the question now is why you're here, Caltoran? Are you following me?"

"Call it a desire to make sure my successor is ready to assume the role."

Radien gruffed, "I believe I have already told you of my concerns regarding the title you seem quite eager to pass on to me."

"It's not like I'm worthy of it anymore, you know."

"Yes, I do know." Radien sighed. "I don't doubt that, no offense. What I doubt is that of all the people in all the universe, *I'm* the one who has that role. It seems to grandiose for my own good, to call myself Defender, the Universal Defender, Defender of the Universe... the universe is a big place, it hardly needs one person hogging the title of its protector."

"The Defender is not the only line Cynar has

against its foes," Caltoran stated. "I found it to be like the Haji-Son's Exemplar, just on a bigger scale. It does not fall on your shoulders alone to safeguard reality from foes from beyond, and within. But the Defender's is to inspire, to—"

"Caltoran, I'm hardly someone to be inspired by!" Radien cut off. By now, an enormous swarm of creatures from across Klatars'Kall had gathered to feast on the fallen giant mushrooms, keeping attention well away from this argument. "I'm far too vindictive and vengeful to be a good inspiration! What kind of *idiot* looks at what I've done, and said to themselves 'I want to be like *that?!*'"

Radien looked out the ruined building to the chaos in the open streets of the wasteland, forming his next thought carefully before he would speak it. "Nobody in their right mind should be taking inspiration from me, with how many sleepless nights I've spent dreaming of all the ways to bring retribution to the wicked and the vile, of how to deliver pain beyond measure to the iniquitous and the honorless. The universe ill needs more people like *me* in it."

"Then perhaps you will find purpose in assuring that no one in the stars has to feel the way you do." Caltoran said, before letting out a sigh himself, and standing next to Radien, looking out and contemplating the horde that was tearing the fallen giant mushroom to pieces. "Perhaps I am all too eager to know who the next Defender is, so that I no longer have to taint the title with my presence adjacent it."

*The Traitor of the Stars!*

The hoarse voice of the Decayed One from before called to Caltoran, and both he and Radien turned around to meet it. The decrepit creature held its sword out towards the Laksorian former Defender in challenge.

Radien knew that this was Caltoran's score to settle, so he said nothing. Though a Demon was what turned Caltoran's hands against the worlds he once protected, his hands had set them ablaze all the same.

Caltoran did not pull arms. He was not going to defend himself.

"Who have you come to avenge?" he simply asked.

*"Myself!"*

The Decayed One hurled its blade across the room with unnatural speed and accuracy, and to Radien's surprise, it connected. Caltoran was thrown back against the wall and pinned to the stone by what was left of the sword of a Death Worlder in life, whose name had been lost to time, but not his sword, or his skill with it.

Radien was stunned, but this was not why he stood aside. He knew that were he in the place of the Decayed One, he would have done exactly the same.

Caltoran coughed. "What planet?" He managed to sputter, despite the sword embedded in his torso.

The Decayed one made his way to the Laksorian his blade had pinned to the wall. "Varskal III," he said.

Caltoran nodded. "That was one of them, yes..."

The Decayed One yanked his sword from Caltoran's gut, letting him fall to the floor, before storming out of the building. Radien looked to Caltoran, who groaned, before his hands began to glow with swirling green power, stitching the wound closed, and replenishing the blood that was lost.

"Not very good at taking revenge, that one," Radien critiqued as he helped Caltoran stand up.

"How do you figure?"

"He left immediately after striking his blow. Didn't bother to make sure you bled out."

"Not many people think like that, you know."

"If nothing else, it gives me the knowledge to do whatever I do right."

Caltoran brushed the dirt and rubble from his cloak. "You going to tell him that?"

"No, I don't think I will. He got his revenge, no need to ruin that for him. No sense in it, either."

Caltoran nodded as he finished dusting himself off, before hopping off the ledge of the building, and glided away. Though Laksorians obviously did not possess wings, the use of his power and an enchanted cloak allowed Caltoran to overcome this fact.

As Radien looked around, another stone plaque with the runes of old crossed into his vision. Once more, Radien placed his hand on the runes, and once again did the scripture glow red before fading back into the stone wall of the ruined building.

*Deliis Unzhernreli kalska zainarr duul nuatharn, zainarr duul dolgelka Jaltai, duul akar aldir nevtaien.*

*To be a Death Worlder is to know that so long as you still breathe, so long as you still hold your sword, you are never defeated.*

# 11

# KUOLAREK BLACK ZONE

Radien was pretty good at cold. He really was. After all, he had thoroughly enjoyed his time in the Blizzardblade Mountains, training within the hidden peaks he had found. However, Kuolarek Black Zone could sometimes get so cold that it would be impossible to breathe, as oxygen became a liquid during the coldest nights of the year in Kuolarek. How to survive in such a place, then? Well, most power-wielders going into the zone would project a shield around themselves for the duration of their stay, whilst looking for an abandoned shelter beneath the icy plains that sometimes gave way to canyons, remnants of an exile that sought the furthest reaches away from civilization, or a futile attempt at settlement at what felt like the edge of the universe. It was like the frozen version of Jaltai-Vuul.

Upon arrival at Point Deathkiller Station, where Radien was to spend a few days preparing for his excursion into Kuolarek proper, he was met by a Death Worlder who *definitely* was older than he looked.

"Ah, the doer of the Gauntlet!" the old guard said as he invited Radien into the station. "Quickly now, nighttime is the part where even a healthy Zhernreli must take shelter to avoid freezing to death. Kastureth! The Tactician is here!"

What followed was the sound of someone scrambling to their feet, before Radien saw another Death Worlder old guard vault from a platform, acrobatically jumping between strategically-placed struts of metal to land in front of him.

"Kastureth, you've got to cut back on that routine! Your spine is not what it used to be." The Death Worlder who met Radien grunted.

"My spine feels no older than six thousand ASC, you crotchety fool!" Kastureth enthusiastically responded.

"You're only fifty-two hundred ASC, though!" another voice called out from elsewhere.

"What, you *counted?!*" Kastureth barked back.

"*Someone* had to!"

"Pay no mind to these no-fun scoundrels, Tactician," Kastureth encouraged, to which the one standing next to him rolled his eyes, before heading back to his computer screen. "The three of us alone there may be, but we are the strength of three thousand armies!"

"Your glorymongering is going to get your head ripped from your neck, Kastureth," the first Death Worlder retorted.

"Madness! *I* am the one who rips the heads off of my enemy's necks!"

"Ripping heads is *my* trick!" the one from

above returned.

"Ah, I forgot. Yes, my trick is to rip off limbs and beat my foes to death with them. Thank you for the reminder, Alvos."

By this point, Radien was already getting a good look around the station, and could see Alvos at his computer station, putting in an order for more supplies.

"Hey, Varix! That mead from Torvaltyne was pretty good, want me to put another case of it in this requisition order?" Alvos called out to Varix down below, who was checking the armory's weapons, making sure they had enough munitions and were also in decent enough condition to last a holdout.

"If we've got room for it, sure," Varix calmly responded. Alvos proceeded to then add two cases of the mead to the requisition order, to sate the grumpier of the trio that were the garrison at Point Deathkiller. "We also need replacement battery packs for my Laser Lance," Varix then added.

"Have I ever forgotten about ensuring your weapon is powered, old friend?"

"If only because I ensure it."

Alvos laughed at this, proceeding to add the battery packs, since he had almost forgotten. "Ah, we have fun here," he further commented.

Suddenly, the power went out.

"Is this normal?" Radien asked calmly.

"No, not since I upgraded the generator myself!" Kastureth growled. "Weapons ready! It seems there is a saboteur crawling about..."

Radien's hand rested on the Borfblade as the

other two made their way to their weapons, Varix swapping the battery on his Laser Lance for a new one, to make sure it was at full power if there was to be a fight.

"A saboteur? All the way out here?" Alvos questioned. "Much as I do not doubt your electrical skills, Kastureth..."

Kastureth held up his hand to silence the room as he sniffed the air, and then the emergency lights came on. The bunker that was Point Deathkiller Station was dimly lit, but it was better than total darkness.

"It's not the generator," Kastureth realized. "The underground cable to the geothermal plant was cut. Otherwise, these emergency lights would've taken a few extra seconds."

"Why would that be?" Radien questioned.

"Because I designed the systems myself." Kastureth answered. "Specifically to give these sorts of cues."

"I can definitely appreciate this level of planning, but if the sabotage is not coming from within the Station, where then are our foes?" Radien asked next as he drew his sword. Alvos and Varix all were weapons-ready, awaiting the next piece of information about whatever was coming.

Then, Radien heard something. Something he wasn't sure if the others did.

"I hear something," Radien noted. His eyes then flashed amber as he used The Aura's Second Sight to figure out what was going on. "Footsteps, spiked boots on the ice, only kilometers away and approaching at sprinting pace."

"What can survive *sprinting* in this weather?!" Varix wondered aloud.

"Something likely far greater in power than us, I fear," Alvos muttered. Radien's head snapped to glare at the Death Worlder who just mentioned fear. But then, Radien was able to figure out what was approaching. Something that could indeed survive the air-freezing temperatures of Kuolarek Black Zone.

"Demons... I've seen this kind before, in the manuals of Arigen Concarius..."

"Demons?!" Alvos exclaimed. "What are they doing here?!"

"Obviously, trying to establish a foothold at a strongpoint," Radien quickly responded. "They likely think they can quickly overwhelm this place, eliminate its garrison, and begin setting up a permanent base over our corpses."

"*Djalsej!* How many?!"

"I count twelve Frigid Lords, thanks to Second Sight."

"*Ja-jahada Djalsej!*" Alvos continued to curse the rotten luck. One Frigid Lord was bad enough, but twelve... that was something else.

"How can the Lords of Evil spare such a force for only four of us?!" Varix seethed. "I remember a time when even *one* to be sent was a gambit on their part! How much strength have they gained?!"

"Or how desperate are they to try to seize such a remote position?" Radien asked. "What's here that makes Point Deathkiller worth sending twelve

Frigid Lords?!"

A moment passed before Radien spoke up again. "Think quickly now, they're almost upon us! If there weren't something worth contesting here, we'd already have taken the Quickgate to Firatyne and sapped it from the other side by now! No matter how much strength the Dark Six have, twelve Frigid Lords is a *hell* of a lot of firepower to send over a glorified supply bunker!"

The footsteps were getting closer. They were less than a kilometer away now. Radien found himself with only one option left.

*<Nel Jalfjaa, hear me, for I know you are watching this Zhernreli complete the Gauntlet. Twelve Frigid Lords bear down upon us, and these old guard are being struck by forbidden fear. We once spoke of how to balance the will to learn, the refusal of ignorance, and the demands of reason and justice. Refuse ignorance today, and smite these foes before I am slaughtered by unfair odds while trying to convince cowards to fight for their own lives!>*

A massive explosion was heard outside, and the screams of Demons being shredded by golden lightning pierced the air. The Nel Jalfjaa had heard Radien, and taken a stand. Twelve Frigid Lords were no more.

"I would have rather fought them," Radien said as he looked out upon the frozen field that the Frigid Lords now painted with their blood. "I dread the consequences of such contempt for my foes."

The three Death Worlders visibly relaxed as they put their weapons away. Radien was not pleased by their hesitation. Though in his mind of minds he knew that he could not blame these veteran warriors for knowing insurmountable odds when they saw them, his frustration that they almost broke in the face of this danger was growing.

*<The dread is mine, Radien.>* The Nel Jalfjaa announced to the entire station as they rippled into existence within. *<The foes that will be the consequence of today will aim their ire upon me. Much like how Cynar is populated by few and far between Grand Psionic Entities such as myself, so too are the Burning Hells populated with their own veritable gods. Until this new war for reality is over, or I have slain them all, I must exile myself from Raon-Arashal, for this world's sake as they pursue me."*

Alvos's eyes widened with shock. The Nel Jalfjaa was about to leave Raon-Arashal?

"You… I… I wish I could pay my respects to the good omen your presence brings…" Alvos pleaded. "But long have you watched our world, Nel Jalfjaa, and guided the Zhernrel-Vuljar down the path of honor and reason, and now, you must *leave?*"

*<A thousand threads are pulling all at once for my actions today, and for the fact that they were necessary. I will return one day, and Raon-Arashal must stand against whatever storm comes to await me.>*

"This is all too sudden, Nel Jalfjaa." Kastureth pleaded. "First Caltoran burns countless worlds, then The Unmaker nearly subjugates the stars while they are without a Defender, and now… the symbol of our honor leaves us? It's too much, too quickly, Nel Jalfjaa… it's too much, too quickly."

Kastureth's transparency surprised Radien, but he understood how the old warrior felt.

<*What of you, Varix of Firatyne? What piece does the Shroud-Piercer himself think of all this?*> The Nel Jalfjaa asked of the only one who had been silent thus far since the Grand Psionic Entity showed up.

Suddenly, the world froze around Radien. Nothing moved, not even the Nel Jalfjaa. He looked around until he saw a familiar entity who did not obey the laws of linear time, shimmering like a two-dimensional sheet of bismuth in the shape of a person that always faced his eyes.

"Oh, come on!" Radien yelled at the Time Ender. "You too?! You're getting in on this as well?! Allow me to take a page from Kastureth's book as I say this is too much, too quickly!"

"And here I thought you might appreciate my presence, for it means that this tragedy in the making you behold can yet be prevented."

"I don't like what you represent, Time Ender!" Radien spat. "I know the fantasy of a control-Z function in real life just as well as the next guy, but that's a kind of power that if I've got The Aura, I *don't* want to have to call on! *You* represent a level of freedom from consequence that I do *not* like the prospect of indulging in!"

Radien angrily paced around for a bit as he formed his next thought.

"I can't deny that what you've done the last times we've met has prevented some pretty awful shit... but I don't want you to act as my magic crutch, damn it! I don't want you to become the deus ex machina of my every problem! It... it just doesn't feel right!"

After a few more moments of silence, the Time Ender finally spoke.

"Indeed, many would clamor for the kind of power you are saying you despise the principle of. So how does one balance the will to learn, the refusal to ignorance, and the demands of reason and justice?"

Radien groaned. He was annoyed by all the events that had just taken place, all at once, with barely any time to process them as one thing became another. He was annoyed further by the fact that the Time Ender had shown up again like a magic eraser to give Radien unlimited lives and a checkpoint, as it were. He then sat in a nearby chair and pondered, every now and again looking back up at the Time Ender to make sure he wasn't about to suddenly ditch him, just to be a dick on top of all this... today-ness.

"You're making that choice here and now, aren't you?" Radien asked. To this, the otherworldly figure somehow managed to nod its head, and somehow, it made sense despite the strangeness of its physical appearance. "You figured that to side with reason and justice is to give me the do-over, huh?"

"Indeed."

"Why? And why me?"

"Even after all of the time I have spent beyond time, I still have things to learn by watching Cynar. Such as the question of how to balance the will to learn, the refusal to ignorance, and the demands of justice. It is not easy to bring me to such introspection, and should not go unrewarded with the chance to make sure you get the ending you want to today."

"There's more to that, isn't there?" Radien asked.

To this, the shimmering form of the Time Ender coalesced into a different form. This was no longer some ethereal beyond-time entity. The Time Ender clearly was once a species of Cynar, ascended into this strange new form of life.

"We do not obey the laws of linear time, and Cynar knows this well." He said. "Our species hails from well beyond today, when the understanding of life and of the universe allows some to become... of this level of existence."

Radien tilted his head slightly as he processed the words of this species from the future.

"We used to number many, but hubris followed in the wake of ascension, and one by one, it overcame my people, until The Unmaker enthralled the one you destroyed, and that has made me the last, the very last... No matter where I go in time now, I will never see another of my kind again. Though you may see one in your future, they are, all of them, part of my past. But I owe my survival to watching you, Miles Sorvenjar Radien. The morals and values you hold, the honor you demand of yourself, it is why I met no similar fate, and I remain, when no others do."

"I'm just glad you're not *me* from the future, honestly," Radien said with slight levity.

"That would be quite annoying, I must agree."

"Even so, my points stand. Much as I guess someone in your position would figure it's just returning the favor, ensuring optimal survival... as someone who still has to experience time in one direction, it does feel a bit like cheating."

"I understand. Let's not make this a habit, then. That all said... what's your plan this time?"

The Frigid Lords were bearing down on the bunker that was Point Deathkiller Station, merely kilometers away.

"I remember a time when even *one* to be sent was a gambit on their part! How much strength have they gained?!" Varix seethed.

Without hesitation, Radien answered this question with a resolute declaration. "Not enough to overcome us! *Hol-nah Viir! Stand and Fight!*"

"*Anan Volkarn! Time for Battle!*" The three old guards responded.

"*Hol-nah Viir!*"

"*Anan Volkarn!*"

"*Pir Jaltai! By the sword!*"

"*Pir Iklae! By the spear!*"

Claws slammed against the bunker walls.

"*Aurok son-Deyl! Behold our power!*" Everyone called at once.

The Borfblade was the first weapon to draw blood as Radien's sword sliced the claws off of the Frigid Lord who had made the mistake of trying to sink them through the eye-ports of the bunker, exposing them to the bite of Hunderfold Novasteel.

Kastureth cackled with spirit of battle as his hands surged with power, summoning a great warhammer into his hands, crackling with raw energy as he leaped into the air, slamming the head of the hammer onto the head of the Frigid Lord who had just burst through the door, exploding it to pieces.

Four Death Worlders against twelve Frigid Lords. The odds were not in the favor of the Demons.

The Borfblade drove itself right into the eye of a Frigid Lord as the Laser Lance of Varix sliced through the throat of another. Nine more to go.

Alvos pressed a button on the console he sat at, and turrets deployed themselves throughout the station, locking on to three Frigid Lords that had just clawed their way in, and were bearing down towards him. Three shots later, there were only six Demons remaining. Alvos then noticed something on his desk.

"Ooh, forgot I had this bag!" He then grabbed a sealed bag of potato chips from an open drawer on his desk. Potato chips were to a Death World Vulpian, what beef jerky was to an excitable Australian Shepard. Alvos, however, quickly had to fend off the fists of a Frigid Lord from being able to tear the bag open and spill its contents on the floor, expertly dodging and parrying the strikes with only one hand, the other focused on protecting the precious cargo from the one whose claws had been sliced off by the Borfblade.

Noticing a knife on his desk, Alvos grabbed it with his tail, flinging it up into the air, and leaping up with a wheel kick that sent the blade flying into the throat of the Frigid Lord that was very unwisely trying to keep a Death Worlder from his potato chips. Five left.

The five Frigid Lords remaining gathered themselves together as the four warriors of Point Deathkiller assembled next to each other, the two sides facing off against each other. The Frigid Lords thought this would be an easy target. Now, they were making their last stand.

Radien sheathed the Borfblade, and charged a crackling sphere of raw power in his right hand as he dropped back into a low stance that charged this full blast of power, and after a few seconds, unleashed it, to the Frigid Lords scattering out of the way, except for the one that the orb was following, and soon turned into bloody chunks.

Each of the four soon engaged a Frigid Lord each, now that the fight was even in number. The enemy that once attacked was now squarely on the defensive, and they were doomed.

As the corpses of twelve Frigid Lords were hauled out into the wastes of Kuolarek to be dumped unceremoniously into one of the many icy canyons, Radien figured that now was the time to have the conversation that when he tried to have it in the heat of battle, meant that the Time Ender had to interfere to give him the chance to do things right.

"What could they be after?" Radien asked one of the old guard of the station. "Twelve Frigid Lords is a lot to send after a glorified supply bunker in the middle of the coldest region on the planet."

"Hmmm… you are correct," Kastureth surmised aloud. "I find it hard to believe that we, despite our exploits, merit such an assassination squad."

"I'd be quite disappointed, honestly." Alvos commented. "Not even *one* Darkstar for the trio that contains the Shroud-Piercer of Firatyne himself?"

He then looked at Varix, who simply shrugged.

Kastureth laughed aloud to this. "Varix, you are far too humble in your elder years! That weapon of his, Tactician, it has slain more of Raon-Arashal's foes than some species have a number for! Though so many lives taken is nothing to tout on a banner, you'd suspect that Varix is still *seeking* his glory with how little he lauds himself!"

"A little lauding is never inherently wrong, by the way," Alvos added. "Ah, but if you *began* to do so now, you'd lose that other title among our little trio of misfits, our dedicated Grumpfox!"

Radien snorted as Alvos called Varix a *Grumpfox*, of all things. To this, Varix let out a slight grumbling noise.

"Eh, if he minded, he'd've said something," Alvos commented, and Varix nodded a little in response. He just wasn't a particularly talkative fellow, and when he did talk, he was all business. One would suppose that *someone* had to be, in a trio of misfits.

After all, it was Varix who was piloting the Landskimmer, all while Alvos and Kastureth had begun an impromptu '*I'm not booping you*' exchange of words, and playful light punches.

"Tactician, I think you've more than earned the right to know where best to spend your thirty days in Kuolarek for the Gauntlet of Doom, considering how you aided us in that battle," Varix noted as Alvos tackled Kastureth to the ground. "I found an excellent meditation spot to ponder the mysteries of the universe at, on my last excursion."

"Do tell," Radien inquired.

After the Demonic corpses were disposed of, the Landskimmer zoomed across Kuolarek until reaching an otherwise ordinary cavernous lump in the ice. It looked like the kind of tunnel into the ground built by burrowing insects, except this was in the ice, and also large enough for a man to stand in.

"I think someone of your Psionic inclination may find what is within most... informative," Varix said, then seemingly taking a few seconds to figure out what was probably a better word to describe whatever awaited Radien.

"Thanks for the lift, gentlemen," Radien addressed as he hopped out of the Landskimmer. "Good battle back at the station, too."

"I'll say!" Kastureth responded. "I never did finish that requisition order for resupply, we *must* add another case of mead to the order to celebrate!"

"There's already two cases, are you sure we can be asking for more?" Varix questioned.

"For the Shroud-Piercer of Firatyne? We could order a dozen, and they'd be *scrambling* to get that much to us!" Kastureth continued.

"I hope you're not throwing my name's weight around to get better supplies to us, there may be others who need—"

"We are *going* to get some mead in you, you old Grumpfox!" Alvos yelled as the Landskimmer sped off, all while Varix insisted on not using the weight of his name to simply get more mead to Point Deathkiller Station, despite how logistically, it was no issue to the Raon-Arashal Defensive Militarium's Supply Corps.

They certainly were a trio of characters, undoubtedly with many stories to tell.

Radien wandered into the icy cavern that led beneath the freezing winds of Kuolarek, and traveled deeper and deeper, until the outside wind knew no power in the depths. A conjured ball of light followed him, even though his Death Worlder eyes could do quite well in the dark. There was something neat to having the ball of light following him, though comforting just wasn't the right word. Even though he could use the Aura to see through the dark, even though his eyes could naturally find the walls and outlines of what he needed to see, Radien valued being able to behold the entire cavern like this, for reasons he could not explain. Similarly inexplicable was why it just made him feel more fulfilled in its exploration. He could see it all. The calm and cool air that offered sanctuary from the winds of Kuolarek, that could freeze the air in its harshest nights.

And yet, in this cavern, one might never suspect such was awaiting outside.

The Nel Jalfjaa rippled into existence beside Radien once again.

*<A temporal disturbance seems to surround you, Radien.>*

"Trust me, you *don't* want to know."

*<Well, then I suppose you don't really need to hear about what I learned of the tablets you keep finding in every zone.>* The Nel Jalfjaa replied cheekily with its ethereal voice.

"Well, if you insist..."

Radien recounted the events that the Time Ender

prevented.

*<It is no surprise to me, Radien, your disdain for what the Time Ender's aid represents. The balance you seek is not trivially attained.>*

"Sometimes I wonder why I burden myself with the search," Radien admitted. "It feels like the path of most resistance, and it promises seemingly no reward when compared to all the manners in which I could compromise my morals in little, yet constant ways… ways that many times it seems, no one would even be able to tell the difference."

Radien then thought for a moment. "Gah, that made sense in some universe, I'm sure of it."

*<It did in this one, if only for your present company.>*

"I suppose a Grand Psionic Entity would have a higher level of intuition, that lets you figure out what the hell I meant by all *that*. Hell, I'm not even fully sure right now."

*<If it should help, there is a matter we can be more sure upon: The tablets you have been finding across the Black Zones, written in the old Zhernreli runes.>*

"Yes, what did you learn of them?"

*<Well, less learned and more remembered that I knew, that the tablets had something to do with the Prophecy of the Beast of Raon-Arashal.>*

"Sounds foreboding," Radien commented. "Granted, what's been written on them seems to suggest that whatever this Beast of Raon-Arashal is, it is *not* some ancient evil imprisoned deep within the planet."

<*Thankfully, no. At least, as far as I am aware.*>

"How long have you been on this planet for?"

<*If I knew everything there was to know about Raon-Arashal, I wouldn't be here.*>

"Point taken."

<*The Prophecy of the Beast of Raon-Arashal itself is written upon the Red Cliff of Stories within Firenthal. I admit that I'm paraphrasing, but the Beast is the one who knows the ways of the Zhernreli so well, who understands their principles and their culture so intimately, that they wield the verses scattered across the Black Zones to solve Raon-Arashal's oldest riddle.*> The Nel Jalfjaa explained.

"And what is the oldest riddle of Raon-Arashal, pray tell?" Radien asked.

<*That has been the subject of heated scholarly debate for eons, I'm afraid. Some say that it is an ancient puzzle of some kind, that the twenty-two verses are the key to the solution of. Others say that the 'oldest riddle' is simply a metaphor, and the Beast is whoever can take the advice they offer to heart the most. I have no answer to this, myself. Even a single planet is quite large, and even a Grand Psionic Entity like myself can never truly know a place like this inside and out.*>

"Intriguing," Radien processed aloud. "Here I am, finding these verses, purported to be the key to a puzzle that I didn't even know existed... to me, this seems like a mystery to solve *after* the Dark Six are defeated. Even your explanation I feel only scratches the surface of this whole ordeal, if even."

<*Hence, even a single planet is quite large. That, and Raon-Arashal is a unique world among worlds.*>

The Nel Jalfjaa rippled out of existence, leaving Radien to ponder further. In the distance, he could hear the howling winds outside that blew into the cavern's entrance for the first few dozen feet. The stillness of where he stood brought an indescribable satisfaction to him, that seemed to hint that despite the whirlwind that had been the last few hundred years, there was and still would be time for respite, something he never knew on Old Earth. The tyranny of that world may have yet haunted him, but perhaps in completing the Gauntlet of Doom, he may break away from the perpetual dark chapter that was life as a Human.

A familiar stone rectangle embedded on the icy wall of the cavern caught his eye. The runes glowed red to his touch once more.

*Deliis Unzhernreli kalska unuath toreiyn duul'e Nejtoulth akar valzhi pirpask.*

*To be a Death Worlder is to know that a breath taken in spite of your foes shall strengthen the next.*

# 12

# JELKETH BLACK ZONE

Those not from Raon-Arashal called it the Jelketh Sea, but those who lived on Raon-Arashal knew better. The largest surface-level body of water on the planet, it did not have the size needed to call it an ocean, and hardly anyone bothered calling it a sea anyway, because the entire thing was the Jelketh Black Zone. Harsh winds and dire waters throughout, dotted with small islands barely rising up from the depths enough to not be submerged. Even then, many of these islands were simply not viable to stand on, as the tides often saw half of them spend half the day underwater. The only permanent settlement was Tlaenhjem, a converted flotilla that in its early history, was known to migrate due to the waters of Jelketh itself. Nowadays, Dredgestone pillars held the town well above even the highest tides, even if only by a few meters. With a name that translated from the Death Worlder language as 'steel-home', Radien found himself pondering the sea during his seven days of preparation before being shipped off to one of the islands to spend the next thirty, leaning on one of the rails that looked off into the horizon, and also stopped people from tripping over something and falling into the deadly waters below.

Footsteps behind him. Radien made himself ready.

"Good gods, you spent *way* too long around the Humans, Radien," Jarrek commented as he handed him a bottle of Redarian Amber Ale, bought from one of the nearby shops.

"You're not the first to say that, and I doubt you'll be the last. Thanks," Radien replied as he accepted the bottle, before twisting off the top and taking a drink.

"The way you ponder the sea and the horizon, makes me wonder if there were any sailors in your family," Jarrek commented.

Radien shook his head. "My family's best parts were as utterly unremarkable as its worst parts were *Nezhval, honorless.*"

Jarrek let out an 'ooh', acknowledging the fiery words Radien had so casually bestowed on them. "That is not a word lightly used."

"But it is used well, in this case. I'm glad to be all that's left, it means that I can make a name for myself without having to worry about how they'll sap from it, whether by living undeservedly well off of *my* accomplishments, or by draining whatever honor I bring to the name of Radien with their lack of it."

"How do you know you're all that's left? Much as I know what happened between Veralis and Amandrianna, that's all of one part of it. In the centuries I've known you, you haven't spoken once of the rest."

"What's there to speak of? My sister drowned after falling off of a yacht during a party with her friends, but she was a bitch anyway, who really took after her mother in all the worst ways. In some ways, she managed to be even worse. My father lived and died, a broken fool from what Amandrianna's tyranny did to us all. As for my brother, he vanished off the face of the Earth in a manner I envied for the longest time, which is to say completely. He was always an enigmatic fellow, and I admired that. No commitments, no loose ends to leave behind untied."

Jarrek pondered the sea with Radien, waiting for the next part of what his friend had to say.

"Every one of them represented something I despised. Whether the maniacal self-entitlement of my sister, the pathologically manipulative disposition of my mother, the cowardly ignorance of my father, or the envy I had for my brother, that he didn't even have to suffer them."

"Vanished off the face of the Earth, huh?"

"Yeah, he got a gig right out of high school and never looked back. I can't blame him, I would've done the same, considering the alternative. Lucky bastard."

The two continued to ponder the sea.

"By the way, Jarrek, what the hell *were* you doing on Earth, anyway?"

"That's right, Brian and I were there for a bit."

"Yeah, that's how we met. You and Brian in Morphic Illusion turning up at the Fourteen Werewolves for me to rid the world of a group of homophobic hicks."

"Would've dealt with them myself, but with Earth being in the sensitive position of non-interference requirement at the time, it was easier to lure them towards a local power-wielder and let them take care of it. Saw the fight from a window, by the way. Impressive as it was, there was a lot to improve."

"Yeah, I kinda did slip back to a more edgy style in those early days of The Aura. Not like anyone's around to remember it, though."

"*Everyone* has an edgelord phase of power-wielding, so don't despair."

"But still, what *were* you doing on a backwater planet overcrowded by an underdeveloped species, anyway? Veralis said that you had faked your death again for some time off..."

"That does have a ring of truth to it." Jarrek chuckled. "Though it was more like me strolling into Admiral DePirr's office and saying 'I'm gonna go die for a bit, I'll let you know when I survive,' and then flopping on the ground and rolling away all 'oh nooo, I'm dying, how horrible and tragic, horror of horrors...' all while he had to physically fight back bursting out laughing. But the more unofficial part of it was investigating rumors that the *Aura Runner* was spotted in that system, that there was a Deceiver Demon looking to subjugate a whole species, and that there was an inexplicable void in the lifeblood of the universe surrounding not just Earth, but the entire Elder Terra system."

Radien nodded. It was a legitimate explanation, and was also the truth.

"You escaped Earth not a moment too soon, Radien," Jarrek finally divulged. "More hands than even *I* know had cards to play, and you were the wrench that threw yourself into their plans."

"I take that as a compliment."

"As well you should."

Jarrek and Radien continued to ponder the sea as they finished their drinks. Once their bottles were empty and rid of, they simply remained leaning on the rail, watching the horizon as day became night on Raon-Arashal.

When morning came, and now was the time to be marooned on one of the small islands of Jelketh, Radien walked across the island in less than an hour, and then back again, before walking to the center of what was little more than a pile of rocks and sand that only just managed to be above sea level. There was hardly any 'survival' to be done here, though this was the Gauntlet of Doom.

If there was nothing to survive against, then he would train. And train he did, practicing the fundamentals of hand and foot, every punch and kick thrown against the wind, to hone them for when these limbs would need to strike the flesh and bone of his foes.

With all this time to practice, he could practice *everything*. From baring the claws that he sharpened in Jaltai-Vuul, to lacing his empty-handed strikes with his power of The Aura, and doing the same with the Borfblade as he continued to hone the art of channeling the azure energy through the Hunderfold Novasteel, that each slice extended beyond itself, as though carving the very air with its edge.

The cuts that were rough, they became smoother and sharpened, and as day became night, practice would be put to use against the hostile waves that swept across the island he stood on, his fists punching through the waves as his stance stayed solid, his feet anchored upon the rocks, that the water could not move. The largest of waves were met with an azure shield of The Aura, that his hands summoned and his spirit kept strong. Jelketh Black Zone could not claim him.

When the night became day, practice resumed. Empty hand, sword, power through the hands, power through the sword, repeat.

His claws could slice through the sandstone of Jaltai-Vuul, and the waves of Jelketh. They could anchor his feet upon the icy peaks of Kaladorum, or against the waves of Jelketh. Most would feel invincible for this fact. Radien did not. Every day and night that he dueled the waves, he never allowed himself the sin of cockiness, the doom that was overconfidence. Undefeatable, sure. But unkillable? The notion was banished from his mind, and for this awareness, he would be neither defeated nor killed.

Another thirty days had passed. Another Black Zone had been endured, and conquered. And on that last day, Radien saw another stone tablet, that he placed his hand upon, before it vanished into the sandy beach.

*Deliis Unzhernreli jagizh Volarthir-nah volarthir pas-Jagizh.*

*To be a Death Worlder is to train to survive, and survive to train further.*

# 13

# JESSEL-TARN BLACK ZONE

**J**essel-Tarn is a unique one, for sure," Arakai told Radien as they both prepared to enter the zone, Arakai for a regular run of it, Radien for this segment of the Gauntlet of Doom. "I mean, they're all unique by nature, but this one's basically the fun one, second only to Klatars'Kall."

"I've heard that the Nel Jalfjaa placed some kind of Psionic artifact that makes it so, but I don't think anyone gave me the proper lowdown on it," Radien responded.

"Okay, so the entire zone is chock-full of random structures of all kinds, from ancient ruins, to derelict castles and watchtowers, and even abandoned military bases. But they're constantly phasing in and out of existence, spawning in and out of reality full of crazy loot to grab, and hostile denizens that all analysis shows are just projections of raw latent energies that coalesce into different forms, like beasts and Demons and Supernals and other things that go bump in the night, to train against and even be rewarded for it with the valuables that are in these places. It's like... like a..."

"It's like a dungeon crawler?!" Radien asked excitedly.

"Yes! It's exactly like that!" Arakai responded, starting to get charged up as well. Radien immediately realized which zone he'd be regularly returning to, and it was no wonder Arakai made regular runs of the place as well. "One time I was here, I found this random wooden trapdoor in a grassy field, and there was this Monument Breaker guarding a wooden chest right? I take him down, and in the chest is a *dozen* ingots of Archonium! Took 'em to a phase-smith to get this lamellar made!"

Arakai referred to the armor that he wore in battle, that had served him through countless duels and battles across his lifetime.

Radien was definitely getting hyped up to dive into Jessel-Tarn now. "I can already tell that I'm going to have a *blast* in this one."

"I know, right?! Show me what you find when you're finished!"

"Will do! Where are you headed to?"

"Rumor has it that a Kendrosian-style fort popped up a few days ago, I'm gonna see if it's still there. Also, don't worry about structures vanishing while you're still in them. It seems that as long as a place is occupied by at least one person from Cynar proper, they'll stick around at least until they leave."

"I was just about to ask, thanks."

The gate lowered, and Arakai started wandering off towards the Ancient Fortress he was talking about. Radien envied his wander, but he was a worthy ally. He would never allow his envy of another to lead him to ruin. Perhaps one day, Radien would wander like Arakai Selendica.

Radien made his way towards the first structure that caught his eye. It towered over the plains, and the jet-black walls of spikes and turrets, a bladed maze of architecture that knew no yield, only the ominous shadow he cast.

Suddenly, it began to crumble, and soon, it faded from existence. Radien raised an eyebrow. Must've meant that someone else got to it first.

The next structure that caught his eye, he entered.

Fighting his way through a forgotten tower, Radien found little challenge in the miscellaneous hostile denizens, from ancient suits of armor still haunted by the warriors who wore them in life, to spectral weapons of heroes long past, that still longed to taste battle. At the end of the corridor, there was a great Demon. Though Radien knew that this was a projection from the artifact that the Nel Jalfjaa embedded into the land to create Jessel-Tarn, the Borfblade was in his hand faster than most could blink, and he growled in quiet rage as he saw the abomination before him.

"You know who I am, don't you?" the Demon taunted as she placed a hand on the sword that was resting atop a stone plinth. All lights around Radien seemed to go out, and the floor seemed to turn to aged copper, a deep and turquoise green.

"Who are you that I should know?" Radien asked, the Borfblade ready in his left hand.

"You *do* know!" the Demonic projection exclaimed with unnatural excitement. "It has been a *long* time since I have seen one of your blood... And a long time since *Zoln'Slaan Thiild* tasted it..."

The Demoness had spoken a name that Radien did not recognize, but he felt as though he should. Like it was an old enemy of his, known in all but name...

"That name means nothing to me. You have mistaken me for someone else," Radien stated firmly.

"Oh, and you don't even *know* that you know yet, do you? *This* should be fun! It seems you've even gotten a bit of a head start..."

"What are you *talking* about?!" Radien demanded. "You're not even making sense! Or, perhaps that's part of the trick! Either way, it will not work. My blade will taste Demon's blood today, as it has many times before."

"I have no doubt of that, *Greígoth*," the Demoness finished before grabbing the blade from the plinth and leaping off of it towards Radien, and the duel had begun.

Radien spun around and side kicked the leaping strike from the Demon, and the arrested momentum caused her to hit the floor with a loud *thud*, but harder than she had anticipated. Her breath was suddenly wheezy, Radien had crushed an entire side of this foe's ribcage with a single kick.

"He's going to *like* you..."

Radien's patience with this creature was spent. A single swipe of the Borfblade separated head from neck, and the roundhouse kick that followed sent it flying onto the wall, and shattering the accursed Demon's skull.

There was little left but a hunk of inert Demon's head, half-caved in from the impact with the wall.

The body of the Demon began to dissolve into red sparks, red sparks that Radien recognized, when he had slain the Demon Avanchenvaldr, and when he battled them in Hulae, which had left only their weapons and armors behind, clattering onto the ground.

And the blade of this Demon he had just killed clattered to the ground like the others. He looked at its intricacy. Though there was no doubt that the metals were of the kind to make titanium seem like tissue paper, the hilt had a dark silver luster to it, the silver of gunmetal beneath a veneer of pewter. The blade was as steel, save for jet black fullers between the two edges. The pommel stone was of an unnervingly pastel pink, and an eye was affixed within the crossguard's finery, above the handle itself. A spherical white eye, with a blood-red iris and black pupil. It darted around randomly, constantly.

The eye locked its gaze onto Radien, and then the weapon fell apart at the atomic level, fizzling away into nothingness.

The light in the room returned, and behind Radien was an intricately-built chest. With a telekinetic flip of his wrist, he remotely opened it. Just in case this was some cruel mimicry.

But this chest was no Mimic. Its treasure was true. When Radien brought it out from the dungeon, the trapdoor entrance sunk into the ground, before vanishing entirely. Radien turned his head, suddenly seeing the Nel Jalfjaa next to him.

<Do you know what you saw in there?> The Nel Jalfjaa asked.

"Haunted armor, spectral weapons, Demoness of some regard, sword with an eye in it?" Radien recalled.

<Well, you're not wrong. Not sure what I expected, though. What you slew in that dungeon was no small feat.>

"It was a Psionic projection, wasn't it? Not the real thing?"

<Well, yes, but actually no. True, it could not have killed you with a lethal strike. You would have been thrown back to this meadow before the blow landed. But the Demoness you dueled, and made a fool of quite quickly, what it was a facsimile of...>

"One of the Dark Six?" Radien postulated, aiming high.

<Not quite. Each of them have Heralds, their second in command. That was an illusion of Watcher of the Burning Eye, Herald of The Deceiver.>

"Burning Eye?" Radien asked. "Like the eye in the sword?"

<The very same.>

"I've encountered that eye before."

<How is this possible?>

"There was a cult on Nibiru once... the cult of the Chaosmaker... their symbol was the Burning Eye, they had it everywhere."

<Everywhere?> The Nel Jalfjaa hovered still as it processed this. <Radien... it is said that every image of the Burning Eye, is itself a Burning Eye.>

"That can be watched through, right?" Radien

began. "Like the eye in the sword, The Watcher of the Burning Eye can see through it?"

*<No 'the,' just Watcher of the Burning Eye.>*

"Right, right. The symbol of the Burning Eye was everywhere on Nibiru. Posters, billboards, flags, people had them as lapel pins, for fuck's sake!"

*<It is a good thing you destroyed that cult, Radien.>*

"You'll have no argument from me, Nel Jalfjaa. So these Heralds..."

*<What of them?>*

"I'd heard that the Darkstars were second in power and influence only to the Dark Six. But these Heralds that are apparently the right-hand men of the Lords of Evil, it sounds like they would have that title properly."

*<Not exactly. A Herald is not superior in rank to a Darkstar. A Herald is a Darkstar, just with the additional title and responsibilities thereof.>*

"So, akin to the bishops and cardinals of Old Earth, right?"

*<Yes, just less morally corrupt, and far less dangerous to be in the presence of.>*

"Indeed. Thanks for the clarification."

Radien then looked around for the next dungeon to run, or whatever it would take the form of. Between Klatars'Kall and Jessel-Tarn, the Black Zones sure had their fun ones. It seemed as though this one was going to be a 'break' zone, as it were. Though presenting its challenges in its own right, Jessel-Tarn was just damned fun to be in.

Jessel-Tarn seemed to exist to show and remind

that the universe was supposed to be fun, damn it. That existence was meant to fulfill and not be suffered, that the highest crime is to rob the living of purpose, to create a living purgatory was the most capital of them all, where none live, only exist. Jessel-Tarn was the place to go to prove that this was not the point of existence, and that the only correct response to those who bring grey centuries is to make them intimately familiar with the point of a sword, delivered between their ribs and into their vital organs.

Through dungeon and castle, Radien trained and fought the enemies that the Archaeopsionic artifact deep beneath the ground produced. Claiming the many arms and armaments that the projected beasts of legend guarded, it seemed that the main task that would await him between this and the next zone would be sorting through them all, and deciding which ones should populate Torvaltyne's armory, which ones should simply be sold at Fireline Station's many vendors, and which pieces of armor to keep. It was the case that though Radien's weapon was well-decided, he had yet to figure out what armor he would wear to battle. Shields of the Aura were only going to go so far, after all.

Jessel-Tarn was providing the chance for him to at least figure out what he wanted, even if he did not find it here. He certainly wasn't going to be short on materials after thirty days, not to mention the many more times he knew he was going to visit. This place did not just train him to fight many opponents, but also trained him how to do so in many different architectural environments, many different structural battlegrounds that he may encounter. Where the other Black Zones were to train his ability to survive in any natural biome, Jessel-Tarn was showing him the principles of survival and resourcefulness to be used in inhabited areas. Though his ability for social survivalism was already quite honed, Radien would never refuse to have his skills grown, sharpened, honed.

In training, there was purpose. Purpose that until these days in the wider universe, had been denied by the whims and wills of wicked Humans, seeking only to grey the skies with monotony and purgatory alike. The will to destroy such evil was being sharpened into the skill to do so. Even though by now, Radien had made many iniquitous pay their debts in blood, that quest for retribution remained a burning hunger to deliver just vengeance. Jessel-Tarn was showing Radien that vengeance is not the only thing that his training can bring forth, and that he need not only train for vengeance.

On the last day, as he exited another castle formerly populated by the projections of the foes he might face on the battlefield, another stone tablet caught his eye. Once again, the runic script glowed red upon his touch.

*Orvu Un'Raon-Arashal, var Jagizhfuur deliis Valgitay.*

*In the Arena of life, where training is itself glory.*

# 14

# JUUNALL-SKATH BLACK ZONE

Why it was called Juunall-Skath was a mystery. Neither of the words in the conjugation meant anything, they had no translation from the Death World Vulpian language. In fact, they had no translation in any language. Well, technically they *did* have a translation from the Trylaxian language, but it was meaningless. *Juunall* in Trylaxian translated as 'Tax reform,' and *Skath* was 'Convection oven.' Specifically convection, too. The word for a conventional oven in Trylaxian was *Arvin*. Either way, this zone's name really didn't have any meaning to it. It very much was two random sounds put together that sounded like they might do well together. The Trylaxian explanation was also moot due to the fact that Juunall-Skath had its name before the Trylaxian language developed to the point of having dedicated words for 'tax reform' and 'convection oven.'

Some theorized that it meant something in a more ancient precursor language, which coupled with the theory of Raon-Arashal being an artificial planet, created by said precursor race as the ultimate training ground for its warriors, that the Death Worlders merely happened to find themselves upon.

The theory of Raon-Arashal's uniqueness remains a hotly debated topic across the universe, at least within the academic circles that discuss it. The most widely accepted theory is that the Nel Jalfjaa, akin to how they used an Archaeopsionic Artifact to 'create' Jessel-Tarn, used more than one such kind of artifact to 'forge' Raon-Arashal into what it is now. At least, that would be the most widely accepted theory if it were true. The Nel Jalfjaa themselves stated that this was not the case, and that Raon-Arashal was as it is before they arrived. At least, before Klatars'Kall was whatever it was before it was an irradiated industrial wasteland. For reasons unknown, the Nel Jalfjaa never elected to elaborate upon the matter of Klatars'Kall's origin. It was however, known that this is not because the Nel Jalfjaa caused whatever disaster led to its current state. This is known to be the case because the Nel Jalfjaa did not cause it. Nobody's quite sure what did it, but at the very least, many possibilities have been ruled out, narrowing the field down a little.

Regardless, nobody minded Raon-Arashal acting as the ultimate training ground for one's survival skills, especially not the Zhernrel-Vuljar, who developed an entire culture based around being stubbornly difficult to kill as a result of all that training.

Death Worlders like to train, and Miles Radien was no exception. Even among other Death Worlders, he was known to be more of a gym rat than most.

And speaking of training, Juunall-Skath was

another one of the forested Black Zones. Where the forest of Azhenar was more tundra-like, and Bassoron had those infuriatingly unstable 'mountains,' Juunall-Skath was a temperate rainforest, which unfortunately meant rain. And a lot of it. Radien hated rain with a burning passion. Snow at least could be dusted off before it melted, and given that snow is falling, it somewhat means that it won't suddenly get warm enough to melt before you get to wherever you're going. But rain... no, rain's only goal is to make one's day miserable, drilling through even your best rain gear with contemptuous blobs of water from the sky that fall so constantly and in such volume, that there *is* no such thing as rain-proof, at the end of the day. There is only the misery that comes with soaked clothes and drenched hair.

Fortunately, Miles Radien was a power-wielder, and could simply project a six-foot shield in every direction around himself that kept him dry. He had practiced this Weather Shield technique specifically to not have to deal with rain, because *fuck rain.*

Finding a clearing in the trees that revealed a rocky, yet gradual slope, Radien decided that this was the place to train. It was the closest thing he had found to a flat surface for the last few days of wandering Juunall-Skath, every now and again practicing his improvised weapon throwing skills for hunting. Which was to say, tossing a rock at one of the rodents native to the zone to knock it clean off the tree it was climbing, and then roast it.

Though he could easily conjure a fire on the

ground, or just course power through his hand to cook the game, or simply chow down on the spot since his physiology was not so sensitive to the diseases that otherwise come with raw meat, something primal was satisfied in the process he chose to undergo instead. He could not truly describe why, all he knew was that it was this way.

The rocks made for less than helpful footing as Radien trained in this clearing. Though the icy peaks of Kaladorum's Blizzardblade Mountains were slick, they were flat. Jaltai-Vuul's canyons were made of hard, flat stone on their floors. Jelketh was a sandy, but flat beach. These rocks on this hill meant that nowhere was truly flat. So Radien trained balance in this zone, paying close attention to where his feet were at all times, and with every stumble, that was one less time he would stumble on the battlefield. Was it luck that he hadn't had stumbling incidents before? Radien doubted it, as almost every battle he had been in up to then was on either paved ground, or was flat enough to not cause problems. But not all battlefields are rolling plains and grassy knolls, and he knew he needed to be prepared for it. And prepare for it, he did. Not one moment was wasted, whether it was spent training with his sword, his bare hands and feet, or even practicing picking up rocks and hurling them at where he imagined an enemy might stand.

Radien's ear twitched as he heard a twig snap behind him. Something was approaching. His eyes glowed amber as he searched the area with Second Sight.

Turning to face the bush that this unseen potential threat hid within, he held the Borfblade at his side, lowered but ready.

"The stories were true," something commented from within the bush. Second Sight recognized the form as another Death Worlder. "*Jazukiir pirfuur duul, Zhenreli.* Vigilance becomes you, Death Worlder."

"*Duul torvalka deyl.* You honor me," Radien responded. The Death Worlder emerged from the bush, revealing himself. He was younger than Radien, an adolescent at most. This was quite likely the first time he had been to this particular Black Zone. But then again, it was also Radien's.

"This is only the first time I've been in this one," the young warrior said. "Normally I train in Jessel-Tarn."

"I was just in Jessel-Tarn, I can definitely understand why you'd prefer that. It's the fun one."

"No argument here, Bane of The Unmaker."

Radien stopped for a moment. "That's right... I did destroy him. Seems like it was decades ago."

"It *was* decades ago. You do not remember?"

"Oh, I do... I'm just not the sentimental sort. And you can just call me Radien, by the way. And you are?"

"Raivis Kalosrhui."

*Kalosrhui,* a not uncommon Zhernrel-Vuljar surname. It translated as 'son of armor,' and historically belonged to people who really knew how to tank a hit.

"I hope you didn't come all the way to Juunall-Skath just to see me," Radien noted.

"Why is that?"

"Well, it just seems kinda silly, honestly. What

point is there in risking the Bladesparrows and Musclemelter Snakes of this area just to see *one* person that's known to be here because he's doing the Gauntlet of Doom?"

"Your fame precedes you, that is why."

"Fame? What fame?" Radien scoffed instinctively. "What fame could I possibly have for being just another wanderlusting dude with a sword?"

Raivis tilted his head at this. "Siegebreaker of Hulae, Liberator of Killentarn, Scourge of the Planet of Traitors, Bane of The Unmaker... these titles that the worlds you have saved bestowed on you, and you ask what kind of fame you could possibly have?"

Now Radien was confused. "They did *what*?!"

"All that vigilance, and you didn't notice?"

"How could I? I was there at the scene, where there was nothing to notice other than what was before me, that needed be dealt with."

Both Vulpians shared a sigh of reflection.

"It is also the case that it's not something I'm used to... it's not something I ever thought I'd achieve... Titles that precede my name, victories that earned them... Things that for the formative years of my life, I well understood to be naught but fiction."

"I can't imagine where you once must have been trapped, if fulfillment was fiction."

"I hope you never have to, Raivis. That's why I do what I do."

"Will you honor me with a spar?"

"I was about to ask you the same thing."

The two sparred at about half-speed for a few

minutes, gauging what the other knew, and deliberately moving slower than usual, so that they could train the finer points of movement and reaction in this more controlled setting.

Neither Death Worlder was really sure how long the spar lasted for, the rhythm of training was zen-like indeed. Eventually, the two decided to take a break to find something to munch on. The Gauntlet of Doom's rules did not disallow Radien from accepting food from Raivis's backpack, even though Raivis was not doing the Gauntlet of Doom, but instead just exploring the single zone freestyle.

One might wonder from this what stopped people from just having friends or sponsors constantly bring them food and supplies during the Gauntlet of Doom. The answer was honor. One might wonder what good honor is in such a large universe. Such a person would not survive in said universe, among species that reached the stars *because* they understood its value. That, and there was a threshold of aid that was considered cheating, and would thusly disqualify someone from being considered to have completed the Gauntlet of Doom.

Either way, Raivis sharing a snack with Radien did not cross this threshold.

"I hope I do not awaken painful memories when I ask you about the Planet of Traitors, Radien," Raivis began. "But I am curious... If only in an academic sense."

Radien thought for a moment. "I'd say it's been long enough, but something like the Planet of Traitors... I feel like no amount of time is long enough to atone."

"It's not like you slew an innocent species, you know."

"Oh, I know, Raivis," Radien said with a slight groan. "I *know* that every Exiled Chapter Vulpian was no longer themselves when that damn Deoxian Pulse Engine fired. I *know* that they willingly charged it over decades, voluntarily preparing to surrender to the will of the Dark Six. I *know* all this and all that about the circumstances... but I also know that I still did what I did. I still depopulated an entire planet, I still removed from the stars an entire species, even though I *know* that species was already lost, and I was just... breaking empty shells, as it were."

"That's not what I'm curious about," Raivis admitted. "True as it is you never set foot on that world since, you were not the last person to land a ship on that cursed world. Archaeologists, historians, academics... there have been almost a dozen explorations of that planet now, piecing together that fateful day that an entire Vulpian species sealed its own fate, trying to answer questions they know they have no business asking you, for the burden that is what you had to do."

"Where are you going with this, Raivis?"

"The Psionic traces they found. Yours, theirs, the latent signature of the Dark Six... all of it lined up, save for one piece. Something else was also on that world, at the same time as you, preceding you, like a riptide that warned of a tsunami."

Radien sat still for a moment as he processed Raivis's implied inquiry, remembering what he could, and also remembering why so much of it seemed like a blank in his mind.

"I remember hatred, rage… it was like I was back on Earth, and as though I had been locked into a room with everyone I had ever wanted to kill… and I had a sword in my hand and a pistol on my hip to do it with, and a rage that flowed through me as though the gods themselves had said 'go for it, do it, do what you've always dreamed of… crush your enemies.' No thoughts and no words that I spoke to myself, nothing but what was in front of me, targets, targets, targets… Time was no object, only a number in my eyes that my power showed me, that number was how many there were left. And if there were any thoughts, they were only of making that number zero."

Raivis quietly nibbled on some of the cheese in his pack, listening to Radien's recollection.

"The corners of my vision reddened, tendrils of darkness seethed from every one of the Exiled Chapter. It wasn't my Second Sight… it was something else. I don't know what it was. I don't know if it had a name. I don't know if I want to know, because I know I never want that part of me to have its way again. I may have been surrounded by nothing but enemies then, and sure, it meant there was no consequence in unleashing… whatever the hell it was, but I don't want to risk that part of me doing something I'll truly regret."

"Truly regret?" Raivis asked. "It sounds like you at least don't regret The Planet of Traitors, and what you did once they betrayed."

"Gah, how can I?" Radien asked of himself. "All the things I know about that day, and that history knows too... I know I can't be blamed, and I know I can't blame myself, but I can't help but understand that this... conflict, this constant debate that rages within me is all that keeps me from doing it again, in malice."

Raivis grabbed a bag of potato chips from his pack and handed it to Radien. To a Death World Vulpian, potato chips were about the equivalent of offering beef jerky to an excitable border collie.

"I'm only taking that if you've got another bag in there for yourself," Radien commented, to which Raivis showed his opened pack to Radien, revealing the two additional bags within. Radien nodded, and opened the bag to munch on its contents. "That's another thing about it. In the moment, it was so easy. Not in the manner of power over my foes, but in the decision itself. It took no time for me to decide that a whole planet needed to die, and in all the months I was there making it happen, not for one *moment* did I ever doubt what I was doing. Not for a single instant did it stop being so easy to just keep going, to just keep killing them... That's the part that worries me, Raivis. That's where the conflict is. If I can so easily choose to exterminate a whole planet, a whole species... what does that make me, no matter how much they deserved it?"

"Well, if nothing else, the debate keeps you from doing it again in malice," Raivis casually figured. "The universe considers itself lucky that you discovered this part of yourself in circumstances that demanded it."

"Oh, bull*shit* the whole damn universe has any thoughts to spare about *me*, of all people." Radien scoffed, not out of disdain for Raivis or his words, but more in disbelief that something as large as the universe could spare a moment's passing for one of its occupants.

"I meant that more as a metaphorical umbrella term," Raivis clarified. "Obviously not the *entire* thing, there's too much of it to do *that!*"

The two shared a lighthearted laugh and exchange of slightly nihilistic jokes, but this breed of nihilism was of a more optimistic sort than Radien was used to carrying with him all the time. Such a change came with escaping Earth, and the purgatory that it was.

Eventually, Raivis checked his pack again and then stood up. "Well, I should get going. My supplies will last me just long enough to hike back, and though I've got a transponder, I'd rather just hike it."

"I hear that. Hopefully I'll hear more of you, Raivis. Perhaps one day we will be shoulder-to-shoulder one of the many battles to come."

"I will train endlessly, that I may see that day."

"As will I. *Skjeln thej duul'e klatar, skill guide your path*, Raivis."

"*Skjeln thej duul'e klatar*, Radien."

As night eventually fell, the locator beacon on Radien's backpack beeped to show that pickup was on its way. Though he had observed it before, he couldn't help but think to himself again that these days were passing quite quickly. Maybe it was because of the constant rhythm of training, that made it seem to go faster. At the very least, it sure *felt* like he was training, and that he was making progress for it. His skills were becoming sharper, like his claws had become in Jaltai-Vuul.

Facing a large rock, Radien bared those claws and swiped them at the stone. Like dragging a sharpened nail through talc, his claws easily sliced through the granite. He then noticed another tablet on the stone, next to where he had just tested the sharpness of his claws. Once again, the runes glowed red to the touch with an ethereal gong.

*Deliis Unzhernreli jagizh deliis Unklornka tsingtarn jasaln-nah deliis Unjasaln nej klornka tsingtarn.*

*To be a Death Worlder is to train to be the river to carve mountains, and to be the mountain no river cuts.*

# 15

# MELKETH-IKLAR BLACK ZONE

Melketh-Iklar. The Swamp One. Radien hated deserts, sure, but the one place he actually realized he had never been to before, was a swamp. And this was *definitely* a swamp. The only thing that stopped him from going thigh-high into quickmud was his Telekinetic Platform Cantrip, that summoned spectral 'bricks' just above the bog's surface for his feet to step on, sparing him of the trouble.

Was this cheating? Not really, considering that Aetherian Taxation would eventually mean that he'd have to find *somewhere* solid to rest up at. Until then, Radien could only imagine what this place smelled like. After all, his nose basically didn't work. That was one thing that transferred from his Human form to his Death World Vulpian form, a nose that doesn't work unless he was *really* telling it to. In some ways, this could be considered a gift. It certainly was in this case.

Sustaining the Telekinetic Platforms was becoming more and more difficult not out of the Psionic strain doing so was incurring, but because the same technique being sustained for hours or days at a time can cause side effects mainly relating to one's internal power becoming bored, as it were. After three hours of navigating the swamp a few feet above it, the spectral platforms beneath Radien's feet began to take on different shapes as the Aura itself within him seemingly tried to find a way to amuse itself despite the monotony that was this single task over hours and hours.

Radien didn't notice this until the platform had become a pyramid, but he wasn't stepping on its base.

"*Djalsej!*" Radien cursed as his foot was poked hard by the abrupt point of the platform instead being a pyramid, like he just stepped on a psychic caltrop. Almost losing his footing, Radien threw out his hand and fired a steady jet of raw power to right himself, realizing that his own powers were starting to get a bit bored of this routine.

He then elected to practice the form of flying that he could do, coursing power through his hands and feet to hover above the swamp and move forward as he looked for somewhere to take shelter within. A cave, a large and sturdy tree, anything as long as he wasn't wading through the swamp of Melketh-Iklar. Was it a bog or a swamp? It seemed both were present here, somehow.

Raon-Arashal certainly was a unique world among worlds. It would be, given that it's name translated literally as "Arena of Life." But this was not to be taken in a pretentious manner, like a rose budding in the middle of a Colosseum. This was instead the arena that was life, the battle that was finding purpose despite the dark machinations of foul circumstance.

Radien folded his arms across his chest, and hovered ominously across the swamp. For the aesthetic of it, though. He wasn't actually going to do anything malicious, but it was fun to hover ominously through the air.

He saw a pair of eyes in the murky water.

"No," he told the creature below.

The creature then narrowed its eyes beneath the water, as if to say '*aw, man,*' and swam off to find a more amusing potential prey.

After about two hours of this hovering, Radien switched back to the Telekinetic Platforms, to make sure the Aetherian Taxation didn't screw him over out of utter boredom.

Radien finally found a cave, but its entrance was half-submerged, and he really didn't feel like pressing his back against the stone just to climb or hover inwards. So he instead parked himself atop the stone, looking out into the swamp, as some flying pests vaporized themselves on the shield that surrounded him, like sparks appearing in the air where an unfortunate blood-sucker of some regard made the mistake of getting within six feet of him.

Radien heard a faint humming in the air. It wasn't an insect's wings, it was the wrong frequency. It did, however, feel like a Psionic humming.

Wrapping his hand around the Borfblade, Radien closed his eyes as he waited for the humming to grow louder. Then, he unsheathed the cutlass with a swipe in the air, that tore the very air in two, revealing a portal through time.

"Hang on, I remember you!" the Human on the other side said. "To your credit though, you *did* erase my prior two memories of these conversations. But what the hell's got you peering through time again, making me remember the last encounters, and endangering our future?"

"Hey man, I just swung my sword at a harmonic resonation and the rift opened itself. I had no part in directing it."

"Fair enough, so why then does it lead here?"

"I'm still doing the Gauntlet of Doom, so there's probably still some kind of link to my past that you're a part of that I still have to break the chains of."

"I fail to see how this is an opportunity to do so."

"As do I. What was the most recent significant event for you?"

"Designation Flaming Flood. As much as I just made that term up on the spot, you should know what it means."

Radien nodded to Miles. He did know what it meant. "You're through the worst of it, then."

"I believe you, but I'm afraid I can't go on remembering that once this conversation is done." Miles sighed.

"I know." Radien nodded solemnly. "I preferred the numbness at the time, anyway."

"I'm sure I'll feel the same, once I'm where you are."

Radien then noticed something behind Miles, back on Earth. An approaching vehicle that stopped behind him.

"I certainly don't remember that vehicle," Radien said. Miles turned around to meet it, and saw several suited men climb out, and point at him.

"SWEEPS?!" Radien said. "Since when did I have an encounter with—"

"No time!" Miles yelled, reaching his arm through the portal, and grabbing Radien's. With a great heave, the Death Worlder was pulled to Earth, but centuries in his past, where Miles was present.

"Asshole! What if I can't get back?!"

"I can still see the rift!"

The group of men stood in shock as the biped vulpine argued with the Human, and the two knew that the time to move in was *now*.

Miles leaped forward with a push kick, slamming one of the SWEEPS agents into the car, cracking the passenger window with the back of his head. Radien shoulder rolled forward, coming up with a leaping knee strike that snapped the back of another's head so hard and suddenly, it broke several vertebrae and cut the spinal cord with the bone fragments.

Miles then grabbed the arm of another SWEEPS agent who had just pointed a tranquilizer gun at him, breaking it with his elbow, which he then slammed into the enemy's ribs, and then jaw, before a roundhouse kick to the body put him out of commission.

Radien evaded the roundhouse kick of the last one, sidestepping it with his own low roundhouse that slammed into the side of his foe's leg, breaking it harshly *and* dislocating the hip joint it was attached to. Another kick like that to the other leg, and then a snapping front kick to the chin ended the threat.

"Lose their car, if you can!" Miles instructed, and Radien quickly grabbed it with the Aura and heaved it through the rift, its occupants trailing behind in the telekinetic grab, and a splash was heard, that of the car, and the bodies landing in the swamp of Melketh-Iklar.

"That's gonna be hard to explain to the Perawls," Radien realized with a slight cringe, one of not wanting to have to deal with the ramifications of this temporal interference.

"Whatever trick you did to erase my memory of the last conversations we had, do it again for this, you'll have to cover the whole neighborhood just to be safe."

"Can do." Radien nodded. "But if I'm seeing you again, what part of my time as you do I still need to reconcile with?"

"Maybe those guys?" Miles theorized. "You recognized them, after all."

"Only in retrospect, I've encountered them as me, but I never did as you."

"Rather, you don't remember that you did, and I dragged your ass into the fray to help me out."

"Regardless, I hope this is the last time I have to see you. No offense, I'm just kinda sick of it."

"None taken. Erase my memory of this all the same, we cannot risk jeopardizing your timeline."

"I agree," Radien affirmed. "I am curious, by the way... what were you doing before going to the woods this time? Judging by the fact you're going to meditate in there, I'd say it's a little past six PM for you."

Miles nodded. "I was working on painting a shield."

"A shield?" Radien realized. "White background? Laurel leaves around the circumference just before the trim? Sigil of two dragons with tails in a Celtic knot?"

"Yeah, that's the one! I just got done with painting the linework. Why do you ask, does that one actually sell or something?"

"No, it's just... finished the linework... that means it starts tomorrow for you."

"Tomorrow? It starts?" Miles raised an eyebrow.

"All of it," Radien said matter of factly. "What starts you on the path that leads to me... it starts tomorrow. The whole damn universe, that all starts tomorrow for you."

Miles chuckled. "Well, there's no harm in erasing my memory of this, is there? Clearly I'll remember, just the long way 'round. Besides, I have no plans to die today, so what's waiting until tomorrow?"

"Nobody does—"

"It was a defiant statement, you twat!"

The two laughed it off as Radien prepared the necessary spell.

"He *always* did that," Radien reminisced.

"And he always knew what I meant all the same."

"Which is why he did it. Skill guide your path, Miles Sorvenjar Radien."

"Skill guide your path... I like that one."

Radien hopped back through the rift, tossing the azure sphere behind him that would make the whole neighborhood forget the events that just transpired, including the Human Miles.

As the rift began to fade, and its view was but one way, Radien saw Miles solemnly walk towards the woods as though nothing had transpired, and the hope that he once had never existed.

"The stars await, Miles Radien. What's one more day?" Radien sent off.

He looked back at the 21st-century Earth minivan, and four dead Humans around it. Actually, only three dead. The one that took a roundhouse to the body and a few elbows after his own was broken was still alive.

Radien lifted him up from the swamp, dragging him to dry land to interrogate him.

"Why were you after him?!" Radien demanded.

The SWEEPS operative tried to chomp down on a cyanide tooth, but Radien yanked the poison from his mouth with telekinesis.

"You're not the first to fail at that trick in front of me, now *answer my question, mortal!*"

Radien's eyes began to crackle with azure lightning.

"Orders! It was orders! Just orders, please!" the Human pleaded.

"You'll find that the Nuremberg Defense *doesn't* work with me, Human! Now answer my question, and answer it *fully*, before I tear it from your mind!"

"Okay, okay! The orders were to take the kid, and bring him to a site outside JBLM! That's all I know, I don't know why they wanted him!"

"*Kid?!* That man was twenty-nine years old!"

The Human yelled in pain as Radien's grip had

shattered his clavicle.

"I can heal that, but only if you give me answers!"

"Fuck! I know, I know! I read his file! Twenty-nine, trained fighter—"

"I *know* all of that, are you telling me there's nothing more you can give me?!"

"I've told you all I know! You said you'd heal my collarbone!"

Radien quickly mended the broken clavicle with The Aura.

"My elbow! My elbow!"

"I never said anything about your *elbow*, unless you've got something more useful to tell me, we're finished here!"

"Fuck!"

The pain this Human was undergoing now that the adrenaline was out of his system was making him useless. But there was nothing more he could tell him, so Radien tossed him into the swamp, just as the creature he had told off hours before leaped up to grab the screaming bastard.

"Yeah, you can have him," Radien said. "The others too, if you want. Maybe it'll mean I won't have to explain this to the Perawls."

The swamp creature gleefully glided off in the water to feast on the dead Humans. As for the van... that would have to be left to chance, it seemed. He figured he'd rather do that than blow it up, and ruin the otherwise perfectly swell day that the Melketh Swampcrawler was having.

As Radien continued to explore the Melketh-Iklar

Black Zone, the Swampcrawler continued to follow him from the depths, every now and again air bubbles popping up on the water's surface as the creature trailed him from a safe distance. Why it was called a Swampcrawler despite being a fish was anyone's guess. But that's what the Raon-Arashal Almanac of Deadly Creatures called it, and that was its name. Most likely it was because an idiot named it, and unfortunately, they were the first to, so it stuck.

A morbid curiosity overcame Radien, and he decided to use the Aura to tap into the universe around him, so that he could hear just what was going on in this Swampcrawler's head, since the bugger was still following him.

*Fish, fish, fish, I'm a motha' fuckin' fish... ooh, what's that over there? Oh, just a twig, phooey. Suck my shaaaark, I'm a diiiiick... wait, that's not how it goes. Food-source continues to hover ominously. I don't even know what that means but somehow that word fits... ow, fuck, I bonked into a rock.*

Radien really wasn't sure what he was expecting.

Finding another surface to park himself on, he did just that, staring out into the murky water , where the Swampcrawler was swimming around within in circles, seemingly waiting for Radien to toss him another Human corpse to snack on.

The *clunk* of the a metal haft behind him caught Radien's attention. A familiar Hykentiu warrior had managed to track him down in Melketh-Iklar.

"Miirkae," Radien greeted as he stood up. "Any reason you're out here, of all places?"

"Haven't been to this one in a while. I've always preferred the ones that have water in them, even if it's the water of a swamp."

"Makes sense, but now I've got to wonder why you bothered to find me."

"Well, I get the feeling you're the kind of guy who really hates people checking in on him…"

"You'd be correct."

"Therefore, my answer is curiosity as to how you're handling the zones so far, and not out of any doubt that you're prevailing."

"As long as that's the truth, I've no problem with that explanation."

"Good thing it's the truth, then."

Miirkae peered over Radien's shoulder and noticed the Swampcrawler.

"Seems you're making friends out here."

"He's been following me for most of my time here, and has kept at it since I fed him the corpses of some attempted ambushers."

"Aye, that would do it. This ground is clearly solid enough, spar?"

Radien's ears perked up when he heard the word 'spar,' like if you had just said 'park' near an excitable husky.

The two squared off, with an audience of one Swampcrawler. After each fighter performed their respective salutes, they took up stances.

A few measuring jabs from Miirkae's spear were parried lightly before he moved in with a more determined thrust that Radien evaded, only for Miirkae to then plant his foot into Radien's side with a follow-up roundhouse kick. Radien was able to take the hit, but it was a solid strike. Radien closed the distance and tried to bind the Hykentiu's weapon out of usefulness, but to this, Miirkae responded by splitting the weapon at its haft, forming two one-handed spikes instead of one double-pointed spear. The metal clangs against the Borfblade could be heard for dozens of meters as Radien evaded the flurry as best he could, while parrying what could not be evaded, and using his free hand to jab into the crease of Miirkae's elbows when it could, and at the crease in his shoulder to stop strikes from fully swinging through. The defense held, whether by evasion, parry, or open-handed defensive strike. But Radien was still on the defensive. This needed to change if he was going to last much longer.

With one of Miirkae's hands trapped by his free hand, and the other in a weapon bind, the two struggled for a moment before Radien swiftly kicked the Hykentiu's shin, which though Miirkae was able to duck his leg out of the way of, it left him off-balance, for Radien to throw over his shoulders. Radien pointed his cutlass at Miirkae, demanding he yield. Miirkae crescent kicked the Borfblade straight out of Radien's hand, and now both fighters would have to settle things with the weapons the gods gave them.

Baring his claws, Radien began a flurry of strikes and swipes that Miirkae was put on the defensive by, until a spinning side kick nearly threw the Hykentiu off of the rock, but Radien grabbed his arm to keep him from falling into the territory of the Swampcrawler.

After pulling him back onto solid ground, the two recovered their weapons as they chatted.

"To be fair, the Swampcrawler wouldn't have gotten me," Miirkae informed.

"Didn't want to risk it, all the same," Radien noted, and Miirkae nodded. The Swampcrawler at least seemed to be amused by the show of force.

The two saluted each other again with their weapons, and Miirkae wandered off. A few seconds after Radien heard the sound of Miirkae warping out of the Black Zone, he noticed another stone tablet in the ground, with its runes that glowed red with a *bong* sound once he placed his hand upon it.

*Deliis Unzhernreli jagizh kalska vel deliis Jasaln-nah vel deliis klornka.*

*To be a Death Worlder is to train to know when to be the mountain, and when to be the river.*

# 16

# NERANDI BLACK ZONE

**N**erandi had been a solid candidate for where to build Torvaltyne Bastion, until Kaladorum was inevitably chosen for the fact of the Blizzardblade Mountains, and that it didn't rain in Kaladorum.

True as it was that Radien could trivialize the rainfall of Nerandi with a telekinetic shield, one tailor-made for sticking it to the rain, he still hated it just as much as he did when he had no such power, which is to say, immensely.

Even when he took refuge in a rocky cavern and stared at the rainy landscape to ponder, he still found himself hating it, even though he had the power to make it no factor.

*Fools*, he thought of those who enjoyed the rain. Snow at least can be brushed off of oneself before returning indoors, but rain must drill through whatever clothes you wear just to make your day that much more miserable. In the end, nothing is rain-proof. Not if the rain is so determined enough. And Radien knew *well* how determined the rain can be to destroy your plans.

"I can't bring myself to see it like some do." He thought aloud to himself. "I can't find any comfort in listening to it fall."

<It seems we are more alike than one might suspect,> the Nel Jalfjaa said as it rippled into existence next to him. <Even a Grand Psionic Entity has preferred weathers... and the opposite.>

"I find myself curious, Nel Jalfjaa... were you ever one of a species of Cynar, or have you always been a non-euclidean mass of yellow-orange light with incomprehensible power at your command?"

<Now that is a question I have never heard anyone ask me... how strange.>

"That no one asked you?"

<That I do not know the answer at this time. Seems like it should be impossible for a Grand Psionic Entity to have a faulty memory, but here I am, unable to recall if I had a mortal past.>

"You're not the only one. The Aura Prism also had a memory futz at one point I had to rectify by reliving it as its subject. Told me to just do as I would, and turns out that's exactly what happened in history, when Kirinaultr sacrificed herself to destroy the Sehlsaln Anchor, to end the First War for Reality for good."

<I am impressed that the Prism trusted you enough to delve into their memory to ensure its correctness. I also find it incredibly on-point, the manner in which they enlisted your help.>

Radien then reflected on his reliving of that part of the past. "Now that I think on it... it almost seems unreal, how quickly the decision was made, how swiftly Kirinaultr knew in her mind of minds that this was her final battle, even if it didn't feel like it in the moment."

*<Do go on...>*

"I lived Kirinaultr's final moments, an ancient warrior and Defender, and in those moments, there could be no doubt of what had to be done. It seemed to play out so simply in the moment, almost too simply, and yet..."

Radien's words trailed off as he couldn't think of any more. After a few seconds, he managed to finish the sentence. "...It just felt like any other battle. It only happened to be the last."

*<Would you go any other way?>*

"I'd rather not go at all," Radien said, then snapping his fingers and igniting a blazing blue sphere of the Aura in his hand. "This power makes that possible, and no longer do I have to constantly worry about the pressure an insultingly short lifespan puts on me. I have time to match my ambition now, I have broken the chains. I know I'm not invincible, but I also know I don't need to be. I only need to not have to worry about time."

*<If I do have a past from before I was a Grand Psionic Entity, I wouldn't be surprised if I felt the same way.>*

The Nel Jalfjaa rippled out of existence, leaving Radien to ponder, mostly about how much he hated the rain.

"Rain is a cage," he said aloud to himself. "It cages one indoors, or under cover. No matter the size, a cage is still a cage."

Summoning a ball of light to toss into the darkness of the cavern ahead, Radien moved deeper into the rocky cavern. A few hundred feet away from its entrance, Radien found nothing but wall. Soon, the entire layout of this cavern was known.

"This is a solid cave, though," Radien thought aloud. "Good cave. Very good cave. Cave out of ten, would cave again."

The rain continued to fall outside, and Radien had seen enough of it. Dropping back into a deep stance, he charged his power in his hands, cursing the rain as the azure sphere of the Aura grew. With a final yell, Radien unleashed it, guiding the orb of power into the clouds, and detonating it.

The effect was almost immediate, as the rain that was still falling when the clouds had been split still needed to hit the ground. But once it was done, so was the rain.

"Fuck rain."

And that was all Radien needed to say on the matter. Fuck rain, indeed.

Even with the rain gone, Radien found himself not particularly eager to leave this cave he had found. After all, it was a very neat little cave to loaf in and generally scheme in the darkness. Had he not already found his sanctum within the Blizzardblade peaks, he would have likely made it here.

Speaking of his sanctum, Radien figured that now was as good a time as any to plan it out. Remembering the place within Kaladorum's peaks in his mind, Radien visualized what he would put where, running through dozens of designs in his mind's eye, all of which forbade forcing the land to conform to the home, and instead ensuring that the design of the manor would conform to the land. Tunneling into the mountain itself to carve out the structure counted, as far as he was concerned. It wasn't like he was severing the tops of the peaks off to place the house upon the precipices. Instead, his sanctum would be built into the mountain, and the frozen peak that he trained upon would be a training ground indeed, with weapon racks in the cavern that he camped within and spoke to the Nel Jalfjaa as well.

Radien wanted to learn it all, he wanted to become skilled with every weapon, able to pick up anything and wield it with competence. His thirst for martial knowledge seemed insatiable, his will and desire to train so paramount, that he was planning the training areas of what would be his personal home before he was planning out its kitchen. Torvaltyne Bastion was a fortress indeed, but Radien knew that he needed somewhere where the solitude would grant him solace. And in the frigid peaks of the Blizzardblade Mountains, Radien had found a solace in solitude that he once could only dream of.

Raon-Arashal's policy on claiming land was built mainly around the universal law of 'don't be a dick'. The *Ja-Anan Volarthirs,* or *Elder Survivors* who built their homes within the Black Zones all abided by this, considering that a lack of honor in doing so would have their heads on pikes before the year was over. Nerandi, though offering this solid cavern and a nearby forest, wasn't the same as the mountains. It also rained often in

Nerandi, which was a deal-breaker for Radien. At least in Kaladorum, the precipitation would be snow instead. He preferred snow to rain any day.

Arena, kitchen, bedroom. What else would the home of a Death World Vulpian need?

Radien suddenly felt as though a strong current of the winds of magic themselves was passing through this cavern, and he opened his mind to peer into it. Resting on his thighs in a meditative position at the mouth of the cave, he closed his eyes and opened the eye of his mind to see what the eyes could not.

*Where Jaltai-Vuul's winds threw my power into flux, here these winds bring the blood of the universe to this world like arteries...*

Radien thought to himself to allow the will of the Aura to speak to him. It had found the strength to do so before, and he knew that in this new, more attuned form, he could do better.

*If the power of the universe itself has a message, let me hear it.*

Radien found himself at the base of a stony hill, still within Nerandi. An old man with an eyepatch stood before him, a spear in hand, and crow on his shoulder.

"I know you," Radien growled. "You have a lot of ignorance to answer for."

"Ignorance? I stand before you now, and you speak of *ignorance*, like a disgruntled child?" the old man's voice boomed, but Radien did not falter.

"I do speak of your ignorance!" Radien responded with resolute will. "And if I am a disgruntled child, then that stands as testimony to your failure, that your children have grown up bitter and resentful for your absence, for the absence of your guidance, the absence of your voice, of your presence!"

A wind began to pick up at the old man's back, blowing against Radien. But the Death Worlder stood his ground, and did not falter as the old man spoke. "You think yourself entitled to my guidance? You believe that I owe you my wisdom, that you are owed my voice?!"

"What am I owed, if not that?!" Radien questioned fiercely. "It's not like I was told anything else other than that I am wrong for having a mind of my own, for having a will of my own, so if I am not owed your voice to guide my morals and tell me what is right, what am I owed when all I have been told is that I am wrong?!"

Radien began to generate a wind at his back with his power, and in the middle these currents of air met, as the two approached each other slowly, apprehensively, in a manner that clearly suggested that they did not truly wish to come to blows with each other, but were prepared to all the same.

"What do you want, a reward for enduring the trifles of life?!" the old man finally said, and to this, Radien threw up an eyebrow.

"Do not think to tell me that recompense is forbidden!" Radien demanded. "I exist, do I not?! I have the right to a peaceful one, I would demand *that!*"

"You dare demand of me?!" the old man said, but slightly shaky in his tone. He was faltering at the skepticism Radien imposed upon him.

"Who will I demand it of, if not you?" Radien questioned. "Will I demand it of your children?! Will I demand it of your sires?! You cannot tell me that I may demand nothing, lest you admit your determination to the cause of ignorance, the *capital* dishonor!"

The old man slammed the pommel of his spear into the ground to command the wind against Radien, but the two remained evenly matched.

"Have you nothing better to do than command the wind against me while acting as though I have no right to demand justice and reason?! Why else do you stand before me only now, after I've had to heal my scars exclusively on my own?!" Radien continued, and then he grinned with defiance as he let loose the words he had been waiting to say for a very long time, if ever he got the chance. "Tell me, Allfather, do you keep one eye covered so that you may always gaze into the Spiritrealm, or so that you may keep one eye conveniently blind to Midgard's tribulations?!"

"How dare you, impudent one!" the old man finally roared, and placed his spear into his hands in an offensive grip and thrust it out at Radien. But he was ready for it, and his claws parried the weapon to the side as the Death Worlder closed the distance, holding his claws at the old man's throat. He paused for a moment, tempted to drive those sharpened ends into his foe's throat, but then resolved to stomping on the haft of the spear to yank it out of his hands, and pin it to the floor.

"If decency is impudence, then let me be a brat!" Radien declared, elbowing the old man across his jaw. "If honor is treason, then I shall be eternally a one-man rebellion! Though I've always known the gods fallible even as the indecent and ignoble alike have tried to screech at me otherwise, but that you stand before me now tells me you *have* existed all this time, and have a *lot* of absence and ignorance to answer for!"

The old man looked at the blood that was bleeding from his mouth, with the shock of one who hadn't seen their own blood in a long time. But Radien's testimony continued, he wouldn't stop now, his verbal assault pressed its attack.

"And if you do *not* exist, and are only here as a manifestation of my mind's eye as a current of the universe's lifeblood flows through my veins when I made myself open to it, I must question why you come to me in *this* insulting form, as though you seek to rectify your absence by giving me a false visage to vent upon! Either way, your name is cursed!"

The old man looked to Radien, breathing in and out, realizing he had been bested today. "I have no excuse..." he admitted.

Radien did not let his guard down, his claws were still bared. He was ready to find out that this was a trick.

"I have no excuse," the old man repeated. "I cannot justify the absence of honor on your world, when those like me exist to teach it. I cannot excuse the forsaking of decency on your world, when those like me exist to enforce it... I have no excuse, Death Worlder. I have no excuse for the injustice you suffered for the circumstance of your birth... born among a species that proudly forsakes honor and decency both, condemned to a lifetime among the witless stampers of their feet against the common good..."

"Make no mistake!" Radien yelled. "Whether you

truly are Odin, or just a projection of the Aura taking his form so that my mind can comprehend this vision, make no mistake! I grew up believing there *was no common good!* That which others call *common* decency and *common* sense, I refused to call such because it was so rare! Because it was so *absent!*"

"You have my admission, Death Worlder!" The old man pleaded. "What more do you want?!"

"*Retribution! Reparation!*" Radien yelled, before swiping at the old man's throat with his claws. "Bleed out onto the ground, old fool! Watch your blood be spilled onto the dirt, and in those minutes, know that no amount of shock and suffering you feel can come close to what it was like to live on Earth!" Radien continued his verbal disassembly of this vision in front of him, he continued to enact his justice upon the powers of the universe that let Earth become so awful. "For every drop that you watch fall on the ground, slow it down tenfold, feel every second of pain, every second of suffering as time slows around you and you feel nothing but the bleeding and the hemorrhaging, and know that what you're feeling in a thousand of the slowest hours is not even what it felt like to spend one *day* on the planet of purgatory!"

Radien's eyes began to crackle with azure fury as he demanded the gods themselves to feel his pain.

"Remember forever every second that you hurt in these moments, let these moments last for millennia for you, and swear to me that you'll never let *anyone else* feel this way again!"

"I swear! I swear! Please, make it stop!" the old

man pleaded through gurgled coughs and barely-taken breaths.

"No," Radien declared. "I will watch you bleed out, and I will watch you do so without emotion, without a second thought to your life."

Though only a minute passed of the old man sprawled out before Radien, sputtering and coughing as he felt a thousand hours of exsanguination in the slowest sixty seconds of his life.

Radien then healed his wound, and stood him back onto his feet. The old man was stunned, flabbergasted at the fact he was still alive.

"Now you know what it's like," Radien growled. "Never let anyone feel like that again."

The old man nodded shakily, still feeling his throat, barely able to believe that he was not still mortally wounded. The haft of his spear struck the ground, and the old man exploded into a murder of crows that flew away, disappearing into the cloudy sky. Though Radien had just split those clouds mere minutes ago, they had already reformed, and the rain soon began to fall, bouncing off of the telekinetic shield that kept him dry as he wandered his way back to the cave he had found.

Just after he arrived back at the cave Nel Jalfjaa rippled into existence again, but said nothing, as its visit was brief. It rippled out of existence, leaving behind a bottle of mead for Radien to ponder over. He certainly wasn't going to protest a bottle of mead.

"I should carry an ever-filling flask on my hip," Radien pondered as he telekinetically popped the cork out and took a swig. "Constantly full of mead, or perhaps gin."

He then thought for a moment. "No, if its a flask, slivovitz. Actually... one for slivovitz, the other, mead. I've got two hips, anyway."

The rest of the time in Nerandi was spent planning how to enchant a pair of flasks to do exactly that. He knew where he'd have them on his person, and what he'd make the flasks out of. He even knew what would be engraved onto their surface. Mead on his left hip, engraved with the words *steel and doom.* On his right hip, slivovitz, the words *skill and stone.* He also wanted to enhance his metabolism, that alcohol would be his Elixir. Psionic scholars on Gelvetori had perfected the art of Elixir Cantrips, where imbibing a particular liquid would make your wounds close in seconds, or cure diseases. Whatever liquid that was, it would become like health potions. Radien certainly liked the idea of booze being his Elixir, to that end.

On the wall of the cavern he had been planning all this in, another stone tablet was visible. Radien placed his hand upon it like he had the others, and the runes glowed red as a harmonic *bong* was heard, but only by him, since he was the only living soul around to hear it.

*Sejvol gel Nel Jakshoth-nah Zanchin Tlaen akar zhollka ves esis deliis Zhenreli.*

*Those who have a heart of storm and a mind of steel shall learn what it is to be a Death Worlder.*

"I only know enough to know that I still have much to learn..." Radien thought aloud. "And I want to learn it all."

# 17
# OUNRAL BLACK ZONE

Where the other Black Zones all were on the surface of Raon-Arashal, Ounral was subterranean, with entrances primarily along the River Karn, though there were access points in Kuolarek and nearby Azhenar.

Arriving at the Survival Station that would serve as where he'd rest up for the week before entering, Radien met with the base's commander.

"I never did catch a sign outside that showed the name of this base, by the way," Radien said to Brigadier Voriiz, after the two saluted each other with the Death Worlder salute.

"*Duulmoor. Your mother,*" the Brigadier replied.

"Gods, I hope not. She had no honor!" Radien replied instinctively.

"*Duulmoor!*" Garen Voriiz replied. The two then waited, raising eyebrows at each other before Garen snorted and finally started laughing. "Gods, that never gets old! They told me that I would get so tired of having named this place Fort Duulmoor, but they're still wrong after two thousand ASC!"

Radien chuckled as well. He figured there *had* to be something more to the bit, considering the Brigadier's reply.

Garen chuckled all the way to Fort Duulmoor's tavern, where the two mutually pondered over drinks.

"By the way, Tactician, have you read Arch-Militant Desh's dissertation on the Red Cliff of Stories?"

"Not as of yet, why?"

"You're going to hate it."

"Does he reach a pretentious conclusion that would make me tell him to go touch some of the grass in the Prismgrass Fields?"

Brigadier Voriiz nodded heartily as he took a drink from his stein.

"Am I going to want to construct a device called a Pretensionite Detector that will start beeping wildly when I point it at him?"

Voriiz nodded again. "When you do, try to get it on video. I'm going to want to see his reaction."

"I'll probably wait until I make Major or Wing Commander before doing that, just to ensure that the High Commandant won't dismiss me for academically feuding with an Arch-Militant."

"My request stands, Tactician."

"I'll make sure to remember to do just that, Brigadier, don't worry."

"Tell me, Tactician, when you go into Ounral, what is your plan?" Garen asked, with an odd sense of personhood to his question. It was as if he was wondering whether Radien would abide by the plan he once himself had when he first entered the Zone.

"Wherever the Landskimmer drops me, it's gonna be at the entrance of one of the caves that leads into Ounral. I will then walk its path, and then I will walk until a trial faces me. Then, I shall conquer that trial."

Garen nodded. "Which entrance? Apherus? Olerus? Norus? Vatergus?"

Radien chuckled as he sipped his mead. "I have no idea what those names mean, but I hope someday, I'll find out. That day will be well beyond this, when I have already conquered this Black Zone and have a victory worth speaking of to my name."

Garen raised an eyebrow. He then eyed the bartender, until he looked over to acknowledge that Garen had an order to be placed. "A replacement for my drink, and another for the Scourge of the Planet of Traitors, on me! Just as is the rest of his tab!"

Now it was Radien raising an eyebrow.

"Siegebreaker of Hulae, Liberator of Killentarn, Scourge of the Planet of Traitors, Bane of The Unmaker, and yet you speak of having yet to have a worthwhile victory?" Garen questioned. "What kind of upbringing is so vile and without catharsis that even now you feel as though you have yet to shake off its taint?"

"One spent on Earth, obviously," Radien replied.

Ounral Black Zone soon awaited, and Radien was entering via the Olerus Channel, a cave system that after a few hours of wandering, was now solidly within the subterranean domain of Ounral.

The book that Agranz had given him back in Dromos-Balth had proven useful in identifying which lichens on the stone walls were edible, and which ones were very much not. The ball of light he had summoned to light up the cavern was also proving useful. It seemed that the bulk of his time in Ounral would be spent exploring these caverns. Radien had been granted a Recall Beacon to warp out back to Fort Duulmoor once the thirty days were up, seeing as how the maze-like caverns made it quite difficult for one to be extracted from the zone by a third party.

Radien remained mobile, never stopping for more than a few minutes at a time to take a look at something interesting along the walls. The reason for the necessity to stay moving were the very architects of the tunnels of Ounral: The *Oun-Thuunc*. Subterranean tunneling worms that varied greatly in size, who never strayed beyond the depths of Raon-Arashal's rock, to the thanks of countless. Every hole, every tunnel was created by one of these worms whose name translated from the Zhernreli-Orul as 'cave sphincters.' Sometimes, Radien would notice a cluster of small holes in the rock wall, indicating that a juvenile nest of the creatures was once there. Hundreds of tiny pores in the stone that each indicated one of these worms, but only one from such a nest would grow large enough to create the tunnel that Radien stood within. Such a violently carnivorous species only seemed to gain sustenance from its own kin, or the unlucky and unaware fool who was unprepared. Sometimes, carcasses of creatures nearer to the surface would tumble down into the tunnels of Ounral, but this was rare and could not be counted on by the Oun-Thuunc.

In the early days of Death World Vulpian civilization, before the advent of materials that could sustain against the conditions of the surface long-term, these tunnels were used as the roadways between cities and settlements, and all who traversed them had to be ready to flee from one of these mindless burrowers. The most common form of escaping them was to duck into a smaller tunnel that ran perpendicular to the one you were having to get out of, as the Oun-Thuunc did not possess the biological or mental capacity for sharp, maneuvering turns to catch prey. If there was a side pocket to dive into, that was your only chance of survival. Running in a straight line down the tunnel out of panic is exactly how people die when confronted by the Oun-Thuunc, doomed to be among the forever vanished and traceless that the tunnels' overlords claimed.

On the Red Cliff of Stories back in Firenthal, there was a doomsday prophecy written that described the Oun-Thuunc migrating to the surface, scouring the planet of life.

Radien suddenly heard the stone beneath him crack.

"Muscovite," Radien realized. "I just hope it's a quick drop—"

The floor gave way, and Radien tumbled down with a surprised yelp as his feet hit the stone floor first, but not before falling a little over two hundred meters.

Groaning and cursing at his shattered legs, Radien's left hand swirled with azure power as he put the bones back together. "Agh, quickly, quickly, before the shock wears off..." he commented to himself as the power of the Aura healed his wounds, ideally before the pain would set in of his legs being obliterated by the fall.

Fortunately, this was the case, and Radien was soon able to stand again, as though nothing had happened.

"And this is why I took the Aura," he said to himself as he examined his legs, making sure he had healed them correctly. "Blasting my enemies to smithereens is honestly secondary to being able to heal myself. Without a sword, I can use my hands. But without this power... my durability is insultingly limited."

Granted, saying this was somewhat an injustice to the physiology of Death World Vulpians. There were not many species that could survive a fall of two hundred seven meters, let alone walk away from it. The natural ability of Death Worlders to heal is also nothing to sniff at. Had he not had the Aura, Radien *could* have simply set his shins relatively straight, and waited in a corner for the next twenty days for things to naturally heal up enough that he could start walking again, and eventually hobble to the surface for proper medical care, that would at which point, simply be based around making sure that the bones didn't heal wrong, and plugging them back into place properly.

Even so, the Aura was a boon indeed, that made sure that this was rendered no factor.

The ball of light that followed him around soon lit up the entire cavern. Two hundred seven meters in diameter, and only stalactites along its ceiling, no stalagmites across the floor.

This tunnel had been formed by a mythologically

massive Oun-Thuunc, and its ceiling hadn't been touched in eons as a result. The deeper beneath the surface Radien was, the larger the Oun-Thuunc tunnels had become. What even more disturbing was the fact that whatever dug the tunnel was likely still alive, as it would have no predators in this realm.

It was also entirely likely that its carcass would be further down towards the mantle of Raon-Arashal, eventually having burned itself to death upon the rocks as it made its way further and further into the depths, that its ever-growing size demanded.

Radien kept himself alert as he continued to wander the tunnel, soon hearing the sound of gnashing teeth against hardened carapace. The duel of two Oun-Thuunc worms was nearby, and considering the size of this tunnel, Radien really did not feel like trying to be audience to it. Perhaps another time, when he was more confident that he could survive such an encounter without having to regrow a limb or two.

*Strange,* Radien thought to himself as he entered an offshoot tunnel large enough to stand in, that led in a vaguely downward direction. "I've no problem facing down Demons several times my size, but some tunneling worms have me on such a defensive? Perhaps it is because they are but mindless worms that makes them so much more unnerving..."

Radien's steps were careful, as he didn't want to accidentally fall through the floor again. But he soon noticed something very odd indeed. A red glow from one of the tunnels that was only big enough for him to poke his head into. At first, he tried very hard to see if he could peer through the tunnel without actually wedging any part of his body through, at risk of being snuck up on by the winner of the duel in the larger tunnel. However, it became clear that he would have to at least get on all fours to get a good look inside.

Better than actually sticking his head through the crevasse, he thought, and cautiously peered in.

The glow seemed to emanate from a hidden source, around a corner within the stone that his gaze could not see into, so Radien decided to throw in the technological towel, so to speak.

In Jessel-Tarn, he had picked up a set of spherical camera drones in one of the dungeons, that could be rolled into a tight spot such as this. Since the Gauntlet of Doom's rules allowed him to bring anything he had fairly acquired from a previous zone into subsequent ones, it was kosher for him to have these.

He only then realized that this fact of the rules was why so many people started with Jessel-Tarn. Oh well.

Tossing one of the spherical camera drones into the tunnel, Radien listened to it rattle and roll down the stone. The sound of rolling stopped, but then a few metallic *tinks* made it clear that it had fallen into a wider clearing. Reaching out with The Aura, Radien looked through the drone's camera to see where it had found itself. Perhaps this room would be big enough to stand up in, and he could blink-jump right to the camera drone to see what that red glow was coming from for himself.

The feed from the camera seemed impossible, and Radien knew he had to see this for himself. Warping into the room from where this crimson glow originated, Radien felt as though it would take days just to process what was before him: A massive stone door, intricately carved with glowing red symbols like those seen on the Red Cliff of Stories, and twenty-two wedges carved into the rock whose jet-black stone was only interrupted by thin veins of gold and silver, and the red runes that gave this place its glow. Scattered across the ground were twenty-two stone wedges, each bearing a symbol on them, that Radien wasn't sure whether or not he recognized. The grandness of this stone wall of red, black and gold dwarfed Radien, extending all the way up to the ceiling of this cavern, the empty places upon the wall similar in size to the stone wedges on the floor.

"I've seen something like this... a Prophecy Wheel Lock," Radien thought aloud. "Like the one on the Planet of Traitors from before, but much bigger... and a lot more vague."

Radien wasn't sure whether to think of this as a door or a wall, as it seemed to be both. A wall that acted as door? A door so massive, it was the wall? Regardless, its size could not be ignored, nor could the intricacy of the carvings that surrounded the empty spaces. Verses describing in grandiose detail, the value of victory and defiance, but other than listing virtues and naming heroes of ancient times, there was no outright hint of what went where.

This puzzle's instructions were clear, but its solution was hidden. Twenty-two different wedges meant an absurd number of possible combinations, too many to brute force before the star Raon-Arashal orbited would burn out.

"This is a mystery for another day, that much I know," Radien said to himself as he burned the location of this place into his mind, so that he could warp back here when the time had come to solve this puzzle. "Maybe once the Dark Six are destroyed and this war is over, I will find the time to solve it."

It was unclear what this door guarded. Was it keeping something in, or keeping the rest of the universe out? What could even be behind it that warranted such a wondrous construction to separate its domain from the rest of creation?

Also, what stopped the Oun-Thuunc from devouring their way through it? What made this stone different from the rest of the rocks of Raon-Arashal's planetary crust, other than the fact that this grand door had been made from it?

It seemed he was about to find out, as the sound of stone being ground and chewed up by the jaws of the winner of the duel between Oun-Thuuncs from earlier was tunneling its way through the rock, and Radien barely had enough time to get out of the way before it burst through.

The Borfblade in his hands faster than most could blink, Radien shoulder rolled out of the path of this Oun-Thuunc whose diameter placed it at the same height as Radien, which meant that this one was at least several thousand years old, having grown to this size through brutality and violence alone, as brutal as it was single-minded. Grow, become larger, consume. This was the doctrine of the Oun-Thuunc. At least, it would be if these creatures were capable of thought on that level.

Radien had to dodge roll out of the way again as the great worm charged towards him, seeking to make prey of this Death Worlder, and once it realized that its quarry was no longer in front of it, the Oun-Thuunc whipped around to face him again, Radien once again having to behold the sight of the circles of teeth that had spent thousands of years sharpening themselves on rocks being devoured, on the hardened carapaces of other Oun-Thuuncs being devoured, and the grinding of the shield-like plates of exoskeleton made Radien's ears twitch with annoyance.

But in this sudden turn of direction, the Oun-Thuunc's tail slammed against the stone door that had previously been demanding Radien's attention, and both he and the Oun-Thuunc learned what prevented the great burrowers from simply destroying this masterwork of stonecarving.

Like an electric fence with a vengeance, the stone door coursed an incomprehensibly strong current of pure electron-based punishment through the creature that dared try to force itself through, and the Oun-Thuunc was hurled against the other side of the stone wall, crashing onto the floor of the cavern, convulsing as arcs of blue lightning chiseled the nearby wall as it fried the Oun-Thuunc from the inside out, the hardened carapace now acting like a blast furnace's walls, immolating the great worm's insides.

Eventually, the thrashing stopped. Radien cautiously approached the carcass and knocked on the exoskeleton with his knuckles, testing its hardness. It could *definitely* be used as armor plating, or a shield.

This was further proven by the fact that the Borfblade bounced right off of it when he tried to slice off a section to test its hardness, like it had against the hide of the Akraknahal from Jaltai-Vuul. Even coursing raw power through his fingertips like a cutting torch took minutes just to pierce through.

The Oun-Thuunc's plating was surprisingly light for its toughness, and it was *extremely* tough. Perhaps the lightness was more a product of the strength of his Death Worlder muscles, but this creature's carapace was something Radien could not ignore, as he spent weeks painstakingly carving sections of plate from the dead Oun-Thuunc, and fashioning them into armor plates for his shoulders, elbows, and knees. The important joints that often found themselves targets would be covered by Oun-Thuunc Plating, and Radien wondered if there was perhaps a way to further treat the material into looking a bit more impressive than the beige bone armor of its natural color, whilst still showing that this was made from one of the Great Tunnelers, and a big one at that.

The beacon on his pack beeped. He had found himself on the last day after spending so long in this room, pondering the door and working on this armor.

With the Aura coursing through his fingertips like a laser engraver, Radien etched his symbol into the face of the left shoulderplate, that only needed to have straps looped through it before it was ready for use. Veralis likely had some Demonhide Leather he could use for this, as she still had plenty left over from making her armor out of the stuff. It was very much the case that she looked pretty badass when wearing it, as it offered the protection of such a durable hide, but didn't hide the muscles that she had built over a lifetime of training when she donned her battlegear.

And now, it seemed, Radien was starting to forge his own. Progress was progress, and over the final day, he began to work on the Oun-Thuunc's carcass to create a plated gauntlet for his right hand. As he arranged the interlocking pieces on the ground and checked over which parts he still needed before securing a Demonhide Leather glove, he saw a stone tablet in the wall. Another one of them, with another verse in the Zhernreli runes, that glowed red to the touch with a harmonic bong.

*Enkyr pashnoth Unsengjavald arel Unsengneshaldtorvej.*

*Only beyond the end of dreams lies the end of nightmares.*

# 18

# SATARAKAAL BLACK ZONE

Radien did not bring the Oun-Thuunc armor that he had begun crafting in Ounral, because the Demonhide Leather that Veralis did indeed possess was not itself acquired during the Gauntlet, and as such was disqualified from being used. Of course, this was what Radien had anticipated, and left the armor-in-progress in Veralis's hands to bring to Torvaltyne, and leave in his office so that he could get to it upon his return. It was at this point that Radien found himself retroactively regretting not taking the entire carcass with him, since apparently Oun-Thuunc plating is just that valuable for armors and shields. It was still the case that the massive stone door wasn't going anywhere, and likely neither was the dead Oun-Thuunc that learned the hard way why much larger Oun-Thuunc hadn't claimed the door yet. The door itself, however, Radien omitted from his recollection of Ounral when he brought Veralis up to speed at Vesharim Station, the settlement in which he was preparing to enter Satarakaal.

"You're doing quite well," Veralis said, to Radien's

confusion. "The Gauntlet of Doom is not an easy trial."

"I figured as much, that's why I chose to do it," Radien responded as he sipped from his pint glass. "It is good to hear that I'm doing it right so far."

"How old are you now, Radien? How many hundreds of years have you lived beyond the lifespan of your birth species? And yet you're still chasing stars, running from one to the next with pure eagerness to see what each one of them looks like."

"Is that a good thing or a bad thing?" Radien asked as one of his ears lowered.

"It's a very Radien thing, and I think that's good."

Radien shrugged. What Veralis said was not lies, and he could not dispute that, despite how difficult it was to believe that she would say that of *him*, out of everyone in the universe.

The ale before him offered no answers, only the wisdom of silence.

"I'll have to ponder that," he said after a few moments of just listening to himself breathe. "Thank you, Veralis. I am honored to call you my ally, and I hope that I can continue to be worthy of your friendship in the battles to come."

The first night in Satarakaal was met with a strange harmonic hum that was without pattern, as though glass chimes gently clinked together. Radien wasn't sure if he was fond of this sound. Looking at his feet, he noticed that the grass he stood upon was not of any color he understood grass to be. This grass was like a field of prisms, all refracting and reflecting the moonlight in a natural glow that lit up this entire field. The

Prismgrass Fields. Radien had found them, and stood within, the gem-like blades of grass brushing gently against the metal tip of the Borfblade's scabbard. His hand rested on the bell of his closest ally, Radien pondered the field.

The Nel Jalfjaa rippled into existence next to him.

"Is there any particular reason you're so damned curious about me? Or is there nothing better to do right now?" Radien asked, though not in an accusatory manner.

<I remembered more about the prophecy of the Beast of Raon-Arashal, thought you ought to know.>

"Ah, fair enough. I'm listening."

<On the Red Cliff of Stories, the prophecy reads:

*Gijavik, Unzhernreli gen kals Kadaroth,*
*Truly, a Death Worlder must know the Ways,*

*Ungikaulet, Ungiorgaen, Ungivarash, Ungikavarges*
*The Disciplines, the Oaths, the Tenants, the Creeds,*

*Fuurka-Saln dolgelka Jadeyl Nel Jalfjaa*
*Pillars that bind the Self to the Soul.*

*Var jagizh akar deliis-nah zhollka akar shalka, Unzhernreli akar zhollka Unshal-en*

*Where to train is to be, and to learn is to live, The Death Worlder will learn to live as one.*

*Un Jagizh-Nurelzi, var Unzholl kalska*
*These training grounds, where the lessons be taught,*

*Valgitayien-Velzaanjaltai-Raon-Arashal akar zhollka*
*The Beast of Raon-Arashal will learn*

*Unvikja enrel Ja-Jahadenpas Orulzanchin-Djellthar*
*The answer to this world's oldest riddle.>*

"What this riddle is, I hear, is hotly debated."

<Whoever told you this is quite correct.>

"Could it possibly refer to the massive stone door in Ounral, with the twenty-two slotted Prophecy Wheel Lock?" Radien theorized aloud.

<The what now?>

"Did you not know about the massive stone door, deep within Ounral? There's a Prophecy Wheel Lock of twenty-two slots, and it is also shielded by a force field strong enough to fry a six foot diameter Oun-Thuunc."

<I will return later.>

The Nel Jalfjaa rippled out of existence without another word. Radien was not sure whether or not this meant that the Nel Jalfjaa was aware of the door's existence.

Radien continued to ponder the Prismgrass fields of Satarakaal, listening to the sounds of the chiming blades of bioluminescent glow that gave this place its name.

"I always hated wind chimes back on Earth..." Radien thought to himself. "But I cannot ignore that this was most likely because my greatest enemy from that time couldn't get enough of them. I guess that's also why I hate candles so much."

Radien continued to wander the Prismgrass Fields, once again examining his legs that he had just remembered had taken a hell of a fall in Ounral. Yet, they were healed as though no wound had been inflicted. It had happened in seconds, an injury that would otherwise have spelled the end of his life as he knew it, even if he were to survive. The Aura was a boon indeed, and it meant that the old weaknesses of flesh had been left behind, in the dust where they belonged, never to be suffered again.

"From the moment I first comprehended the weakness of my flesh, it disgusted me," Radien ruminated as he looked upon his arms, noticing that the scars that were once upon them when he was a Human were absent. No longer, substituted instead by the new bones, the new flesh and fur of a Death World Vulpian. "I craved the strength and certainty of steel... but now that I am Death Worlder, now that this body can heal and endure on the level that my ambitions demand, my bones are as steel, even if they are not the blessed metal that knows not the faltering of a crude biomass that fools call a temple, and bind themselves to the chains of tradition that demands they allow themselves the decay and betrayal that mortality entails."

The wind blew through the Prismgrass Fields again, the chiming of the blades ringing in a harmonic that Radien still couldn't figure out whether or not he liked.

"Defiance becomes me, more so than ever. I had longed to become one with the Machine out of necessity, because that would have been what it took to defy the weakness of flesh. But now, with The Aura, now, as a Death Worlder, the only steel I need is the steel on my hip, the steel in my hands during my time of need."

Radien pulled the Borfblade from its sheath and into his hands, beginning to practice with it, the sharpness of the Novasteel whistling through the night air as he trained without falter, and was not bound by fatigue to stop. The stamina of a Death Worlder, the defiance of Radien, and the unbreaking will of a warrior all were on full display as he trained for thirty nights in Satarakaal's Prismgrass Field, without a single moment of pause, a month-long display of skill and stamina, with strength that knew no falter, and the open air itself would bear witness to the unbreaking will of Miles Sorvenjar Radien. Not one strike was flubbed, not one bolt fired from his right hand was faulty, and not one swing of sword, fist or foot was made in error.

Thirty days of training, constant training, never stopping, never faltering, never fading. Suddenly, Radien's sword struck against rival steel.

Radien stepped back in surprise as he saw who had come to visit him.

"Uh... hi, Veralis."

"Hello, Radien."

"Need something?"

"A good spar."

"Works for me."

The two began slowly at first, testing just what kinds of speed they could match. Though Radien and Veralis had sparred in the past, they hadn't done so with their weapons. The twin axes of Veralis Stratenheim, versus the cutlass and Psionic Off-Hand of Miles Radien.

However, this spar would prove itself to be a short one, as another visitor, far less welcome, had shown up at this sacred site on Raon-Arashal. Well, another is the wrong word to use, because that suggests there was only one. There were two. Two Darkstar Demons had found their way here.

"I think we've caught our quarry at an opportune time, Golvartegon," one of them said.

"How long has this Death Worlder been practicing for, anyway?" the other questioned openly. "He has drained his energy on the empty air, and now we need only put down an exhausted and spent fighter."

"I think you'll find that thirty days of training is only the tip of the iceberg of what I can do!" Radien declared defiantly, as he pointed the Borfblade towards his foes.

Veralis stamped on the ground once with her foot, summoning a dome of raw energy around them. "No one flees this fight!" she similarly declared. "If only because I have no intention of letting two Darkstars escape our blades!"

The two Darkstars, unfettered, took up stances as the four combatants squared off, prepared for this fight to the death.

Radien charged forward with a leaping stab, that was parried by his foe's own infernal Gladius, and responded to by a swift thrust to the chest, that Radien evaded.

The foe that stood against Veralis was met with suddenly having to go on the defensive as a hundred eighty-eight centimeters of athletically build and densely-muscled Cynofrax Vulpian unleashed a flurry of swings and strikes with the axes Käyner and Käynvi, that left little room for counterattack, if any at all.

Radien's exchange with his opponent continued, one of the school of Cutlass and Psionic Off-Hand, the other of Gladius and Scutum. The shield of his enemy did most of the defending, being sure to stay in front of Radien, not allowing the Borfblade to meet the flesh of his foe. But Radien had the range advantage against a Gladius, and the constant attack would eventually summon a faltered defense, that he needed only press forward to find, and then capitalize upon. Only one problem, a big-ass shield that he had yet to be able to maneuver around.

Veralis was now on the defensive against her opponent, who had begun his own advancing flurry of blade.

The Borfblade bounced off of the Demonic Scutum, again, and Radien grunted as he threw the sword on the ground, and held his hand out, daring his foe to come for him.

Evading the stab that was aimed at his chest, he then grabbed the Demon's hand, and with claws bared, sliced through it, before tearing it off with a heave. The Demon yelled in pain as he held his shield in front of a once again advancing Radien as he desperately regrew the lost limb with his dark power.

Every step forward was also a pushing kick that battered the shield of his enemy as he kept trying to break this defense with the pursuing combination of front, roundhouse, side, front, roundhouse, side, repeat. Even if the shield was blocking it, the force was battering the Demon's remaining arm and threatening to crack its bones.

Veralis, meanwhile, had quite enough of her enemy's attack, deciding that now was the time to show her own toughness. Deliberately allowing the sword of her foe to slam against her armor, she grabbed the blade that was trying to dig through the Demonhide Leather spaulder, gripping it with all her might, though her foe tried to wriggle the blade out of her grip, slicing into her hand. It mattered not to her. Keeping as firm a grip on the weapon as she could, the distracted Demon seemed to forget that he had another sword in his other hand, and was beginning to panic at his trapped weapon, so he did not notice her using her free hand to slam Käynvi into his ribs, and then his thigh, dragging it through and yanking the wounded Demon forward and forcing him to suddenly do the splits on the ground.

Retrieving Käyner, she then slammed the axe into the skull of the Darkstar, splitting it cleanly in half vertically. But the weapon kept going, soon slicing into the Demon's heart, and Veralis pulled the axe out through the chest of her doomed foe, the heart flying across the ground, now dislodged by just how much Demon this axe had just cloven through. With one foe dead, Veralis quickly focused her efforts on healing her hand that had just been sliced up a bit by the weapon it grappled with.

The Demon that Radien was fighting had regrown its hand, and the two were now engaged in combat of fist and foot, the Scutum on the ground with dents and cracks across its face from the sheer force of impact that Radien had been imparting on it with his assault.

"You think yourself the mountain?!" Radien yelled. "Then I strike you as the sea!" As a fearsome roundhouse kick broke the arm of his opponent who had tried to block it. "And if you think yourself the sea, then I strike you as the mountain!"

Dropping down for a low sweep, Radien's heel slammed through the Demon's ankle, shattering it and sending him to the ground, blood seeping from the bruises into the Prismgrass of the field.

Radien grabbed his exhausted foe, hoisting him up, and crushing his collarbone with the sheer force of his grip.

"Her axes are Hunderfold Delvonen Hypersteel, so your friend won't be coming back," Radien explained to his doomed foe. "My sword is Hunderfold Novasteel, so no Demon felled by it shall return either! Avanchenvaldr was only the first blood that the Borfblade tasted, and it will spill oceans more before this war is over!"

The Darkstar coughed and sputtered, unable to defend itself at all, as Radien's eyes sparked with azure fury, arcs of Psionic lightning proving the presence his fury.

"You're going to deliver the Dark Six a message for me, and that's why these claws, sharpened on the canyon stone of Jaltai-Vuul will strike the final blow today! I need you need to return to the Burning Hells to tell your masters that you were sent crawling back to them by Miles Sorvenjar Radien! I am steel and I am doom, I am skill and I am stone! Let your legions descend upon me, I shall tear them asunder and ask if that was all!"

Radien bared the claws on his free hand that wasn't holding this Demon in place, and jammed them into the skull of his foe, grabbing onto and then tearing out a chunk of brain matter as he pulled his hand out of the Darkstar's head.

The Demon Veralis had felled disintegrated into red sparks, and the one that Radien had killed fell apart as blackened ash.

"A bold challenge," Veralis said. "When that Demon comes back to Cynar, he'll be looking for you, you know."

"Good," Radien replied. "That means he'll be too distracted to hurt someone else."

"I always knew there was a reason I liked you." She chuckled in response, retrieving her axes.

Radien sheathed the Borfblade as he then stopped for a moment, processing what Veralis had said. "Huh. I will—"

"Have to ponder that?" Veralis finished teasingly, before continuing to giggle as she headed off, noticing that the locator beacon on Radien's backpack was beeping.

Once she was out of earshot, Radien voiced his thoughts aloud to the empty air. "Much as I'm glad I remain consistently me, I also don't like being predictable."

The harmonic bong of one of the stone tablets rang out, and Radien noticed that he had stepped on it.

*Deliis Unzhernreli jagizh djozernaaverash ves akar fuur djalanan-nah jagelka Valgitay akarka.*

*To be a Death Worlder is to train to destroy that which would create suffering, and claim the glory of doing so.*

# 19

# SATHVO-KATH BLACK ZONE

Another seven days resting and preparing between Black Zones, another seven days of reading up on what to expect within them, and brooding mysteriously in a dark corner of the local pub or tavern.

To his surprise, he was approached. That surprise was soon over when he recognized who was approaching.

"Demons in Satarakaal isn't something that goes unnoticed, let alone when said Demons get absolutely humiliated," Arch-Militant Jalnar Veks began as he sat down with Radien. "I know you're a bit busy to be filing a proper report of the incident, Tactician, so that's why I'm here, to just hear it from you."

"Two Darkstars, only one of them said their name. Golvartegon, I believe. Carried two swords, his partner had Gladius and Scutum."

Jalnar typed that name into the datapad he was carrying, cross-referencing the name and weapon choice with what was known of the Demons, however little it may have been.

"Nothing on either of those Darkstars. Was a long shot, anyway. The amount of information we've got on who's who is annoyingly lackluster, as those tomes you recovered from the Field of Unreality are still in the process of being digitized," Jalnar said with a shake of his head.

"Well, Golvartegon was killed by a Hunderfold Blade, so he won't be a problem anymore."

"And the other?"

Radien sipped from his pint glass before answering. "I sent him back to Hell by my claws, and told him to deliver a message, that the Demons will learn to fear my name."

Jalnar nodded with approval. "Much as I understand the need to have a little flair, I suggest avoid telling Arch-Militant Desh about that. He'd chastise you for not just killing the guy with your Hunderfold sword."

"I wouldn't blame him, honestly," Radien said. "Not long ago, I would have done exactly the same."

"One thing about Pelikarn Desh, is that he takes the professional part of our profession to another level. One that honestly gets pretty annoying at times. But he *is* an Arch-Militant, and he earned that title by way *of* that adherence to maximum practicality."

"I can respect that," Radien said.

"Oh, almost forgot," Arch-Militant Veks said as he reached into his jacket and grabbed a circular pendant of onyx, with a ruby in the middle. "You don't exactly strike me as a guy who stands too much on ceremony, but feel free to correct me if I'm wrong for the next one."

Once Veks set the pendant on the table between

them, Radien looked at it. A commendation unique to the Raon-Arashal Defensive Militarium, known as the Circle of Spite. Tradition dictated that it be given to those who despite tremendous odds stacked against them, were victorious in the end. "Officially, that's yours because of the duel. Two Darkstars is nothing to sniff at, even if the numbers are made even by Scion Stratenheim. Between us, I think your actions in Hulae are more appropriate for it. Either way, it's yours."

Radien studied the medal's simple design as Jalnar stood up, soon noticing the confusion behind the thousand-yard stare that Radien was imparting to the token of commendation.

"What part of it aren't you used to?" he asked. "Accomplishment, or recognition?"

"I want to say both, but I guess at this point it's just the recognition," Radien answered. "I realize it also doesn't help that I remember growing up in a time and place where medals like these were bathed in controversy and divisiveness, like the blood they often were."

Radien then looked up at Jalnar, who was clearly about to comment. "Before you say it, I know. I spent too long around Humans. No one understands that fact more than I do. So tell me, Arch-Militant, what's the difference between a trophy of victory, and a monument to meaningless death?"

Jalnar sat back down, motioning for another drink to the passing server. He then unpinned the one of the two medallions from his jacket, and placed them on the table for Radien to take a closer look at. It wasn't a uniform jacket he was wearing, but the pendants were still present, albeit in a more casual setting that only those in the know understood the meaning of.

"This one was given to me after the Siege of Zolth, on Talvakorrik. I was on loan over there, learning from some of their master engineers, when Demonic sappers suddenly made their move and tried to take the city. It was a lot like Hulae, to that end. Ripping portals open by way of sacrificial servants, swarming in and trying to establish a foothold. So I started fighting, and didn't stop, just like what you did in Hulae."

It was a Sunburst Medallion. Many planets recognized and awarded it, it was one of the more universally recognized ones for valor and gallantry. It was given to those who wasted no time in taking action against a threat that made itself known, and the bright orange stone in the middle represented the fury of an exploding sun, that had been brought to bear against an invader who thought they could have their way. It was the recipient of a Sunburst Medallion who had proven such an invader wrong to think this.

"When I first heard about Hulae, it was already over, and the battle had been won, because some madlad locked them all into the arena with him, cut them all down, refused to elaborate, and left. That Hajivakk girl, Synval-Kolderan, she turned down a Sunburst Medallion afterwards because she said it belonged to someone else, you know."

"I didn't know she did that, no," Radien said matter of factly, only afterwards realizing that he hadn't actually been asked whether or not he was aware of it.

"She also said that Sunburst Medallion was the wrong commendation for Hulae. I agreed, whoever pulled that off was due for a Circle of Spite. Eventually, word reached my ears that Miles Radien was the Siegebreaker of Hulae, and I learned this two days after you showed me the handmade banner of Torvaltyne Bastion that *you* made, and that's when I realized that Raon-Arashal had just gained a powerful ally."

"I'm only one person, how can my alliance alone be so significant to a world so vast? Let alone the entire universe?" Radien continued to question.

"Tactician, I know it may seem hard for you to believe, but there aren't a lot of people out there who can summon the spite to win a whole battle on his own, overthrow two different tyrants, build his own castle and and paint its banners himself, forge his own armor from the plating of an Oun-Thuunc, directly challenge the Lords of Evil themselves, and still stand at the end of the day like he's just getting started. I've seen a lot of warriors and posers claiming to be them over my time, so believe me when I say that I can tell when someone's only just getting started. That Circle of Spite right there, that's the first of what *will* be many. As for the difference between trophies of victory and monuments of death... Warriors know the difference, they can tell when the medal on someone's shelf was earned by way of valor or devilry, and whether or not it was for the right side, for the right reasons. There is no medal in history that has gone to *only* those who deserve it. There have been those who proudly display a Sunburst Medallion who I'd love nothing more than to tear their throats out, and those who keep it in a dusty corner when they are ones who represent what it *should* mean to carry it."

Jalnar then took the medallion that was his, and placed it back on his jacket. It was not brazenly displayed, but instead rested respectably on the line between pride and humility. "It falls on the shoulders of warriors who understand honor and principle to define the difference between marks of valor and monuments to sin, and to plant their feet on the right side of history."

On the jagged cliffs of Sathvo-Kath, Radien trained his balance, leaping from rock to rock with the precision he demanded of himself, the balls of his feet bounding from precipice to precipice, the calluses upon them hardening further and further until they were as hard as the stone itself.

Once he finally landed on a more substantial plateau platform, he took a breather to not only gather himself, but also take a look at his surroundings, and observe the scenery he had found himself in. The rose stone of Sathvo-Kath's causeway had provided a natural acrobatics training ground, the ancient rivers and creeks that once flowed through having eroded them into place, a serendipitous creation of Raon-Arashal, which only proved further why this world was named 'the arena of life.' Upon these hallowed training grounds of an entire planet, Radien did train.

How many ankles had these rocks twisted and broken? How many skeletons lay at the bottoms of these valleys, of trainees and prospects who failed? It did not matter to Radien. That was then, and there was a battle to be fought out there, there was no time to lament the fallen, who strayed from the path, who could not embody its principles, who for whatever reason, are what the carrion picked clean at the bottom of the valleys, what lay frozen in the fields of Kuolarek, and buried beneath the dunes of Jaltai-Vuul. What mattered now, was that he must train. He must train, so that he does not join the skeletons at the bottom of the chasm. He must train, so that he is among those who fought the battle and won, and so that his is not among the endless names of the nameless who failed. He must train, as even if he dies a worthy death, surrounded by the broken corpses of his foes, he still has been taken out of the battle, and he *must* survive to see the new dawn, to destroy more of his foes. Though heavy is the burden of the survivor, he must survive, even if because no one else will.

By all that he was, all that he will become, he will reclaim his name from the dishonor of the names before his, making it his own by claim of claw, by right of steel, and by the training that made his claws as steel.

When a rock scraped him, Radien healed it with the Aura. When a strike flubbed, Radien corrected himself. When a mismade maneuver sprained or tore a ligament, he healed it and thanked that he had this power, and that as a Death World Vulpian, his body had this strength.

The only time he picked up such injuries was when impacts were of the kind that would shatter a human shin or tear off an arm. And yet, Radien suffered only trivial bruises, that cleared so quickly, either because his new body could heal naturally so quickly, or because with the power of the Aura that he had been granted access to by the Aura Prism once so long ago, he healed them in seconds.

And yet, Radien still cursed with every wound, demanding higher precision of himself, higher vigilance, higher perception, so that these weaknesses were nonexistent and these wounds would become similarly such. His drive to train, his will to learn, to eradicate mistakes, it burned like a kilonova. In his mind of minds, Radien also knew that he would stand against such a burning tide, if only it was asked of him. He would learn every trick in every book, if it promised that he would survive the tide. He vowed that no wound would destroy him, he vowed that no amount of training would be enough. There would only be 'insufficient' and 'barely adequate.' He must train, to stand against the darkness, even if he stands alone. The Oldest Truth, it was a fire that both burned and cauterized. It stitched what wounds would otherwise cut the very soul, and kept at bay the tears that were forbidden to be shed.

*The Oldest Truth, the fact that has been known since fact could be known, is that I stand alone, but this is not a bad thing.*

*I cannot allow it to become a bad thing, for the strength in solitude is that no one can betray me when I'm all that's there.*

*I am steel and I am doom, I am skill and I am stone, and though it is the oldest truth that I stand alone...*

*This is not a bad thing.*

The oldest truth is that he stands alone, but he will still stand, he will stand against the darkness.

And on the final day, Radien once again found a granite tablet in the rose stone walls of Sathvo-Kath like he did the other Black Zones, and once again, the runes glowed with a harmonic bong to the touch.

*Deliis Unzhernreli jagizh ginufuurka-nah japasanan, tais nejtarnka, esis gisehlkais pirpask Jatarn.*

*To be a Death Worlder is to train precision and speed, that even a miss is a feint that ensures the next strike is true.*

# 20

# TERIOTH BLACK ZONE

Terioth marked the first of the final four Black Zones that Radien was to stay within for the Gauntlet of Doom. After this, Turelion, followed by Zralanan, and finally Relanon. Relanon was to be last, specifically because of the local flora that was, by all accounts, 'fun.' Relanon was home to the Myzeriath Lichen, a species unique to Raon-Arashal, whose dried form was considered similarly fun. What this title entailed could likely be left to the imagination without consequence or falsehood.

However, Radien was currently in Terioth, and not Relanon. Terioth was home to forested fields, pocked by great clearings of meadow, fields of stumps upon which a layer of grass had managed to grow. Radien found himself pondering the fire that he had made. A pile of sticks and tinder would keep the fire alive so long as he fed it fuel, but the fuel it had been given, it would last until the dawn.

Radien pondered the fire. What would he do of it,

this fire that would only last for so long as he commanded it, brought forth by fuel alone? It seemed wrong to bring its life by fuel alone, sticks and twigs alike, leaves that though they made smoke whose greenness gave away his position, did not matter, if only for the size of this Black Zone, or the skill of his blade. If a fool wished to challenge him because he existed, the Borfblade would meet them.

Though his sword was in his hand in every situation, he asked himself, what if it were not?

What would he do on that day, knowing what he did, what he could?

Dozens of ways the battles played out in his head, as he thought, as he pondered, as he ran those battles in hid head and he wondered which of them he might win, or at least survive, to become a constant thorn in his enemy's side.

How many ways could he become the bane of his enemy?

How many heads could he make roll?

Progress was progress, every step forward, very much a step, even if he was only able to fell one foe a day, a dozen days passed meant a dozen foes felled.

He sat, he planned, he pondered, and he prepared, training his mind as he trained his body. Both would need to be in their peak state for what may very well be the next centuries to come. But with The Aura, it meant that he would at least see them. Time no longer bound him, mortality's limits, conquered. But perhaps he had crossed the line of overthinking, he soon realized as he questioned the practicality in thinking of things in this manner. Then again, not every pondering session was going to be a winner.

Like how he trained balance in Sathvo-Kath, he similarly trained balance in Turelion, across the stumps and the fallen logs that revealed why this place existed, this out of place meadow in the middle of the forest.

The Aura also made it so that Radien did not need to sleep. As less and less needs limited him, by way of training or his power, Radien knew no falter. Everything was sharpening like sword on whetstone, and his claws seemed to be able to cut the very air around him, like his sword could. Every now and again as he wandered Terioth, he grabbed a stone and tossed it into the air, obliterating it with a blast of the Aura from his palm. Sometimes, he would break it with his fist instead as it fell.

Soon, he came across a great quarry. The cliffs were of a gleaming red stone, akin to what was on the Red Cliff of Stories. But the Red Cliff of Stories was not a natural phenomenon. Perhaps the stone used in the Red Cliff of Stories came from here. It appeared to be the same kind of stone.

Radien grabbed a chunk of the rock, studying it over. The reds and pinks made the stone look like a chunk of meat.

"Forbidden bacon," he commented.

In the distance, Radien could make out a form atop the nearby hill. At least, the hill on the other side of this valley.

His eyes glowed amber, and he was soon able to see who was meeting him here. The Demon from

Satarakaal, that he had killed with his claws, had returned. This only proved the necessity of killing them with Hunderfold blades.

The Darkstar was once again armed with his Infernal Gladius and Nightplate Scutum, engraved with a blazing green sigil of Demonic nature. Why it was green, Radien did not know. He had never seen that symbol before, and so he burned it into his mind so that he could draw it from memory later in order to search for it at The Hideout, or wherever might have the information he would seek.

He looked over towards his foe who had sent him back to Hell in disgrace.

"Send a message to the masters, of all the insulting demands," the Demon said to himself. "Let us see what this insolent Death Worlder is made of when—*did he just take a fucking bite out of that rock?!*"

On the other side of the valley, Radien was showing off the strength of a Death Worlder's jaws and teeth. "Regrettably, this does *not* taste like Hajivakk Gem Candies. How irksome," he grumbled. "Might make for a good party trick, though." He then tossed what was left of the rock aside, before spitting out the crunched-up fragments. Much as the digestive system of a Death Worlder could probably handle it, he really didn't feel like testing his Irongut Cantrip today. "Well?!" he shouted across the vale, challenging his foe. "Did you deliver my message, or am I going to have to do this with my claws again?!"

With a great and mighty leap, the Darkstar traversed the distance by the sheer power of its hatred, crushing a boulder with its landing. "Your insolence is at its end, Death Worlder!" it growled. "Presume to order me like some paltry messenger at your peril, you uncouth—*hurk!*"

The Demon's head was suddenly caved in by a bowling ball-sized rock that Radien had just chucked at it. Though Radien had yet to learn his name, this Darkstar had fallen to ash before he even hit the ground, his weapons disintegrating with him.

"I stand corrected about the claw thing, I guess... well, *that* was just in case you hadn't gotten around to it yet."

As he eyed the rocks in the quarry, he picked another one up, and looked over at a much larger stone about twenty meters away, and chucked the rock in his hand at the boulder that was now a makeshift target. He didn't hit it quite dead-on, it bounced off the top. One more thing to train. Though the Aura could nudge his arm into the right spots to make sure his aim was true, Radien also wanted to be able to throw with accuracy without it, just in case. Though there were few technologies or techniques that could drain a power-wielder of their ability to do so, they did exist, and Radien wanted to be ready for that possibility.

If he was going to be traveling the universe and helping out where he could, he would need to be ready.

Radien heard footsteps behind him. No way had that Demon come back already. He chucked another rock towards it, and a familiar Vulpian caught it.

"Is it too much to assume you can recognize my footsteps?" Arakai asked as he held the rock in front of his face, having stopped its path with his catch.

"Perhaps one day I'll be able to," Radien replied.

"To be fair, it's a somewhat overrated skill, for the amount of effort it takes to learn," Arakai concluded, casually clenching his fist and shattering the rock, letting the fragments fall onto the stones beneath his feet. "You know, you should never train alone, it only habitualizes mistakes."

"What else am I to do?" Radien asked.

Arakai looked around for a fist-sized rock. Once he found one, he picked it up, then looked to Radien. "Train with me."

Arakai tossed the rock underhand towards him, and Radien fired a bolt of the Aura from his palm to obliterate it in the air. Arakai nodded, and grabbed another. This time, an overhand throw sent it speeding towards the Death Worlder, who met it with his fist, shattering it into a million pieces.

Arakai grabbed two more, throwing one towards Radien in an arc that seemed impossible for a rock of that shape, but Arakai had telekinesis of his own to assist. The other was sent directly towards him, that the two would impact simultaneously and hitting different targets. A lightning-quick draw of the Borfblade transitioned into a horizontal slash that sliced through both incoming stones.

Seemingly with the go-ahead to up the ante, Arakai began grabbing and throwing rocks at Radien for him to deal with, hurling some of them overhand at blinding speed and tossing others underhand to go with them. Some curved slightly in their path, and some were hard to tell the trajectory of just from the way Arakai threw them. Radien began slicing through them with the Borfblade at first, some of them he blasted with The Aura. One hit his outstretched palm and shattered upon it, and he kicked another into smithereens. The barrage continued, and even though Radien was fending it off quite admirably, some were still sneaking through and meeting their targets. But Radien was not so easily swayed, and could quickly heal the bruises with his power as he took what impacts he could, and rendered inert the ones he didn't want to risk.

"Evasions, Radien! You don't have to tank every hit you can't parry!"

Radien took the advice, and began dodging the rocks being hurled that he couldn't slice out of the air with his sword, using the strength of his Death Worlder muscles to acrobatically tumble through the air to avoid what Arakai was trying to hit him with.

Once Arakai had his fill of throwing rocks at Radien, he drew one of his two swords and the next part of this spar began. Though the blade could have ignited with the silver fire that it was imbued with, there was no need. This was training. After a few measuring jabs and quick slices aimed for limbs to try to attack the corner's of Radien's guard, Arakai had to evade an umbrella strike from the Borfblade, that would've cut the top of his skull clean off were this a real fight, and Radien were actually trying to kill him. The follow-through slash was blocked successfully as well, and now the swords were in a bind. Arakai reached for the second one at his hip, to which Radien responded by striking him in the chest with a palm to force him back, and out of the reach of a cut that would come with the draw.

The two faced off, all weapons drawn. Arakai's twin single-edged straightswords, Radien with his cutlass in one hand, and a crackling blue sphere in the other. They then sheathed their swords, and each held out a hand as they slowly inched towards each other, and once the backs of their hands rested against each other, this next test began.

Radien thrust forward with his palm, which Arakai shoved out of the way with his hand, moving in to counter. Radien allowed the motion of his arm away from its target to carry into a push of Arakai's hand down and away, pinning it to the side, and the two looked at each other in the stalemate, wondering who was going to involve their other arm first. Radien spun around with an elbow, which Arakai ducked under as he lashed his heel out and swept Radien's legs from beneath him. Slapping the ground with his palms before he hit in order to mitigate the impact, Radien shattered more rocks to dust with the force of it, rolling to the side to evade Arakai's heel coming down from above, carried through by the swinging motion of the sweep mere instants ago. Both combatants stood themselves up, and squared off again.

Where once they inched towards each other with their hands, they now did so with their swords. As soon as the blades touched, they began a delicate balance of pushing and riding, the metal ringing as they slid across each other, trying to find out where the wrist might falter and where the hand might not know where to move, blades in a state of perpetual gliding across and against each other, seeking where there was falter. But evasion and movement assured that neither would meet their mark as the two found themselves evenly matched. Arakai found himself thrilled that someone finally was meeting his skill, and Radien was thrilled that he even had the chance to test himself against another.

Seconds turned to minutes as the two dueled in this manner, this test of kinesthetic awareness and blade control stretching into the minutes as the two remained just as conscious as their footing, making sure that they didn't suddenly roll their ankles on a rock.

Finally, Arakai stepped back. The two stood for a moment, and Arakai then sheathed his sword, breathing in and out calmly as he thought about the spar he just had with Radien. "It's been a long time since I've had a spar go on for that long."

Radien shrugged. "It's been a while since I've had someone to spar with."

Arakai tilted his head. "All the centuries you've seen by now, and you still gawk at the willingness of others to test their skills against yours?"

Radien let out a sighing laugh of sorts. "I guess it'll never stop being a surprise to me... I remember all too well what it felt like to be eternally denied."

"Eternal is a strong word to be using, especially now that your lifespan could be such," Arakai reminded.

Radien nodded. "I agree. But I cannot ignore that what I felt all that time ago, no matter how short it becomes by comparison... it was all I knew up until then. Denial of training, denial of purpose, clawing at life itself to grab what little of either I could get ahold of... Even when I found it, in what little quantities I could hoard... it just felt *wrong*. And not because I had it, but because this was what I had to do to get it."

Arakai nodded. "I understand."

Radien felt shocked, his eyebrows furrowing at this so sudden and casual understanding.

To this, Arakai chuckled. "Oh, what a world, what a world you grew up on, wasn't it? Earth's name already lives in infamy among the planets that the Humans have settled upon beyond its shackles. Already, Earth is an enigma of evil."

Radien's head snapped towards Arakai as he mentioned enigmatic evil. "Evil must *never* become an enigma. That's how it returns, how it resurfaces. In the ethereal image of a supposedly dead past is how it becomes trivialized in the present, as its perpetrators adopt different symbols to ruin with their taint, and idiots allow it because they can't recognize evil unless it wears the armbands and crosses that took a prior generation of war to understand were the colors of the enemy."

"You'll have no argument from me, Radien." Arakai nodded as he produced a bottle from his pocket. However, this pocket was nowhere near large enough to fit such a bottle, at least from the outside. It was quite clear that this was some regard of a bag of holding, where the space within was larger than the outside, like how the Aura Runner was, yet confined to a smaller space. He then produced two glasses from the same belt pouch, and Radien found himself thinking about what he might put on a hip pouch of holding, like he had once thought of hip flasks of healing booze.

"First bottle from Torvaltyne's meadery," Arakai explained. "Rather, a bottle from the first run."

"That's right, I did commission a meadery to be built there..." Radien took a look at the bottle, and the label upon it. *Defender's Aegis*, the mead was called. A straight mead, of honey, a few choice spices, and fermentation. Though the months that it had spent fermenting would make it particularly strong, it was to be watered down enough to reach a certain alcohol content, and eventually, after enough fermenting, aging, mixing and testing, it would be what it was supposed to be.

After Arakai poured a glass for each of them, they sat down on rocks large enough to sit upon and tasted the mead.

"Oh, good. They did what I told them to, what they knew how to do... make good mead," Radien commented.

Arakai cupped his glass in his palms as he sighed in reflection. "Oh, yes, this is a good one. You brought good brewers on board, no doubt."

"I'm glad I did right."

"Don't act so surprised, Radien." Arakai chuckled. "You brought good men and women into the fold. For every master you recruited, you brought a dozen apprentices, eager to learn how to become the next masters. How can you be shocked that picking good men and helping them do their best worked?"

"Well..."

"Don't tell me, I know—grew up on Earth."

Radien simply shrugged his shoulders and tilted his head knowingly as he took another sip. Arakai's tone was not one of annoyance or frustration at the repetitive relevancy of Radien's plight, but one of quiet understanding of what it feels like to be late to the cosmic party, where all the adventures had been had, all the glory claimed. But where Radien came from a place of stagnation, Arakai's was more in an Alexandrian sense, where his privilege was a bitter one that saw his predecessor leaving nothing left for him to aspire to. Arakai was the son of Ikakorest the Stargazer, a famed warrior-wanderer whose name carried the weight that comes with being a famed warrior-wanderer, and overall wiseman.

"Long have I felt as though I was condemned to Ikakorest's shadow, my feats being merely extensions of his own," Arakai explained himself. "I know that you can't relate to having favorable relations with direct genetic relatives, but I'm willing to bet you at least comprehend what I'm on about here."

Radien nodded. "What I can relate to is when said direct genetic relatives see their descendants solely as extensions of themselves, unable to comprehend the sentience of their offspring, let alone respect their autonomy. I know what it is to live in an ominous shadow, but I envy your heritage, because it is at least a proud one."

"I think we both know that envy doesn't suit either of us," Arakai added, and Radien agreed.

The two decided to have the rest of the mead

together, pondering the quarry. Radien grabbed one of the crimson stones from the ground, and began shaping it into a sphere with his claws.

When the bottle was empty, Arakai took his leave, bound for Jessel-Tarn once again. It was indeed the fun one.

Days passed as Radien chipped away at the stone, forming it into a rough sphere. He figured he could smooth it down once he returned to Torvaltyne, and had access to the tools therein.

Among the rocks that made this quarry look like a beef mine, a granite tablet caught Radien's eye, its contrast making its presence obvious.

With a harmonic *bong* to follow his touch, the runes glowed a deep red once more.

*Deliis Unzhernreli jagizh jagelka altjatlaen, pir gelka biin pir kals zanchin.*

*To be a Death Worlder is to train to wield all weapons, whether held in hand or known in mind.*

# 21

# TURELION BLACK ZONE

Turelion, by all accounts, was an oddball among the Black Zones. Though some of them were quite similar in makeup and dangers within, and others were quite unique in their own way, Turelion was itself an oddity, even when compared to the rest.

This was because the Black Zones all presented great danger in the physical realm by way of the sheer hostility of terrain, flora, fauna, and weather. However, Turelion was a danger of the psychic variety. Like many things on Raon-Arashal, the origin of the phenomenon was unknown. What was known, however, was its effects, that could easily make Turelion the most dangerous of all, especially for one who is prepared exclusively to face physical peril, rather than psychic peril.

What is the difference between psychic and Psionic, anyway? To the lay mind, it would seem as though they are synonymous. And yet, it is just as obviously different to those who have studied and learned how to wield the cosmic powers that be. One can only wonder the sheer torment that it must have been to exist on a planet upon which these powers had no presence, an emptiness in the universe itself that left those trapped within just as empty in their very souls.

Radien didn't have to wonder, though.

But that was then. Now, he faced Turelion. And he had studied, he had learned how to wield the cosmic powers that be. The denial was long over, yet the searing drain lingered in his mind, creating this constant need to act, to train, to partake within the universe that he was now a part of, without cease and without break.

It was as though Radien still anticipated that at any moment, he might be rocketed away from all this, awakening from a cruelly wondrous dream and finding himself back in a bed he had grown tired of sleeping in, on a world he had grown tired of living in. And with every moment that he spent here, continuing to learn and hone his skills, it may yet grant him that many more weapons to wield back in what would become his waking life, if it turned out this all indeed was a dream. Even if this was a dream, perhaps there might be a way to bring something back from it.

But he also knew that if this was a dream, it had all been so vivid and so real in the here and now... he found himself understanding that it would be unlikely that he could live in a universe where the one he now occupied was merely fiction. As he spent more and more time on Raon-Arashal, he could only understand this further. As he trained, effectively, even, and as he rapidly healed any wound caused in his training, he only understood further that if this all vanished, he would not be able to live with that fact.

The Aura itself may have already made its decision clear when he defeated The Unmaker and became Death World Vulpian, but the cruelty of Earth whose unseen scars that remained made him unable to ignore that there may be more powerful, crueler forces in creation that would love little more than to see him ruined, for the sake of the entertainment that would come from such a hideous and heinous rug-pull.

A wave of energy was sent from Radien's fist as he slammed it into the ground, shuddering the dirt and the grass as he demanded that these darker thoughts be banished from his mind. This was not the time for them. It would never be time for them again, because he had escaped. The Opponent Unbeatable could not tear him away from the endless wonder of the stars. The Planet of Traitors could not make him tear himself away from it all out of shame. The Unmaker could not turn the stars under his thumb and drain them of the wonder that Radien still wanted to explore.

Just as he knew all of this was true, Miles Sorvenjar Radien also knew that the Dark Six would not burn the endless wonder to ashes. After all, what's an endless tide of enemies to someone who counts his blessings when his problems exist in a form that can be punched? Long had Radien wished that the solution was his sword, and now it *was*.

Every step forward, very much a step forward.

The steps forward he had been taking in Turelion, however, saw him in a place he did not recognize. It seemed that in letting his mind wander in this manner, his feet had wandered into a strange place indeed. It reminded him of the canyon in Jaltai-Vuul he trained within, but instead of dense sandstone, the walls that surrounded him and the nearby cave that was before him were made of what could best be described as 'Shadow Selenite' considering the dark luster of the stone, and its overall look. Radien could not recall the given name of the mineral itself. If it had none, then he may have just invented it in Shadow Selenite. When he ran his claws across it, they did scratch the stone, though an eerie ring became of it. Perhaps Shadow Selenite would be a misnomer, then. Regardless, Radien took a moment to look around at this place he had somehow managed to wander into. The sky above was dark, it was a deep enough hole in the ground to make it so. No telling if it was night or day down here.

The ringing of the crystal echoed through the canyon-crater, and Radien couldn't help but feel like he wasn't alone. The scraping of a blade against the stone caught his attention.

A Gladius was scratching the crystal walls now.

"Well, here we are again," Radien called out, not even having gripped the Borfblade's hilt yet. "Did you deliver my message yet?"

"Steel and doom, skill and stone..." the Demon spat, mockingly. "I can only wonder how much deserved ridicule that title has earned you over the years."

"That's for me to keep in my past, and you to never find out."

The Darkstar slashed vertically with its Gladius,

carving a path through the still air that aimed for Radien's skull. Radien simply evaded the attack, and when the follow-up thrust was similarly sidestepped, he grabbed the Demon's hand and yanked it forward, bringing the palm of his other hand into its elbow, breaking the arm. The Demon groaned in pain.

"That looks pretty bad… let me set that for you!" Radien taunted as he then struck the break from the other side, breaking it even worse. He then picked up the Gladius, examining it. This was not a Hunderfold blade. Then again, Demons didn't need to carry them. It would actually be quite foolish, as a matter of fact, for them to carry on themselves one of the only weapons they were truly vulnerable to.

"Tell me, how bad of a mark is it on your record if you get sent back to Hell by way of your own weapon?"

The Demon said nothing, it only focused on healing its arm, which seemed to be going slower than it had before, like this Darkstar was psionically exhausted, even though this duel had only just begun. How much energy did it expend just tracking down Radien again, so soon after being resurrected in its home dimension?

"I guess you're about to find out," Radien finished, before jamming the Gladius into his foe's chest, before yanking it out and then embedding it into the Demon's skull with the same vertical strike it had opened with, just in a different order this time.

The Darkstar fell motionless to the ground, its body and weapon soon falling apart into ash. It would return to Hell, and eventually, back to Cynar, seeking its rival again. A rival who did not even know this foe's name. It mattered not to Radien. An enemy is an enemy, and they must all die the same.

Turelion's trial had yet to truly beset itself against him, though. As Radien climbed out of the strange mineral crater he had wandered into, he noticed that the winds above were carrying with them other mineral shards that were tearing through the air like shrapnel, promising to slice to ribbons anyone unfortunate enough to be caught in them.

Radien stuck his right hand above the lip of the crater, and soon cursed in pain as he retracted it, a shard of crystal embedded in his palm, sticking out to the other side. Sliding down the crystalline walls was no picnic either, as that too seemed to shred his palms. But with The Aura, all he had to do was remove the debris, and concentrate. The wounds stitched themselves clean, like they had never been inflicted. Even so, it was not a fun time. It was as though all the pain and soreness of the healing process was compressed into mere moments, a searing that died away as quickly as it had first come. This was the drawback of using his powers in this manner, that though it was honestly more reliable than trying to chance it with traditional techniques and medicines, was a lot less comfortable. Radien also remembered that Jarrek and Arakai both possessed cybernetic implants to aid in the regeneration process, without the same stinging that comes inherently with using Psionic power. Granted, Psionics were not as vulnerable to faults and software bugs. Double granted, cybernetic implants these days were exceptionally reliable, and if one were to break their Autoregenerator Implant, they would damn near have had to set out to do so.

When his hands and forearm had finished healing, Radien grunted, remembering that he had planned to also create himself an Elixir Autopsionic Cantrip, in which a type of liquid could be used to fuel the regeneration to a quicker and less painful extent.

Naturally, the time in Turelion was mainly spent in meditation, honing the Elixir Cantrip to let alcohol be his Elixir. When it was finished and fully set, booze would heal his wounds.

When he opened his eyes, he noticed that the slicing crystal winds of Turelion had subsided. After climbing out of the crater-canyon, he could see the ground was littered with the crystals that had been flying through the air like locusts. The crunching of the minerals beneath his footsteps permeated the otherwise silent air.

Through the fields of Turelion, Radien wandered. He wandered until he noticed what looked like a dust devil, but instead of dust, it was made of the crystals that had only hours ago, been sailing through the air like a tide of glass shards.

The swirling miniature vortex coalesced into a more solid form, but it was only more solid in the sense that it was all interconnected like the skeleton of a pufferfish. A spinning orb of these mildly energetic crystal shards, that seemed to be moving with a will of its own.

Radien watched as it approached him, before lashing out with several shards, and the arm that he quickly raised to block it was cut deeply, but the durability of a Death Worlder was not to be underestimated.

Despite the surprising move, Radien quickly drew the Borfblade, deflecting the next several strikes as his forearm stitched itself back to health. The Crystal Devil started taking to launching pieces of itself at him, which Radien began deflecting with slashes from his cutlass, and evading the ones he couldn't parry.

The Crystal Devil lost more and more mass as it mindlessly continued its attack, flinging shard after shard at Radien, to no avail. Not one of them was hitting him, now that he was in his rhythm of battle. One of the crystals bounced off of his sword in a manner that created sparks, and the Crystal Devil's aim was feral yet tactical, flinging pieces of itself at his head, his chest, his sides, his legs, a few of them even were aimed at his feet. All were dodged or parried.

Soon, the assault began to dwindle. After a few dozen more halfhearted flings that were met with deflections and evasions just like the rest, there was nothing left of the Crystal Devil.

"Intriguing," Radien commented. He then whipped around to face whatever it was that had just stepped on some shards behind him.

"A field of bones is what you stand on, Death Worlder," a strange entity uttered with a voice that sounded like if the chiseling of tool on stone could speak. Like a humanoid construct of interlocking obsidian shards, Radien could only speculate upon what he had just encountered.

"You... You can't be a... can you?" Radien wondered aloud.

"I am Orsidia of Prismos," the being announced. "Last of the Shard."

Radien readied himself again. He had heard legends of the evils of Shard. "The transgressions of the Shard against life itself are legendary, as is the suffering they inflicted! Have you come to fight me? I wouldn't mind erasing the last of a species of slavers!"

"I won't be the last forever, Death Worlder." Orsidia said as she produced a two-handed blade that seemed to be made of obsidian, but was presumably a much less brittle mineral that merely looked the part. A solid black gem was embedded in the forte of the blade, that was as black as the rest of the sword, and its owner. "But that is irrelevant to you, for you won't be worrying of it much longer."

Orsidia seemed to say this with almost an annoyed groan, as though she had grown more bored of interlopers than anything else.

The two squared off, and Radien was prepared to fight a foe well-trained enough to be bored of men like him.

After a few seconds of waiting, Radien's patience was over. He moved forward with a leaping stab that Orsidia ducked beneath, forcing Radien to quickly blink-jump a few feet back in order to avoid impaling himself on her blade.

"A do-over?" Orsidia scoffed. "Very brave..."

Radien had to remind himself that Orsidia was trying to goad him into making a mistake by attacking in anger. He took a few breaths, and then decided on a different opening move, an umbrella strike followed by a slash at her head that was the natural transition of the wrist movement, and a thrust after that. Though Orsidia parried them all, she was on the defensive, and Radien pressed the attack with four more slashes, two diagonal and two horizontal, all aiming to carve his opponent's torso to cutlets. After another stab aimed for her midsection, Radien parried a riposte and sliced vertically at Orsidia's head, which she sidestepped and tried to reply with a stab at Radien's ribs, which Radien parried and moved out of the line of aggression of, responding with a low swipe at Orsidia's legs. Though she jumped the slash initially, Radien followed through with a spinning side kick that connected while Orsidia was still airborne, knocking her backwards and off-balance. Radien pressed the attack again, slicing horizontally at Orsidia's neck, which she stumbled backwards out of the way of, before planting her sword in the ground for balance and lashing out with a snapping front kick that Radien dodged with a quick movement of his chest out of the way. As he turned back towards his opponent, Radien let the movement carry a vicious roundhouse kick right to Orsidia's head, enough to knock her flat on the ground, and make Radien finish a three hundred sixty degree turn just from how fast and powerful the kick was. He then fired a bolt of the Aura at the grounded Orsidia, and she barely raised her sword in time to absorb the blast. The assault continued, and Orsidia was blocking these bolts with the gem embedded in her black blade, and Radien somehow understood what this meant.

His hunch would prove correct, as the bolts that

the blade absorbed were soon hurled back to him in a single purple-black mass of Void energy, that the Death Worlder had to do the splits on the ground just to duck out of the way of in time. He then reached out with his right hand, ensnaring the projectile with the Aura as it flew past, and with a precise movement with his arm and wrist, sent it right back at her. Orsidia had no choice but to cleave the blob of death in half with her sword, but the explosion of energy that followed knocked her to the ground again.

"Holy shit, I didn't know I could to the splits!" Radien commented to himself.

A weakened and fatigued Orsidia quickly got to her feet, groaning in annoyance at the interloper before her. As Radien moved in for the kill, Orsidia realized that she couldn't win this duel. So she warped out.

"Coward! Face me, Orsidia!" Radien yelled at the now empty air.

Though Orsidia had indeed fled from the duel, she had done so in a somewhat rough manner, as it were. Sudden teleportations like that were plays of desperation, as common convention and courtesy across the universe was that jumping from planet to planet was considered very rude, and the vast majority of people just didn't use teleportation as their primary method of transport. Naturally, she left a trace behind, that Radien began to try to follow.

But he still had about five more days to spend in Turelion. If he left now, the Gauntlet of Doom would be over. But if he did not leave to alert someone of the presence of a Shard, let alone the last one, let alone a creature as clearly dangerous as Orsidia of Prismos, that was a five-days head start for her to run, recuperate, and prepare her next move.

However, Radien also knew that this, Turelion, was home stretch. Only Zralanan and Relanon remained after this. It would be another matter if he had this encounter in Jaltai-Vuul, where the Gauntlet had only just begun. He couldn't break this streak now, not for anything. He would have to settle for something else.

To this end, Radien reached out with his mind.

<Techbooth, hear me,> he called to his ship's AI computer.

*I STAND READY.*

<I have just dueled a being identifying herself as Orsidia of Prismos. She has escaped. Alert Disciple of Shadow Jorvask of this development, she is the most likely one to know how to follow up on this.>

*SENDING MESSAGE TO DOS JORVASK'S COMM-LINK... MESSAGE SENT.*

<I've still got a few days to spend in Turelion, but I'm sure she knows that.>

Those few days were spent mostly in contemplation of the foe he just faced, once Radien found another one of those holes in the ground that provided cover from the crystal storms. Radien couldn't help but feel like his encounter with Orsidia had just rekindled intergalactic-level drama. As he listened to shards of crystal whistling through the wind, he saw on the ground next to him another granite tablet. If nothing else, seeing its runes glow red to the touch and hearing that harmonic *bong* brought a level of solace to be found in consistency.

*Deliis Unzhrenreli jagizh fuurnejtarn-nah tlaendeyl, tais tarnka esis nejtarn pirilka nej doriath duul.*

*To be a Death Worlder is to train evasion and endurance, that even a hit is a miss from how little it sways you.*

# 22

# Zralanan Black Zone

As Radien pondered a pint of Redarian Amber Ale at Volgivert Station, he was approached by a familiar Redarian.

"Orsidia of Prismos?" Micah asked urgently, but calmly.

"That's the name she gave me. Orsidia of Prismos, Last of the Shard."

"Look something like this?" Micah asked next, handing Radien a datapad.

"Yeah, that's the one. Carried a single-edged two-hander as well, intricately designed forte with embellishments. I think the gem in it was a Black Star of Korvideyl."

"The sword is called Shadowrend," Micah informed. "You fought her, too?"

"I had her on the ropes, and she warped out. Trace ended up on Zharekk, but she was already in the wind."

Micah raised her eyebrows when she heard that

Radien had the upper hand in the fight. "That datapad is all you need to know about her. I've already informed the Shadow Houses of Nathineyl that she's turned up. Considering her motives, she's gonna be in hiding for a while, though."

Radien read the dossier as Micah got herself a drink of her own.

### ORSIDIA OF PRISMOS

*Species:* Shard

*Age:* At least 1.5 Billion ASC

*Planet of Origin:* Terevetz – Beloran Waste

*Orsidia of Prismos was created in what was initially believed to be an abandoned genetics laboratory on the ruined planet of Terevetz. Both she and the Shard scientists who created her were discovered during a salvage survey being conducted by Laksor Gentech, at which point a battle broke out between the two sides, resulting in what was initially thought to be their mutual annihilation. However, Orsidia was the sole survivor of the battle, and documents later recovered from the laboratory revealed that she is the culmination of the Shard's hate.*

Radien raised an eyebrow at the last sentence. Normally these reports didn't editorialize, they weren't supposed to.

*Investigation of the lab with the intent to discern the nature of Orsidia's creation revealed that she was created using gene-sequences of the Shard's deadliest warriors and assassins, and was also being telepathically indoctrinated with the principles of Shard ideology, i.e., supremacism and belief that enslaving species perceived to be lesser as a divine right of the Shard. Scattered reports of encounters with Orsidia over the ages have gleaned the following:*

*-Orsidia possesses the kinesthetic awareness of Tormal of Alabasteron.*

*-Orsidia possesses the stealth of Amthesa of Shard.*

*-Orsidia possesses the martial skill of Renveesh, First Sword of Prismos.*

*-Orsidia possesses the analytical cunning of Silf the Jade.*

"I assume these names all mean something that adds up to Orsidia being the sum of the Shard's best," Radien commented.

"I can vouch for Amthesa of Shard being a slippery bastard. I was the one who killed her, after all."

Radien raised an eyebrow. As far as he was aware, the Shard had been presumed extinct for a long time.

"Stragglers of the Shard elite have popped up from time to time, even recently, and I guess right now. So it seems unlikely that Orsidia is truly the last, as you say."

"Orsidia called herself the last of the Shard when I encountered her," Radien pointed out.

"That does change things. Whenever a species is on its last hundred, all of its members become innately aware of how close they are to being the very last, and also when they become such."

Radien remembered that he had read of this phenomenon once. It was not known how it happened, but it was apparent that every sentient species in Cynar possessed this 'last ditch defense' against extinction, to become aware of such a level of endangerment. If Radien were the last of the Death World Vulpians, even if he had spent the last five thousand years in a cave never seeing or interacting with the outside world, he would become aware of when he was among the last hundred, the last fifty, the last ten, and finally the very last.

Radien continued to read Orsidia's dossier.

*After Orsidia of Prismos assassinated Thayvek Rentarili, two simultaneous orders were issued by the Conclave of Sentience regarding her demanded fate. One order was for her execution. But another, far more lucrative bounty was offered that remains to this day, demanding that Orsidia be condemned to the Realms of Torment.*

Radien raised an eyebrow again. "Interesting demand from the Conclave, considering the time. The Realms of Torment were a young hypothesis back then."

"And they remain unconfirmed in viability, probably for the best," Micah commented. "The universe was quite excited to see if they worked, and Orsidia was the perfect first subject, having killed the Kendrosian who penned the Pillars Three. To this day, it's hard to argue against Orsidia being tossed into one of them, if ever they become feasible.”

“The Pillars Three were everything the Shard hated. It would've been enough to drive Orsidia out of hiding just to kill the Defender who ratified them.”

“It was indeed.”

Micah took a drink from her glass, now that she had one in her hand. Radien continued to peruse the dossier, that mostly detailed other medium to high-profile assassinations that Orsidia had conducted. Having gotten the gist of things, Radien set the datapad onto the table and stretched.

“Assassin of Defenders or not, I can't help but think she won't be much of a threat until after this war with the Dark Six is over,” Radien surmised. “The Shard hung back during the first, I don't see why their last remnant would hang back during the second. Besides, she's clearly out of practice if I was able to put her on the ropes.”

Micah nodded. “She's deadly, and she may be a fascist, but she's not stupid.”

“Well, that's a surprise, considering how stupid fascists are. I mean, that's how they even become them in the first place, stupidity.”

Micah nearly spat out her drink as she giggled at the comment, nodding once again once she had gotten ahold of herself. “Radien, I consider myself lucky to have a friend who knows how to properly banter.”

To this, Radien was confused. “I, uh... I'll have to ponder that.”

“I've no doubt you will,” Micah said, taking another drink from her glass. “Or perhaps that's just the ale talking."

"In vino, veritas, as it was once said," Radien commented. "In wine, truth."

"Then that just means you can't deny it. You're just gonna have to live with the fact that I consider myself lucky to have you as a friend, and that I consider you one."

Radien shrugged. "I consider myself lucky to *have* friends."

"Don't make me tackle-snug you like I did in Mev-Rossar's Cave."

"Okay, I won't."

The two each took drinks from their glasses, eyeing each other and wondering if someone was going to do something. Neither made a move.

"Micah, I do need to save my energy for Zralanan Black Zone, you know."

"Yes, yes, I know. I'm looking forward to the Survivor's Ceremony once you're done."

"Well, let's not start taking victory laps until we've crossed the finish line."

"Either way, there'd better be Myzeriath."

If Radien's cheeks could be seen from beneath the fur, they would be noticeably red. Myzeriath, the infamous purple lichen native exclusively to the Relanon Black Zone. A universal seasoning that enhanced the already present flavors of any dish that it was put on, but that was not its primary purpose. Myzeriath's notoriety came from the fact that it was an extraordinarily potent aphrodisiac, and its ability to enhance and turbo-charge choice systems of whoever ingested it meant that a couple on Myzeriath could go at it for several days in a row behind closed doors.

The Survivor's Ceremony itself, the party that comes after someone completes the Gauntlet of Doom, can traditionally have a 'second part' after the main merriment has concluded, in which Myzeriath is brought out for the room. It was known that the Warrior's Gate pub in Kendradeyne had its entire third story dedicated to private rooms in which this section could take place.

To say that there were stories of the potency of Myzeriath would understate things quite heavily. It was not for the faint of heart or endurance.

Further training awaited in Zralanan Black Zone, home of the River of Ash and Blood, named so for the frequent volcanic eruptions in the area, and the fact that the nearby river flowed deep and ruby red as it cut through the grey plains that so continuously were subject to the ashfall. As Radien made his way around, ash sprinkling onto the telekinetic shield that surrounded him, he couldn't help but remember what this looked quite familiar to. The rumbling beneath his feet, the knowledge of what that meant, and in the distance, the mountain banishing an entire side of itself in great eruption, as he covered his ears and waited for the sound, hoping that it might save him from going deaf, though the risk of hearing damage seemed minimal at this distance.

Back on Earth was his mind as he yelled to passers-by to cover their ears and get ready to get to high ground.

*Abandon the cars, there's too many on the road!*

He remembered his own voice barking the order to *Just go, go, go already!*

*Grab a bike or something! Hell, just get out of the valley on foot if you have to! You've only got enough time if you start moving now! Follow me! To me! I know the way, damn it!*

No one was listening. They were just grabbing what they could from nearby stores and getting into their cars to make off with the loot. But none of them would survive. He would, however. He knew how critical these next moments were as gunshots rang out from nearby, as anarchy began to sweep through the city, a whole valley that would soon be erased from existence because of what was coming.

So little warning before the eruption long overdue, what could have made it so? What was it that made Rainier give no warning, and for it, no quarter?

*Fine! Die buried in the lahar if you must!*

Within the day, every town between the mountain and the Sound were no more. The death toll, catastrophic. What aid was being summoned was as confused as it was disorganized, where even to begin?

What few made it to the high ground had only endured the easy part, as Miles made his way north and then northwest, trying to get to the other side of the Cascades, just to keep his lungs away from the ash.

The refugee camps that he passed, he passed through just to avoid that many *people* there. He knew he had the strength to make it to the next if he had to. And so he kept passing them by, cursing that no one listened, they just wanted to take advantage of the disaster, thinking they had time because they had cars... never even realizing that so many on the road meant nobody was going anywhere. Those who were not immediately killed were trapped in their cars under feet of ash, awaiting inevitable death by either thirst or the poisoned air.

It took until he was only a few hours outside of Spokane before he finally found somewhere not so inundated with people that it made him sick. Not out of pity, but disgust for Humans, and an excessive amount thereof.

Only after getting off his bike did he realize how long he had been pedaling for, collapsing as his legs refused to go any further. Cursing as the pain of soreness seemed to ignite fires in his muscles, he was immediately set upon by medical staff, who asked him his name, his age, where he was from.

"Auburn, I came from Auburn. I was in the valley but close enough to the hill to make it," he told them, to their shock. This explained why his legs were so tired, but he had biked non-stop from there on pure adrenaline?

A reporter who was passing by couldn't wait to get an eyewitness account from ground zero.

"I tried to tell them to get to high ground, to just start moving, but they wouldn't listen..." Miles told her, to the camera she held. "They just started looting like crazy. I saw one guy guzzling down a bottle of Jack Fire he grabbed from Saar's, four guys came running out of one of the pawn shops, spraying bullets at everything they saw, just to try to experience the thrill of it before the end... pure anarchy as everyone knew they were going to die, and yet, I on my bike did not, because I knew what to do… I tried to tell them, fuck's sake… I need a drink."

A nearby volunteer who had been listening handed Miles a flask, having heard that he was in Auburn, and that he had biked all the way here. "Shouldn't there have been a few weeks of earthquakes?" Miles then wondered aloud. "Sure it was overdue for an eruption, but where was all the warning volcanoes tend to give beforehand?"

Radien snapped himself out of this vision of the past, ordering himself to focus on the task at hand. But rage was overcoming him, and his eyes were starting to crackle with azure fury as he seethed with hatred of the idiots who could've lived, choosing not to in the name of opportunistic dishonor.

With a curse and a yell, Radien slammed his palm into the ground, and a great column of ash erupted all around him, decades of built-up volcanic runoff all exploding into the air at once. Yanking the Borfblade from its sheath, Radien began swinging wildly at the falling ash, yelling incomprehensibly and firing off blue lightning from his body as he couldn't control anything about what he was doing.

Like when he gave into the rage on Kalivan Tor, he gave into the rage in Zralanan Black Zone, but there was nothing to lock on to, the burning red in his vision closing in as it could not find anything to unleash upon, instead unleashing upon the air and the ground, making great plumes of ash leap into the air with the explosions and pumice stones were cut into halves, thirds, quarters, eighths... he had to hit *something*, and with no foe to focus his rage upon, anything near him was a target.

The Borfblade began slamming against the ground, like he was trying to break either the ground, or his sword with the fury of his strikes. But the Novasteel blade did not yield, and Radien had begun carving the very rock away, leaving behind streaks of magma as the friction and heat melted them, and Radien's feral rage did not yield to the sight of him carving a new vent into the volcano itself, his strikes tunneling through the rock as he saw nothing but red.

In the tide of rage, something else stood out. A dark form. A Demonic form. That same damned Darkstar that had been following him since Satarakaal, and Radien wasted no time charging forth towards his foe with blinding speed, slamming into the Demon with a vicious body check that had crossed hundreds of meters within the blink of an eye. As swiftly as countless foes on The Planet of Traitors had been dispatched, Radien had torn the head off this Demon with his bare hands, and heaved it into the air, before striking it with a roundhouse kick as it came back down, and it was as if an explosive charge had been implanted in the very brain of the Demon with how many pieces it exploded into with the force of the impact of Radien's foot.

Then, everything seemed to blank out. He found himself laying on the trunk of a dead tree, lightly covered in ash. Wondering how he had not suffocated under the ashfall, Radien remembered that he had the lungs of a Death World Vulpian now, and a little ash wouldn't sway them. He did also notice that he was almost completely drained of his natural reserves of Psionic power. In layman's terms, he was out of mana. An impressive and equally disturbing feat. The locator beacon on his pack beeped as it signaled that his time here was almost finished.

Radien was still panting as he sat on the trunk, memories of that day still fresh in his mind as they had been so forcibly recalled.

*<What kinds of memories need be unburied to enter a rage such as yours, rivaled only by that of entire armies?>* The Nel Jalfjaa rippled into existence as it asked that question of Radien, the words echoing in his head.

"Permit me to show rather than tell," Radien said, concentrating and letting the recollection of those fateful hours and days return. The Nel Jalfjaa saw through the eyes of the Human of Earth long ago, only able to watch as opportunism and greed born of ignorant despair consumed not just the city he stood in at the time, but all of the cities that had already been erased along the path of Rainier's lahars, and Auburn was only on the tail end before it all dumped into the Puget Sound, and even caused a fair amount of flood damage on the other side from the wave that resulted from all that debris displacing all that water.

"Survivor's guilt does not become me, Nel Jalfjaa. I never had it, and I never will. So what do you call the frustration that comes not with surviving while so few or none others did, but the fact that the idiocy of everyone around you ensured it? My only solace is that the dead were fools."

*<You never did strike me as the type to be guilty of*

*your survival. Even I do not have that answer, for I do not have that perspective. I admit it freely, for mine is a power that could halt such a volcano's eruption in its tracks with hardly any effort, a power I have been privileged to have for so long, I cannot even comprehend what you had to endure that day.>*

"That day, that month, that year... I went viral, to use a term of the time. I became the face of those who survived Rainier's wrath, but the world eventually found other disasters to inundate the headlines with. Though... now that I think of it, I think it's because I didn't have an agenda to push with that eruption as the backdrop. I didn't point the cameras at my face and say it was the punishment of some breathless god, what happened. I guess Earth got lucky, to that end. I find myself unable to help but wonder what cursed timeline we would've gotten if someone with an axe to grind was in my shoes... so the world moved on. True as it was that the cities were never really rebuilt and by the time I left that stupid planet, there were still scavengers making daily runs to the areas, the world at large moved on in due time."

*<And after that?>*

"After that, the months were numb. I didn't keep track of time. I didn't feel like thinking about anything in particular. To occupy my mind, I began moving my hands in the ways that used to bring me satisfaction in creating. I'd head to those woods just to ponder, to meditate, to ask why of the universe. And then, another fateful day befell me. Talgoron showed up in the *Aura Runner,* and I knew I'd be a fool to question what had been thrust upon me. I've always said that my life was purgatory for so long, and that Talgoron was what stopped that. But honestly? Rainier exploding and my surviving it was what brought me out of purgatory, even if into limbo instead. Funny thing, we all kinda knew it was gonna happen at some point. It was long overdue. But what nobody expected was the *suddenness* of it. Normally, volcanoes are polite enough to give you a few weeks warning with earthquakes and such." Radien laid back on the trunk he sat upon, stretching himself as he groaned with annoyance at his past, and the dismissal of it as such.

<*My incomprehension of what it must have been like is matched only by my admiration of the stalwart stoicism with which you met it.*>

Radien thought on the Nel Jalfjaa's words as it rippled out of existence. He would remember them, for it was a worthy compliment. One given by a Grand Psionic Entity was not to be sniffed at. Once he sat up from the trunk, he noticed a familiar stone tablet with through a thinner layer of dust than what covered the rest of the ground. Brushing the ash off to read the runes was a touch enough to make them glow that familiar crimson hue.

*Deliis Unzhernreli kalska jazukiir kos alndka kallej-nah toulth.*

*To be a Death Worlder is to know that vigilance can see both ally and enemy.*

"There were no allies that day, only those with ulterior motives behind their illusions of sympathy," Radien said to himself. "The Oldest Truth... always."

# 23

# RELANON BLACK ZONE

The truest sense of the term 'home stretch', Relanon. Satarakaal was considered a break during them, Relanon even more so. A Gauntlet of Doom-specific rule was that one could not do Satarakaal, followed by Relanon, or vice versa. This was not out of belief that two 'break zones' in a row was unfair, but the fact that it was inadvisable. Many fatalities have been recorded when doers of the Gauntlet have done those two zones first, and then been less alert when traversing the next one. In almost all contemporary instances of the Gauntlet being done, Relanon is saved for last.

With Zralanan finished, it seemed as though people were already preparing for the ceremony to follow the completion of the Gauntlet of Doom. Radien remained baffled at this, because the Gauntlet was not yet completed. He still had a whole month remaining. In Relanon, sure, but that's still a whole month away. What was it that meant he was receiving messages from Torvaltyne Bastion about how they were preparing to celebrate? Why was the Warrior's Gate pub already getting itself ready to be the venue? What was so significant about *him* doing the Gauntlet? This was a trial done by many Death Worlders and even non-Death Worlders, what was it about Radien doing it that meant all of Raon-Arashal seemed to be spectating and waiting for the news?

These questions were asked by Radien to Dorg of Gliropa as the two sat together in one of Fort Stone's taverns, the Survival Station along Relanon's outskirts Radien was preparing for entry into the zone at.

"It may have to do with the fact that you're the first person to undergo, let alone complete the Gauntlet after the whole Caltoran incident," Dorg casually postulated.

"I'm what now?!"

"The first to undergo, let alone complete the Gauntlet after Caltoran was corrupted."

Radien paused. It seemed... fundamentally incorrect. "Okay, I can believe that nobody was doing it while Caltoran was *actively* corrupted, but he was destroyed! And that was over half a millennia ago, now! You mean to tell me that in nearly seven hundred years, *nobody's* even *started* the Gauntlet?"

Dorg shrugged. Hard as it was to believe, it was the case.

"Needless to say, Raon-Arashal has taken notice of the person breaking the silence."

"Then a silence-breaker I shall be! I breathe defiance and feast on spite!" Radien declared, lifting his glass.

"To defiance and spite, then!" Dorg agreed as he raised his, and the two clinked them together before draining them. To defiance and spite, indeed.

Radien still had the guidebook that Agranz had given him back in Dromos-Balth, with detailed pictures of many of the mind-altering plants and fungi that existed naturally within Relanon, and Radien could already feel his mind 'relaxing' somewhat just from the spores that were in the air of all these different plants, many of which were harvested for their recreational purposes. However, though Radien was encountered several of them, he deliberately chose not to imbibe them, if only because he was still in the Gauntlet of Doom, and this close to the end, he really didn't feel like risking anything, even if there was so little risk in doing so.

A nagging feeling in his head also told him that the Darkstar might turn up again. It had done so in every zone since Satarakaal, even with how quick some of those visits were, interrupted by whatever Radien did to send it back to Hell in disgrace.

As Radien explored a cave he had found, he decided to ponder within it, among the spore-laced air of Relanon, a naturally calming phenomenon that seemed to allow the very mind to vent out whatever was clogging it, in the metaphorical sense, of course. No plant in Relanon was so potent that brain matter would begin oozing out of the ears.

Thirty feet from the mouth of the cave, Radien sat and pondered, until he heard dragging footsteps, and exhausted pants. Radien's eyes slowly opened as he knew *exactly* who was there.

The Darkstar had returned, but it seemed... broken. Its Infernal Gladius was still sheathed, and its shield was dragging across the stone. Soon, the shield clattered to the ground, and the Darkstar fell to its knees as Radien stood up to meet it again.

"Do you know what it's like, being torn apart alive?" The Darkstar groaned. "Being reincarnated in Hell after a merely mortal blade sends us back, it is as though we are torn apart and rebuilt, and though the pain is nonexistent when we walk again, the memory of it remains."

Radien was silent as he waited for the Demon to retrieve its armaments.

"There are those of us who have died hundreds, thousands of times, but never five times so close together... it is an unenviable record to hold."

Radien had no comment. He had thought of some, sure, but he chose not to voice them to this Darkstar. He had no desire to give it the satisfaction of a clever response.

"I cannot best you, Death Worlder," the Darkstar finally admitted. "Five times I have tried, and failed. The first time, I thought was a fluke. A product of underestimation. And then the second time came, then the third, fourth, and then... the *fifth.*"

"You caught me at the wrong time in Zralanan," Radien finally commented.

"I cannot agree more..." The Darkstar shuddered as it recalled the fate it met when it tracked down Radien within the previous Black Zone, so recently, too.

Radien's left hand gripped the Borfblade, ready to

finish the job.

"Wait! Stay your blade!" the Darkstar desperately implored. "I know I cannot best you, so let me serve you instead!"

Radien raised an eyebrow as he had also raised his hand, ready to slice this Demon with a blade that would see it fall forever. "You mean to tell me that you want to switch sides?"

"Yes! Yes, I turn my backs on my former masters!" the Demon pleaded, almost convincingly. "There is nothing they can teach me, but your skill so clearly outclasses mine, let me become your disciple!"

"You're trying to tell me that you're no longer loyal to the Dark Six?"

"Destruction upon them! Destruction upon the Dark Six, yes!"

"You mean to tell me, that you renounce your servitude towards them, that you *defect?*"

"I renounce it all! I claim reformation, I submit myself to the cause of bringing doom upon them!"

Radien lowered himself to meet the Demon on its knees eye-to-eye, and said one word to it: *"Liar."*

The Darkstar gasped as Hunderfold Novasteel pierced through its chest and out its back.

"You cannot test me with these lies, Demon!" Radien growled. "If your words were true, you *never* would have been loyal to the Dark Six in the first place! There *are* no ex-loyalists to the cause of evil! There is *no such thing* as 'I was bad, but now I'm good!' You cannot infiltrate us, *Nejtoulth!*"

The Darkstar was at a loss for words as its ruse

was torn asunder by Radien's words, as surely as its fate was sealed by Radien's blade.

"Your lies claiming reformation are wasted on me! Let the last words you ever hear be this: *You are defeated!*"

Radien pulled the Borfblade out of the Darkstar's chest, kicking it onto the ground to sputter its last breaths and die, before disintegrating into the red sparks of a Demon's final death. Breathing in and out as calmly as he could in the face of such a disgusting and pathetic attempt at deception.

Returning to the cavern to meditate and ponder, Radien hoped that as many of his enemies as possible heard what he just told that Demon. He hoped that they would know that there would be no fooling him. He knew well that there was indeed no such thing as an ex-loyalist to an evil cause, and that anyone trying to say otherwise was either a privileged fool who knew nothing of strife, or an outright liar, an infiltrator. Never anything else. Never. Anything. Else.

*<There is but one final thing that binds you to the past,>* the Nel Jalfjaa explained as it rippled into existence next to him. *<I know how uncertainty clouds your mind, Radien.>*

"I hope you're not referring to how I just handled that Demon," Radien commented. "That was about as far from uncertainty as it gets."

*<We both know that is not why I am here. You are not the only one who has had the time over your Gauntlet of Doom to think inwards.>*

Radien slowly nodded. "You know what I seek, to

that end?"

<*What you seek is not within Cynar, but I can use my power, as a gatekeeper and keymaster between Cynar and Auros, to allow you to break that final chain.*>

Radien breathed in and out. "I've heard you've done this plenty of times before, so... I stand ready."

<*Though few remember this fact, the Gauntlet of Doom is more than a mere trial of survivalism. Throughout the history of the Zhernrel-Vuljar, the Gauntlet has been a ritual of self-affirmation. Before entering, the past stood behind you, waiting for the moment to strike against your present, and your future. As you entered and conquered each zone in the present, fragment after fragment of that past burned away in the crucible. On this, the other side of the Gauntlet, you alone have traversed through. Your past has not. Who you are, however, remains as the tempered and hardened, truest version of Miles Sorvenjar Radien. No other version could survive the Gauntlet,*> the Nel Jalfjaa explained, just before Radien's vision flashed completely white, then black, then reasserted itself. Radien stood in a small village within a tundra forest. The morning fog was just beginning to clear from the log huts, some with thatched roofs, others with shingled roofs. A stone path allowed for the entire village to be traversed on foot, though this place was empty. In the center of town, there was a large tree, surrounded by a stone plinth to sit on and discuss the day and its happenings. A tavern was nearby, that also must've held the brewery and meadery within. Likely a distillery, too, considering its size. It was the largest building in the village, an oddly large structure for a village so small.

The village was empty, save for one person that Radien recognized.

"*Oldefar?* Great-Grandfather?" Radien asked aloud, as he felt himself having returned to his old Human form, if only so that this old man could recognize his great-grandson. The old man stood up quickly, as though dreading the youth of the descendant that stood before him.

"*Jeg bare på besøk.* I'm just visiting," Radien quickly reassured.

"We have no need to speak in old tongues here," the old man informed. "But that is a relief, that you haven't come because it was your time."

"I don't understand what this place is," Radien said. "It doesn't look like anything in the old stories... or any stories, for that matter."

The old man nodded as youth seemed to return to him. It was clear that now, Radien was seeing his ancestor as he was when he was at his physical peak, his most fit state.

"Where's everyone else?" Radien asked.

"Either out and about or moved on," the man informed. "Otherwise, accounted for, even if not present."

Radien breathed in and out. "Do you know what's brought me here?"

"Some kind of rite of passage trial, I figure, being that you're only visiting."

Radien nodded in response. "To cut the last link in the chain of my past, so I can move forward with what's next for me."

"I see."

"I don't think you do."

Radien reached a hand out and placed it on his great-grandfather's temple, suddenly showing him rapid-fire the memories of his entire lifetime, like summarizing the experience he'd had so far, from the earliest memories on Earth, to the adolescence spent dreaming of nomadic days that seemed impossible to ever reach, to the day Rainier gave no warning, the numb months afterward, the arrival of Talgoron and the relief he felt upon leaving Earth, to the glories he earned in battle against the foes of the universe, and even what happened on The Planet of Traitors, the event that had the name Kalivan Tor stricken from reference. The campaign of The Unmaker, Radien's regeneration into Death World Vulpian, and now the Gauntlet of Doom, up until this visit to this in-between realm just now. As soon as his great-grandfather opened his eyes, he saw Radien as he was now, the Death Worlder, with the Borfblade on his hip, wearing his black t-shirt and olive green cargo pants.

"You've done well for yourself," the man said, impressed.

"No thanks to your efforts..." Radien growled. "You fell for a damned lie! A lie I would've easily pierced, and for it, you condemned your children *and* theirs to the grey death that *you* placed them in! *You* sentenced your descendants to purgatory!"

The wind began to pick up in the village, a backwind that pushed against the man that at first, Radien almost felt honored to meet, that was quickly being replaced with rage at his idiocy and incompetence.

"Because of an idiot's choice *you* made, I've had to claw my way, kicking and screaming at glass ceiling after glass ceiling that saw me in a cage, too small to stand up in and too narrow to lie down in, decided long before I had such a miserable existence forced upon me, because *someone, somewhere along the line, fucking fell for a gods-damned lie!*"

The wind continued to pick up as Radien seethed, and one of the thatched roof houses began to groan as the straw that made it up was stressed to the point of nearly tearing off.

"*You fell for the lie, and I had to pick up the pieces of what was shattered!*"

The roof of that house finally tore off, flying across the town and into a nearby hill. The logs themselves groaned and creaked, before splitting and splintering, one of them bouncing off of the tree at the center of the village, that remained unflinching despite the wind Radien summoned, and the debris it was generating. Radien's great-grandfather began to age again as he was backed up against one of the buildings made of stone instead of wood.

"*You're right!*" the old man cried out, to Radien's surprise. The wind began to die down, as Radien didn't expect to be told he was right. "You're right, damn it!"

The old man was barely holding back sobs as he tried as hard as he could to remain as strong as he could. "There's no way around it, no arguing it, not this time... you're right... you're... you're just *right*."

He managed to stand himself up before his next

words. "No word in any tongue I know can apologize enough for my foolishness. Likely, no tongue that exists in any language can even begin to describe my regret for what I condemned not only you to, but your father, and his as well. What I condemned my sons to, for falling for the lie that you're right, should've been so easily pierced by anyone else..."

Radien just stood there, shocked that he was being told he was right.

"My only solace is that despite it all, you stand where you do now, with a fine blade at your side, having proudly renounced the parts of you that you despise, and fully realizing the man you've wanted to be."

"I wasn't expecting you to tell me I'm right," Radien finally admitted.

"I saw in the memories you showed me how all you've heard in your time is how wrong you are, and how you're always wrong, but you're right. And you and I both know I'm not the first to tell you that."

"It has yet to stop surprising me," Radien added.

The old man chuckled. "You really are the son of your fathers, then. We've always been surprised at generosity."

The two stood there in the town for a moment, before looking at the ruined house that had been utterly flattened. "I will have to rebuild that house, rock for rock, plank by plank, and nail by nail, with these old and arthritic hands."

Radien shook his head. "That's not enough and we both know it."

Radien thrust his palms forward, and a great wave

of force suddenly blasted forward, and the entire village, save for the tree and the plinth and benches that surrounded it, exploded all at once in a great flood of dislodged and shattered rock, wood and metal. When the rubble settled, only the tree and its sectioned area remained.

"You will rebuild every building in this village, stone for stone, plank for plank and nail for nail until it is complete once again. But you may do so with the strength of your youthful arms and back. That is the allowance I will grant you. Only when you have rebuilt this place as it once was, can you rest again."

Youth returned to the old man as Radien allowed it to, granting his great-grandfather the strength he once knew for this immense task that was set before him. Even as he prepared to leave this place and re-enter Cynar, he couldn't help but question the wisdom of giving him that allowance. He still debated whether or not to allow that advantage to someone who failed so egregiously.

"Gods, do I know *that* look," the young man said as he looked back at the Death Worlder. "Even if it's not on a Human's face, I know that look, the look of doubt for if you've delivered harsh enough of a sentence for such an incredible transgression. You're not the only person of your bloodline to have worn that look. And having that look beamed at me... that I think, cuts deeper than however much pain you could deliver with that sword you carry."

"It's a good sword, one would be wise not to doubt how much it can cut."

"It *looks* like a good sword, and I don't doubt it at all. Despite that, I still know what I've said."

Radien nodded as the young man sifted through the debris, looking for a tool of some kind. There was one around here somewhere. Radien just turned around and left. Restoring his great-grandfather's youth for his task was as much help as he could stand to spare.

Returning to Raon-Arashal, the Nel Jalfjaa floated before him.

<*The grey of your past is slain, Miles Sorvenjar Radien,*> the Nel Jalfjaa reminded. <*You would not have conquered the Gauntlet of Doom if anything short of that were true.*>

"Slain, yes." Radien sighed. "But the memory lingers, reminding me of what I must never allow myself to be subject to again."

<*My impression of you has always been that burden does not become you.*>

"Just as I cannot allow myself to fall to where I once was, *what* I once was, I similarly cannot allow it to burden me in the present, you are right. I fear that if I forsake those memories entirely, I may risk losing what I am now, out of ignorance of what I've risen above. I don't want to lose myself like that, I don't ever want to forget what it means to be Radien. What I do want to do, is abandon its weaknesses, sharpen and hone its strengths, and be the Radien I have always dreamed of being."

<*Your new form—no, your true form now, as a Zhernrel-Vuljar is the door flinging itself open, inviting you to be that Radien now and forevermore.*>

Radien nodded. There could be no doubt. Not anymore. He looked over his arms again, seeing that there were no scars upon them, the old marks of failure that was once upon Human skin had been replaced with the toughened flesh and sand-colored fur of his Death Worlder form, upon bones beneath stone-solid muscle that were stronger than steel.

"For all my time on Earth, I never knew what hope felt like. After I left, I was too busy excitedly taking in the new universe to think about it. Here... now... I think I know what it means. And it doesn't feel Human, and *that* is a compliment upon it."

<Something I have learned about Humans, is that they have a very twisted and maligned interpretation of hope. They think of it as a fragile candlelight, that must be coddled and kept safe from the oppressive dark. The fools. Hope has blood on his knuckles and fire in his eyes. If it dies, it dies only because of such a heinous mistaking of its identity, shunned by those who would otherwise be its beacon, for the insipidness of candles.>

"I hate candles, anyway," Radien commented, picking up his sword and returning it to his hip once he had noticed that it was lying on a stone a few feet away.

<My point exactly,> the Nel Jalfjaa continued. <You are the first to have completed the Gauntlet of Doom since Caltoran was taken from the stars, and you have done so by the blood on your knuckles and the fire in your eyes that saved Hulae, that put to rest The Planet of Traitors, that destroyed The Unmaker. Make no mistake, Miles Sorvenjar Radien, the universe has begun to notice the new flame of defiance that has ignited in

*the dark.>*

Radien knew that the Nel Jalfjaa was aware of Caltoran's true fate, and his exile to the Black Zones. The choice of words was a deliberate one, indeed.

"I still have yet to *complete* the Gauntlet," Radien said.

*<Is that so?>* the Nel Jalfjaa asked cheekily.

Radien then looked to the locator beacon on his pack. It was beeping. The month was almost over, having passed so immediately while Radien was visiting his great-grandfather courtesy of the Nel Jalfjaa's power, and by the time he looked back, the Grand Psionic Entity had rippled out of existence. On the cavern wall behind where they had floated, the last of the granite tablets bearing the verses of the Prophecy of the Beast of Raon-Arashal sat. With Radien's touch, the runes glowed red once again, spelling out this final verse.

*Deliis Unzhernreli jagizh tailarnka alt kalos, pir sejzaa pir zanchin'e-tlaen.*

*To be a Death Worlder is to train to don all armors, whether hardened metal or hardened mind.*

On the nearby wall, Radien noticed a purple growth along the wall. There was no mistaking it. The renowned purple lichen itself, Myzeriath. Carefully, he scraped it off the wall and into a glass vial, pocketing the sample after verifying the find with the guidebook Agranz had given him.

Outside the cavern, the motor of a vehicle could be heard, and the bickering of its occupants. Radien recognized those voices.

"But I must seek the Myzeriath!"

Kastureth insisted.

"Not since the last time you got your claws on Myzeriath!" Varix barked.

"Varix, I thought you *enjoyed* that time..." Alvos commented.

"That's... that's not the point, damn it! It'd take us too long to find any, right, Tactician?"

"Surely," Radien calmly responded as he walked out towards the Pathripper the three old guards were on. What else would these men have but the most well-reputed all-terrain vehicle on Raon-Arashal? It looked like it had been modified, too. Upgraded and enhanced by Alvos, the tinkerer of this trio of misfits. Red and black flame decals adorned the sides, along with the name *Ardjuul-Doriath*, which translated as *corner-damager*. Granted, though calling something the 'corner-damager' in plain Old Earth English would not carry much of a coolness factor, but in the Zhernreli script, it carried a more significant meaning in the art of guerrilla warfare. There could be no doubt that this Pathripper, the *Ardjuul-Doriath*, had many exploits involving the picking off of numerically superior forces until almost nothing remained of them.

"See, Kastureth? I bet the Tactician found nothing within the cavern of the sort! We do not have time to search for Myzeriath today."

Kastureth grumbled as he was denied the chance to search, and once Radien hopped onto the *Ardjuul-Doriath* to be taken back to Fort Stone, he nudged Kastureth's shoulder, and covertly slipped him the vial he had collected in the cavern, with a quick wink to tell him that there's more in the cavern, if he remembered the location. Kastureth's grumbles were replaced by quiet, mischievous chuckles.

The *Ardjuul-Doriath* turned rapidly around, and Varix put the pedal to the metal and sped forth, expertly dodging trees and correcting his speed and angle for whenever there were drops or bumps in the jungle floor.

"Who taught you how to drive this thing?!" Alvos demanded after being nearly thrown off following a sharp turn.

"You did, after you modded the engine and gearbox!"

"Gah, fair enough!"

"Tactician! Five points if you can hit that Bladesparrow over there!" Kastureth dared.

Radien looked at his surroundings as the *Ardjuul-Doriath* continued speeding through Relanon's jungle, and he saw an opportunity in the nearby tree. Positioning himself just right, he leapt from the vehicle, using its momentum to add to his own, and when his feet hit the great tree's trunk, he catapulted himself upwards, his legs acting like the coiled springs they had become in but a moment of transition from Pathripper to tree, and into the path of the Bladesparrow that had alighted on the branch above. With one swift motion, the Borfblade was pulled from its sheath with a single strike that followed, and then returned to the scabbard as he still careened through the air, the two parts of the Bladesparrow falling from the branch, and the branch falling itself, having been carved in two just as cleanly.

"Good *gods*, that was a sight! Reminds me of you

back when you were his age, Varix!" Kastureth exclaimed. "I thought you were just going to throw a knife at it or something! That was *far* more legendary of a move!"

"The training helps!" Radien commented back.

"*Toriyah!* On that, we agree! Onwards, Varix! The doer of the Gauntlet must reach his destination!"

"You're *still* only a Poet of Arms, First Degree, Kastureth! You can't give me orders!" Varix barked back, but not with anger or malice. He was just concentrating on not flipping the *Ardjuul-Doriath* over on a stray root or rock.

"Whatever would we do without our dedicated Grumpfox to rein us in?" Alvos snickered.

"Die, presumably!" Varix shouted back. Kastureth burst out laughing at the snappy and sudden nature of his old friend's comment.

Once the Pathripper vehicle finally made it out of the jungle itself, the ride was much smoother. However, this allowed for even more ridiculous hijinks between the three old guard as they took turns driving, if only because one would say 'I wanna drive now' and then Varix would sigh and remark 'Yes, you do need more practice on this thing'.

Radien was busy pondering just what the hell he'd do once he returned. He wasn't sure what to expect, and at what scale. After all, the fact that these three had come all the way from Point Deathkiller just to be his escort back to Kendradeyne, and then the Warrior's Gate pub, it told him that there might be a bit more pomp to the Survivor's Ceremony that awaited him.

Dorg had been the one to inform him that he was the first person to undergo, let alone complete the gauntlet in several millennia. With Caltoran's corruption and eventual demise placing the universe in a scramble to put out all the fires and count its losses, these parts of life that were anything beyond preparation and repair seemed to fade into the background as damage control became all that there was to do.

It would've been one thing if Caltoran had simply died. Defenders had died before, and the last breath of one is the first breath of their successor. Every time a Defender had fallen previously, there was solace to be taken in that the next was somewhere, waiting to either be found, or to enter the universe's stage on their own accord. Never before had such a protector's hands been turned *against* the very worlds they had saved, and pledged themselves to continue saving. Whoever the next Defender was, it seemed to not matter. The last person to hold the title, rendered extinct over a dozen Conclave species, including two of the most populous and powerful ones there were. The last person to bear the title of Defender destroyed tens, if not hundreds of thousands of worlds. All the eons of training and experience, suddenly in the hands of the enemy. How more vital worlds like Cynofrax, Caren'Das, Laksor, Redaria Prime, Elas'Sotheel and others survived was a strangeness indeed.

Perhaps the Demon who controlled Caltoran knew that such massive targets would become martyrs of planets, and galvanize the universe with even more vengeful will than simply erasing countless smaller, yet inhabited worlds.

Kendrossos Prime was scoured of life, yet the planet remained intact, and to this day could be resettled. But no one did, the world remained a barren wasteland that its natural biosphere had reclaimed. Eluria itself was bathed in fire, and what little was left of the world was soon demolished, pushed into its parent star by Gravity Satellites, just to soften the blow and not subject the people of its sister world Vendrigost to bear the sight of the skeleton in the sky.

The crusade of fire saw not just integrated worlds destroyed, but the bulk of the planets burned to ash were those with species still developing, ones that were on track to join the wider universe, and inevitably become powerful allies of the worlds in the fight against Demons. No wonder the Dark Six wanted them gone.

So it was not just Conclave worlds and species that Caltoran destroyed. The unknown loss that his corruption wreaked was literally immeasurable. How many histories that were confined to one planet, extinguished, never to be found? Irreversibly stolen from the stars were so many worlds whose deaths would not even be known by the rest.

The universe that Miles Radien had entered seemed on the brink of surrender. Perhaps that was why the idiots in Hulae tried to hold a city-wide convention on why Demons could be reasoned with. But even idiocy born of desperation is still idiocy, and the solace Radien took in that he was one of only two survivors of that battle, was that the rest no longer burdened Gliropa with their stupidity and defeatism.

When the *Ardjuul-Doriath* arrived at Kendradeyne's Gate of Stories, Radien braced himself for what was next. He honestly didn't want to see a crowd gathered, if only because it seemed a bit silly to gather a crowd just for his sake. The four Death Worlders disembarked the vehicle, and Varix flipped a switch on it to warp it back to Point Deathkiller's garage.

The gate opened just enough for the four to enter, and the three musketeers in front of him entered first. Radien took a breath, and rounded the corner to enter Kendradeyne, The City of Survivors, a true *Zhernrel-Vuljar* at long last.